JENNY'S STORY

Jenny's STORY

JUDY BAER

TYNDALE HOUSE PUBLISHERS, INC. WHEATON, ILLINOIS

Edited by Curtis H. C. Lundgren

Designed by Jenny Destree

Library of Congress Cataloging-in-Publication Data

Baer, Judy.
   Jenny's story / Judy Baer.
     p. cm.
    ISBN 0-8423-1922-0
    1. Widows—Fiction.   2. Gambling—Fiction.   I. Title.
PS3552.A33 J46 2000
813'.54—dc21   00-025562

Printed in the United States of America

04   03   02   01   00

5   4   3   2   1

To my dear friend Betina Krahn, who taught me that both gardens and people sleep, creep, and eventually leap. Thank you for sharing your home, your wisdom, and even your puppy with me. Your generosity will be forever etched in my memory.

And to Jim and Joanne Jorde, who allowed me to use their home as a haven and provided me with a place for this book to take root and germinate. Your sunshine—both literal and figurative— helped me and my story grow.

And last but definitely not least, to Tom, who is helping me "de-frag" my life so that I have more room for the truly important things. The best is yet to come!

Earth is crammed with Heaven,
And every common bush afire with God.

—ALFRED E. P. DOWLING, *Plants of the Sacred Nativity*, LONDON, 1900

Either the trees were talking in clear, childlike voices or someone was tucked in the branches of the gigantic oak tree overhanging the Morrison backyard. The old tree's leaves rustled with the movements of three small inhabitants tucked deep into the vee of its large limbs.

The platform on which they perched had been built for Libby Morrison by her father, Joe. It was big enough to hold a small rainproof pup tent, a battered cooler, and a set of shelves rescued from the berm on garbage pickup day. The perfect tree house for an idyllic afternoon.

"Do you want more lemonade?" Libby asked primly, hostess of this tea party for her two best friends. She brandished a thermos on loan from her mother.

"Are there more cookies?" Jenny Owens inquired. A robustly healthy child with naturally curling blonde hair, pink cheeks, and eyes the color of cornflowers, she could have been a poster girl for her Scandinavian relatives. Earnest, good-natured, and slow to anger, Jenny's even temper added a basic cheerfulness to the threesome that seldom faltered.

While Libby rooted in the cooler for a tin of frosted molasses cookies, Tia Warden poured herself another cup of lemonade. Then she leaned against a tree limb and raised her small, heart-shaped face to the flecks of sunlight spackling through the leaves. Her dark hair, usually worn in a ponytail or braids, was loose today. Though at the ripe old age of nine years she did not know what a wood nymph was, she strongly resembled one.

"God must have made trees just for kids like us," Tia concluded contentedly as she sipped her drink and watched the leaves dance above her.

"What about squirrels?" Jenny asked. "And birds?"

"We can share." Tia reached into the cookie tin and extracted some crumbs. She left them on the far side of the platform for the nearly tame squirrel that inhabited the tree house when the girls weren't there. More than once, they'd found acorns stored inside their forgotten shoes.

Tia was a delicate, exotic-looking child with her dark hair, pale skin, and deep brown, gently slanted eyes. The organizer of the trio, she implemented lemonade stands, rummage sales for cast-off toys, and most of the childish trouble into which they managed to embroil themselves. Her tenacity and determination were legendary in the neighborhood and among her parents' friends.

Libby was the trio's mother hen. She took it upon herself to see that everyone was fed and comfortable and that rules, when necessary, were followed. She wanted everyone in her small sphere unflaggingly happy. An only child, she was the most coddled and protected of the three, and she had learned her lessons well.

Fortunately for Libby, Jenny was usually happy. An easygoing, loving child, she was content in almost any circumstance. And who could be less than happy today?

"Do you know what Jimmy did to me on Friday?" Tia blurted suddenly, as if some great indignity weighed on her mind.

"Kissed you?" Jenny asked, her blue eyes dancing.

"No! He stole my notebook. I had to chase him all of recess before I caught him." Tia sighed with satisfaction. "I pounded him for it too."

Libby made smooching noises with her lips and Jenny broke into peals of laughter. Tia turned her nose in the air and gave a childish *harrumph*.

Knowing better than to push Tia too far before her fiery temper erupted, Jenny flopped onto her stomach, propped her chin in her hands, and stared at the vast expanse of clear blue sky. "Do you wonder sometimes what's going to happen to us when we grow up?" she mused.

"We'll be taller, silly."

"And we won't all fit into our tree house."

"I know what I'll be," Tia said confidently. "A boss."

"You are already bossy," Libby observed.

"I mean like in a business. My own business. I'm going to sell—" she paused to ponder—"sell something."

"I don't want to grow up," Libby said. "Not yet. I want to stay at home with my mom and dad."

Tia looked at Jenny. "What do you want to be, Jenny?"

Because she'd never really thought about it, even Jenny was surprised by the first words out of her mouth. "I want to be married."

Tia hooted and Libby made more smooching sounds. "Who do you want to marry?" Libby inquired.

Jenny blushed and Tia giggled.

"Jimmy White?"

"No way!"

"Kevin Olden? He always wants to sit next to you at lunch." Libby pressed on.

Tia sat at the edge of the platform, swinging her legs over the edge, her arms resting on the rough wood railing that surrounded it. "I know," she said confidently.

"How could you know?" Libby challenged. "Jenny doesn't even know. Do you, Jenny?"

"She doesn't need to know yet, but I can tell."

"Hah!"

"Double hah!"

"Hah, hah, hah!"

"Jenny," Tia said importantly, "likes Mike Adams. He will be her husband."

Libby and Jenny stared at Tia as if she'd lost her nine-year-old mind.

"He's naughty! He has to stay after school every day and write spelling words!" The obedient Libby spoke as if the boy regularly committed high treason.

"Lots of boys have to do that." Tia flipped her long hair away from her shoulders and curled her arms gracefully around her knees, displaying two large scabs, the result of a recent tumble off her bike.

"Every day?" Libby pursed her lips disapprovingly. "He should be good. I wonder what his father thinks."

She referred to Reverend Adams, pastor of the church the families of all three girls attended. More than once they'd seen Mike being towed out of Sunday school for a serious discussion with his father about his behavior. The girls had once discussed whether or not Pastor Adams always wore that anxious look around his son or if Mike occasionally gave his family a rest from his rebelliousness.

"He'll 'grow out of it,' that's what my mother says. Besides, I think he's kind of cute." Tia cast a sly look at Jenny. "I'll bet you do too."

"I saw Mike and Jenny sitting in a tree, K-I-S-S-I-N-G! First comes love, then comes marriage, then comes Jenny with a baby carriage!" Libby chanted, joining the spirit of the conversation.

Jenny put her hands over her ears and giggled. "You don't know anything!"

Libby stopped mid-chant. "You mean there is someone you do like?"

Jenny blushed and looked away.

"Tell us!" Tia demanded.

"No. You'll blab it all over school."

"We're your best friends in the whole entire world! Don't you trust us?" Libby sounded wounded.

"Then you tell me something about yourselves first."

"I've got an idea." Tia, always the manager, took charge. "Let's promise to be best friends forever and ever. And best friends never tell secrets or say anything to hurt their friends." She thrust out her hand, palm down, to make a pact.

Hesitantly Libby laid her hand on top of Tia's.

Slowly Jenny followed suit.

"Now we're the Best Friends Forever Club," Tia said with satisfaction.

"BFF, that's us!" Then Libby turned to Jenny. "My secret is that Jimmy White tried to kiss me during recess."

Tia and Jenny gave appropriate squeals.

"Gross!" Jenny shuddered.

Tia made wiping motions across her lips. "I don't blame you for not wanting anybody to know that. Yuck!"

The girls turned expectantly to Tia for her revelation.

She screwed her features into an expression of intense concentration. A hint of a blush crawled up her neck as she spoke. "Loren Wold left a present for me in my bike bag."

Libby gave an ear-piercing squeal. "What was it?"

"A bracelet." Tia dropped her gaze and turned fully pink. "I think he got it at Woolworth's with his allowance money."

The girls were all silent for a moment, contemplating the serious nature of this gesture. After that revelation, Jenny's secret didn't seem so shocking after all.

"If I tell you this, you can never repeat it." Jenny took a deep breath, and her friends nodded soberly. "I like Lee Matthews, and I think he likes me."

There, they were out. Secrets that would bind together Best Friends Forever. Little did any of them know the ultimate scope or power of that friendship.

CHAPTER ONE

Persian legend says a man
committed suicide over an untrue report
that his love had died and that where his
blood fell, tulips grew up.

A cliché shouldn't have pushed her over the edge, Jenny Owens Matthews knew, but it did. She went straight down, crashing into tearful hysteria that didn't really subside until Tia Warden and Libby Morrison found her curled in a fetal position on the living-room couch. Then the storm subsided to Jenny's hiccuping and blowing her nose on the edge of a linen-and-lace doily from the nearby coffee table.

"Welcome to the First Day of the Rest of Your Life," a magazine article headline trumpeted from the floor where Jenny'd tossed it. "Reinvent Yourself in the Millennium and Beyond."

"C'mon, Jen, drink this," Libby urged when she emerged from the kitchen armed with a teapot and large mug. She looked as cozy and motherly as she sounded in her faded bibs, soft plaid flannel shirt, and Birkenstocks. "I've already added honey and lemon. And I started a pot of soup with a chicken breast from your refrigerator and some egg noodles I found in a drawer."

"Contrary to your opinion," Tia muttered, "tea and chicken soup do not cure every ailment known to mankind. Especially not those of the heart."

Tia was still dressed in her sleek navy power suit with matching leather pumps, a pristine white blouse, and oh-so-proper pearls. Her hair was pulled tightly back in a chignon, which emphasized the exotic tilt of her eyes and her flawless complexion. Only a slash of bright red lipstick and the flash of long red fingernails as she ran her fingers through Jenny's silken hair gave the slightest hint of color to the ensemble. Her look was as formidable as her touch at the base of Jenny's neck was gentle.

Libby ignored the tart response. After all these years, she knew that Tia sounded the most imperious when she was upset.

Lee Matthews's funeral had been last January, three months past. Both Tia and Libby had hoped that by now Jenny would be finding some order and reason in her life, not sliding deeper into the terrible grief she'd suffered at the death of her husband of twelve years.

Jenny stiffly struggled to sit up. Every joint and muscle in her body mounted an insurrection at being asked to move, and her head pounded with another of her frequent headaches. Crying was not for sissies. It was excruciating work.

"Thanks, Tia, Libby. I'm so grateful you came by. I should have called, but the telephone seemed to be a hundred miles away." She looked ruefully at the cordless model on the nearby table. "I really crashed and burned, didn't I?"

"You might say that," Tia agreed in obvious understatement. "What brought it on?"

"That." Jenny pointed an accusing finger at the magazine. "I was shot down by off-the-rack, two-bit psychology."

Libby picked up the magazine, which fell open to an article entitled "Ten Steps to a New You: The Millennium Message." She looked confused. "What does this have to do with anything? We've been bombarded with this junk for ages."

"Think about it, Lib. 'Welcome to the first day of the rest of your life.' I thought it was a faddish catch phrase years ago, and now it really depresses me. I have no life! Not without Lee. He was the only life I ever needed or wanted. How can I reinvent myself now? Nothing will ever compare to that!"

"You don't think it will," Tia said matter-of-factly. "But you don't know that for sure. The shock and adrenaline that kept you going after Lee's death are wearing off, and reality is setting in. I'd say you're perfectly normal, considering what you've been through."

"Normal? Nothing is *normal* anymore."

"This is your life now," Tia said bluntly, the compassion and pain in her expression softening the harsh words. The truth pained Tia as much as it did her friend. "So what are you going to do about it?"

Tears welled in Jenny's eyes.

"Tia . . . ," Libby warned. "She's had about as much as she can take."

Tia sat down by Jenny and took her hand as gently as if she were handling a newly hatched hummingbird. "Jen, honey, you scare me." Her words were as soft as a caress. "During Lee's funeral you were the Rock of Gibraltar. You comforted the rest of us, made the arrangements no one else could manage, reminded us that Lee was in heaven and happier than the rest of us could ever imagine. You carried us! And now . . ."

"God," Jenny murmured. "That's how I got through the funeral."

"Exactly! But the zest for life has seeped out of you ever since. Jenny, you're fading before our eyes. Where's God for you now?"

Pain and confusion played on Jenny's features. She'd asked the same question. He was there with her as she had seen the life blood pour out of the only man she'd ever loved and was helpless to do anything to stop it. God had given her the words to comfort Lee's aging parents and frantic older sister. And he'd gifted her with the strength to face her own family while they'd mourned the loss of Lee like that of their own son. And then God had disappeared.

"I don't know, Tia. I can't feel God anymore. After the funeral, the relatives, and the thank-you letters, I finally took a deep breath and he was gone."

"Oh, Jen . . . ," Libby murmured.

"Help me find my way back!" Jenny pleaded, her voice cracking. A single tear slipped from the corner of her eye. "All I ever wanted was Lee."

"From the time you were nine years old," Libby agreed.

"He was the desire of my heart, and now . . ." She picked up the discarded magazine to point at the article that had triggered her frenzy. "'Reinvent myself.' Start doing whatever it is Jenny does? Well, what does Jenny do? She cooks. She cleans. She does laundry, shops, and makes a home for her husband. That's what Jenny does. That's who Jenny is. And now her job's been cancelled!"

"We all know that you chose to give one hundred percent to your marriage. You'll find yourself again—with time."

"If that's the case, I should be fine. The only thing I have an abundance of lately is time."

If only they understood how many endless seconds there were between midnight and 6 A.M. She'd been awake to see every one of them. Some nights Jenny lay in bed impotently willing herself to sleep until the early hours of the morning. Every fiber of her body ached with tension, not the relaxation and release for which she longed. She'd started grinding her teeth during the infrequent hours she did sleep, so that she always woke with a dull vicelike headache around her skull, and her jaw muscles grew taut and strained. It was just one more little misery in a litany of them. She'd come to dread nighttime even more than the endless days.

Tia took Jenny's hand. "Where is the Jenny who was always

laughing and never feeling sorry for herself? Where is the person who cooked like a professional chef and planned church banquets without a blink? Who turned the music on full blast so she could dance while she vacuumed? Where's the most vibrant, funny, witty person I've ever known? The more you hibernate inside this house, the harder it's going to be to adjust and to live again."

"When Lee died from the aneurysm, he took my life with him." Jenny's gaze drifted to the kitchen, where she had been forced to watch helplessly as life ebbed from him. "Even the paramedics said they'd never seen anything quite like it. . . ."

"Stop this, Jen," Tia pleaded. "Don't relive it again."

"I can't help it. It's permanently embedded in my brain."

"I'm going to check on the soup," Libby announced. "Tia, can you help me?"

In the kitchen, Tia leaned against the butcher block over which hung a circle of shiny copper kettles.

"Now what?" Tia muttered. "I think she's pedaling backward, Lib."

"She's stumbled on her faith walk. That's not surprising. We all know it's strewn with land mines." Libby's lips twitched in a small smile. "What's that quote? 'I know that God will not give me more than I can handle, but I wish he didn't trust me so much.' Every day I refuse to get out of bed in the morning until I tell myself that nothing will happen that day that together God and I can't manage." She thrust a spoon into the pot and stirred. "These days my own faith walk is more of a faith *stagger* like Jenny's."

The rhythmic click of the spoon against the side of the pan was the only sound in the room as Libby stared absently into the kettle.

"You're handling more than you used to, if my observations are correct," Tia murmured, a note of question in her voice.

Libby nodded but said nothing. For her, her aging parents' mental and physical deterioration was a painful subject. She'd committed herself to being there for them as long as they needed her and had remained steadfast and unshakable in her decision.

"If I were you, I'd be wrung dry of patience and compassion by now," Tia said frankly. Then she grinned. "Of course, my patience is about as long as my attention span."

Libby smiled wanly. "I'm glad your parents are in good health, Tia. Being cared for by you would be like being nursed by a whirlwind. Believe me, there is nothing about the elderly that approximates the speed of a whirlwind."

"They are trying your patience," Tia observed. "Big time."

"No one gets by without some challenges." Libby summarily dismissed her own problems. "Right now Jenny's have to come first for us." Not for a moment did Libby assume that Jenny would have to handle her problems alone. She and Tia were there for her. God was, too, if only Jenny would believe it.

"Are you talking about me?" Like a specter, Jenny floated into the kitchen, her hair tangled, her eyes vague and unfocused. She wore an afghan draped across her shoulders. One corner dragged on the floor. She looked very frail and vulnerable with her blouse unevenly buttoned and a coffee stain on her shirttail. Radiating an air of bleakness, Jenny was a phantom of sorts, a pale shade of her former self.

"Soup's ready," Libby offered, ignoring the question.

"I'm not hungry."

"How much weight have you lost?"

"I don't know."

"Are you taking vitamins? Eating anything at all?"

"I don't remember."

What was food anyway? It all tasted like sawdust and unflavored gelatin these days. Even its textures repulsed her, reminding her of gristle and phlegm. When she swallowed, her esophagus rebelled, threatening to send the food shooting back upward. Anxiety seemed to have taken residence in her gut. There was no room for food to sustain her.

Jenny stared down at the steaming soup mug as if she didn't recognize what it was. A tear dripped into the pale yellow broth. "What am I going to do?"

....

Tia stayed with Jenny until morning. Though Jenny slept little, Tia slept even less. Her time was spent in prayer, knowing that at her home, Libby kept the same vigil.

It was nearly 9 A.M. when Jenny woke. Tia and Libby had exchanged the watch at six that morning so that Tia could go home to shower and dress for work.

"Why are you here?" Jenny asked sleepily when she saw Libby leaning over her with a worried expression on her features. "Wasn't Tia . . ."

"Working. But I don't have to be anywhere special today. Tia told me to take as much time as I needed from the store so I could be available to you. It's nice to have a boss who is also your best friend. Such perks. Mom and Dad are capable of getting their own breakfasts."

Libby began to fold the comforter Jenny had kicked to the floor during her restless night. "I don't know how I'd manage to care for my parents and hold down a job if Tia hadn't hired me on at the store."

"You were afraid to leave me, weren't you?" Jenny accused.

Libby remained silent.

"I don't need a baby-sitter. I'm a grown woman."

"You haven't been the same since Lee died. We have no way of judging whether or not you might—"

"Hurt myself? Put an end to it all? Please, Libby! Give me a break. You know I'd never do something like that."

"I used to know. I'm not so sure now." Libby looked as though she were about to cry. "You've changed, and it scares me."

"Oh, hon, I didn't mean to do this to you." There were tears in

Jenny's eyes too. "I had a bad day yesterday, that's all. Some days are worse than others. Today is going to be better. I know it. I feel it in my bones! I want you to go home and get some sleep. Frankly, you look terrible."

Libby smiled wanly. "Now that's the pot calling the kettle black."

"And if you're going to call me names besides . . ." Jenny mustered a grin. "Scoot. I'll take a shower and eat some breakfast. I'll be fine."

"Are you sure?" Libby had seen this more familiar side of Jenny emerge and then become lost again more than once.

"That I know how to take a shower or eat? Positive."

"But do you know how to 'be fine'?"

Jenny patted the Bible on her bedside stand. "I know where to go for help." Jenny didn't want to admit, even to Libby, the terrifying depth of spiritual void that she'd experienced in the past few weeks. "I just got lost for a while, that's all. And just because I got lost doesn't mean God did." Jenny knew what would comfort Libby. It was what she longed to believe too. Perhaps all she needed was a little more time.

"Scram, my friend," Jenny said, fluttering her hands at Libby as if to dust her right out the door.

"I'll be back," Libby warned.

"Fine. But wait until after lunch. I may soak in the tub until then." Jenny looked down at her fingers. "And do my nails. They look as though I've been using them to scrape texture off walls. Why didn't you tell me how much I'd let myself go? Get out of here so I can get beautiful."

As soon as Libby was gone, Jenny's instinct was to lock the door behind her and crawl back beneath the covers. She would have, too, except the idea of a long hot soak in the tub to ease her aching body was very appealing. Jenny crept into the bathroom, dumped half a jar of bath bubbles into the water, and unbuttoned her nightgown and let it slide to the floor.

The sight in the mirror shocked her. She'd never been heavy, but neither had she been as slight as she was now. She could actually see her ribs, and her upper arms looked like sticks. Her hips were boyishly straight, and her legs appeared longer than ever.

For the first time in weeks, Jenny stepped onto the scale and was shocked to find she was more than twenty pounds thinner than the last time she had weighed. No wonder Libby kept trying to force-feed her chicken soup!

As she eased herself into the water, the warmth and billowing bubbles surrounded her like a cloud. Tomorrow she would drink a shake or eat a candy bar, Jenny decided as she slid beneath the water and felt her pale blonde hair fan out around her.

Maybe Libby and Tia were right. Though today she doubted it, perhaps there was a chance she could learn to live again.

. . . .

She'd dozed off in the tub, Jenny realized. The water was cool, the bubbles had dissipated, and her fingers and toes had turned to small white raisins. After a quick wash and rinse of her hair, Jenny dried off and pulled on a soft flannel dress. Lee had never liked the dress. He'd said it made her look heavy. Nothing could make her look large now. Besides, Jenny liked the way it hid her scrawniness.

Before she could put a comb to her damp hair, the doorbell rang. She started downstairs, stopped halfway to ask herself if she really wanted to see anyone, then gave in to the persistent chimes.

It was George Hardy, the old gentleman who lived down the street. He wore a kindly but worried expression on his deeply hewn features. His blue eyes were buried deep in the folds surrounding them. His granddaughter Kim, a tiny girl with pale hair and large eyes, clung to his big hand.

"Did I get you out of the shower? I can come back later. . . ."

"Not at all. Sorry about the hair, though." Jenny fingered the naturally curling strands. "I haven't dried it yet. Hello, Kim. How are you?"

The little girl watched Jenny somberly. She'd been here several times with her grandfather, and it always took her a few minutes to warm up to strangers.

"Looks mighty fine to me," George said kindly. He was a neighborhood favorite of Jenny's, who had always watched the house when she and Lee were away. George was an extraordinary gardener with lush flower beds and a lawn that both looked and felt like carpet. More than once Jenny had admired his work and been rewarded with a bloom of the moment, whether it be a first spring tulip or a late fall mum. What's more, he was always Johnny-on-the-spot with his first roses of the season, offering them up to her as though they were diamonds. By George's own admission, Jenny knew she was the only one on the street who regularly received any of George's roses. To show her appreciation, she'd purchased a special crystal vase in which to display his offerings.

"Would you like some coffee?"

"Thanks, but I've already had my limit of the leaded stuff," George quipped. "How are you, my dear?"

"Upright. Putting one foot in front of the other. It doesn't sound like much, but it's an improvement over last month."

"It's hard, I know it is. Though my Clara and I had fifty wonderful years together, it just didn't seem like enough. When I lost her, I wished I'd gone too. It takes time to realize that there's still life to be lived, even without a mate."

"I'm not so sure of that as you are, George. I hope you're right."

The old man frowned. "Maybe this isn't the best time to say what I've come to say. . . ."

"Nonsense. Come inside and we'll discuss whatever it is."

"Perhaps you should step outside since that's what I've come to talk about." With a courtly gesture, George waved her by him and into the yard, his granddaughter at his side.

Jenny looked around, wondering what was out here to see. She'd barely glanced at her yard since Lee died in early January. Tia's father had shoveled snow then and was mowing the grass on occasion now. She had considered it no further.

George cleared his throat nervously before speaking. "I know you don't need one more problem on your plate, Jenny, but it's come to my attention that some of the neighbors are discussing the state of your lawn. It's not gossip, mind you, but concern. I know Mr. Warden mows whenever he can, but with the rainy spring weather we've been having, it's hard to keep up.

"Could I be of some help to you? Trimming around the house and trees? Pruning the shrubbery? Your dogwood is getting leggy. What's more, if you allow those plants around the porch to cling too long, they'll rot the wood beneath."

Jenny stared at the dogwood as if seeing it for the very first time. Her plants were growing wild. The dogwood was choking out her miniature lilac and tangling itself in the railing of the porch. "It's huge!" she blurted. "How did that happen?"

George gave a commiserating chuckle. "You've had other things on your mind. And I know Lee did all the yard work. Spring is an important time of the year for a gardener, and this spring has been especially early. It probably never occurred to you that it might need a little attention. Everyone knows how difficult it's been keeping everything together since Lee's death. . . ."

Keeping myself together, was Jenny's first thought. "I am simply mortified at the appearance of this yard!" She blushed until her face was the color of one of George's favorite roses. "I had no idea what an overgrown, unkempt mess it had become." She walked to a flower bed. "There are so many weeds in here that the perennials haven't got a chance. And the pond!" The green sludgy soup occupying Lee's pride and joy horrified Jenny. The fountain was crusty with moss and obviously plugged. Not a dribble of water came out of the tipped urn the boyish statue held.

"What about the fish?" She looked in horror at her neighbor. "Did I kill them?"

"No, of course not. I brought them to my house." George chuckled. "They're thriving in my pond. I'm just glad you didn't miss them or you might have thought there was a fishnapper on the loose."

Jenny took George's hand in both her own and squeezed it gratefully. "Thank you. I'll do something about this right away."

"I didn't mean to make more work for you, lass. I'll just come over with my trimmer and—"

"It's a bigger job than that," Jenny insisted. "I wouldn't dream of asking that much of you. Besides, it will give me something to think about. And when it's done, you can bring the fish back, knowing they won't suffocate in the murk."

"If you're sure . . ." He looked doubtful and a little worried as he beckoned to his granddaughter, who was studying the empty pond. He seemed concerned that he'd put too big a burden on such small, thin shoulders.

"Positive." Jenny stood on her tiptoes and gave the old man a kiss on the cheek. She watched him leave and felt her heart swelling in gratitude to the old gentleman. Even though she and God had not communicated much lately, she realized that he had been sending her human angels to minister to her as she needed them—Libby, Tia, and now George.

CHAPTER TWO

*The nasturtium, in Latin, means "nose twist,"
perhaps for its pungent odor.*

Once inside the house, Jenny headed straight for the telephone. As straight, at least, as she could, given the clutter of unread magazines, green plants left after the funeral, boxes of untouched mail, and all other debris her friends hadn't known where to stow.

For the first time, she actually saw the mess. How had she let things get so out of hand around the house? Her home had once been her pride and joy. Now she couldn't remember the last time she'd had either the energy or the inclination to push the vacuum or pick up a dust rag.

Feeling a bit like Rip van Winkle just waking up from his long sleep, Jenny dug around in drawer after drawer looking for a phone book. She found the dog-eared volume holding open a window with a broken latch.

"Nurseries, gardens, gardeners . . ." She thumbed through the Yellow Pages until she came upon an attractive half-page ad:

"How Does Your Garden Grow? A one-stop shop for the novice or expert gardener. Services offered include landscape design and supplies, shrubs, perennials, nursery stock, fountains, total gardening services, and free consultations."

"The Rolls-Royce of gardeners," she muttered as she punched in the phone numbers. "By the look of things, it's my only chance at salvaging Lee's hard work."

The receptionist was brisk and efficient at discerning Jenny's gardening needs and scheduling an appointment. When Jenny hung up she felt she'd signed on for surgery rather than for a lawn consultation. The lawn she thought she could handle. A surgical procedure to correct the rest of her life would be welcome.

As she wandered into the living room, the searing pain of memory sliced through her. Lee's favorite chair was there, just as he'd left it, with an old bed pillow for a backrest. There were dozens of unread books on the bookshelves flanking the fire-place. An avid reader, Lee was a member of a half dozen book clubs that flooded their mailbox monthly with catalogs and novels. Unopened parcels were stacked all around the chair. It occurred to Jenny that it was her responsibility to cancel the subscriptions now, but it seemed so—final.

It had become easy to ignore problems or to pretend they didn't exist, Jenny realized. It was comforting to pretend that this was all going to be over soon—a celestial mistake that would somehow right itself. Perhaps this denial was why she'd become so remiss about reading her Bible.

With more than a little guilt and remorse, Jenny considered how badly she'd ignored the one book that might give her some comfort. Suddenly she felt herself slipping again into that famil-iar hopelessness, the sense that there was nothing she could do and no one who could pull her out of her despair. Still, out of long habit and a desperate desire for solace, Jenny picked up her Bible.

Curling onto the couch, feet tucked beneath her, she closed her
eyes and opened the book to play Russian roulette with God. Her
thoughts were filled with irony. Would he come through for her?
Or was her nagging suspicion that he had moved on correct?

She opened her eyes and saw that the Bible had fallen open to
Psalms. "OK, Lord," she murmured. "Let's hear what you have to
say." It was a challenge, clear and simple.

> As the deer pants for streams of water, so I long for you,
> O God. I thirst for God, the living God. When can I come
> and stand before him? Day and night, I have only tears
> for food, while my enemies continually taunt me, saying,
> "Where is this God of yours?" . . . Now I am deeply
> discouraged. . . . "O God my rock," I cry, "Why have you
> forsaken me? Why must I wander in darkness, oppressed
> by my enemies?" Their taunts pierce me like a fatal wound.
> They scoff, "Where is this God of yours?" Why am I
> discouraged? Why so sad? I will put my hope in God! I will
> praise him again—my Savior and my God! (Psalm 42:1-3,
> 6, 9-11)

Jenny stared at the passage. "I thirst for God. . . . I am deeply
discouraged. . . . Why have you forsaken me?" Those words,
each so aptly chosen to express utter despair, could have come
from her own heart.

"If you know how I feel, Lord, then why don't you help me?"
Jenny said aloud as angry tears spilled down her cheeks. "You
were there at the beginning, I know you were. But now . . ."

Every muscle in her body was burning. When Jenny couldn't
sit still any longer, she paced the living-room floor until the odd
sensation passed. The dull throb in her head increased. Her body
sent her all sorts of strange, unfamiliar signals these days. Her
whole being was revolting against her. Hard as it was for her to
believe, she had begun to wish for the numbness of those first

days. Then her mind and body had been like a tooth shot full of novocaine. Now the anesthetic of shock was wearing off, and the prickles of pain were attacking relentlessly.

"Maybe I should be grateful," she mumbled to herself. "Maybe it will make me feel real again."

A small scraping sound outside the back door drew her attention. She opened the door and looked out. No one was there. Jenny was about to close it again when she noticed a scrawny dog cowering in the shrubs by the door. The dog was white—or had been once—with patches of reddish brown hair dotting its emaciated body.

Jenny and the dog eyed each other warily. It was difficult to tell which was more afraid. Then the dog gave a small whimper and lay down, his huge liquid eyes fixed on the woman above him.

Jenny's heart melted. "You poor scrawny thing. You're starving. Stay there. Stay. Stay." She backed into the kitchen and glanced around for something to feed the pitiful creature.

A growl in Jenny's midsection reminded her that she hadn't eaten yet either. Jenny never noticed her hunger until she could hear it or until it became great enough to claw like a wild animal at her insides. She ate only to subsist these days. And the poor pup outside didn't even have that luxury.

There was bread on the counter that wasn't too old, which Jenny tore into pieces in a large bowl. She opened a can of prepared chicken gravy and poured it over the bread and tossed it as she might a salad.

Outisde, the dog began to wag its tail ever so slightly, and when it smelled the concoction, it began to shiver with excitement. Jenny leaned over to put the dish on the steps, and the timid animal crept forward.

"I don't think this is on a dog's heart-healthy diet," she murmured. "Sorry, but it's the best I can do." It pained her to watch the shy creature trying to decide whether or not to risk eating while she was there, so Jenny stepped back inside and closed the door.

Now it was her turn. She stared into the interior of the refrigerator as if it were a door to an unknown world. Many of the dishes had globs of whitish mold growing on them. Even had she wanted to open the covered bowls, she doubted she'd be able to recognize their contents.

Jenny jumped when a voice from behind her said, "It looks like a fridge full of petri dishes! What are you doing in there? Science experiments?"

"Tia! You startled me! Don't sneak up on me like that."

Tia stepped around Jenny, pulled a bag of wilted brown-and-gray lettuce with a half inch of murky sludge in the bottom out of the fridge, and stared at it disdainfully. "Sneak up? We rang the front doorbell, called out to you, and stomped across the floor like we were wearing army boots so as not to startle you. And you didn't hear us anyway." Tia opened the door beneath the sink, pulled out the trash can, and dropped the distasteful bag into it.

"Libby's watering your plants in the living room. Poor things. They must think they've been transplanted to Death Valley. Do you realize there is cottage cheese in the refrigerator six weeks past its expiration date? New life forms are running amok in here." Tia began systematically hurling most of the contents into the trash. "What were you staring at in there anyway?"

"I heard my stomach growl, so I thought I'd better eat something."

"Not out of here," Tia concluded. "You'd have food poisoning in a heartbeat. Besides, Libby brought food. You know her, Earth Mother, nurturing, cooking, weaving cloth to sew her clothes . . ."

"Are you making fun of me?" Libby came into the room carrying a casserole with a loaf of freshly baked bread on top. "I do not weave. Just because you're dieting all the time and can't resist my pies, you shouldn't criticize."

Tia snorted. "I don't diet. I eat in a healthy manner that will serve me well all my life!"

"Tofu and seaweed?"

"Whole grains, fruits, and vegetables!"

Right in the middle of their debate, Jenny sat down on a kitchen chair and began to cry.

"Now see what you did!" Libby set down the casserole and began to rub Jenny's shoulder. "Don't cry, Jen; we were just teasing."

Tia rolled her eyes. Being the methodical, left-brained one of the trio had always left her on the fringe when Libby and Jenny were being emotional. Though no less compassionate, Tia was able to see things as they were, not as they felt.

"I think we're witnessing an emotional power surge."

Libby looked from Jenny to Tia and then nodded. "I see."

Tia moved a chair so she could sit down and face Jenny. "What is going on, honey? What's put you in this state? Did we come stomping in and upset your emotional ecosystem? We didn't mean to be thoughtless. I know sometimes I can trudge all over people as if I'm wearing combat boots—"

"It's not you. It's me!" Jenny stared at her friend through eyes brimming with tears. "I'm not sure I can do it. I don't want to live without Lee. Everything is flat. I want Lee back!"

"But you can't have him, honey. Lee's gone." Tia sounded as stricken as Jenny.

"And he's not the only one," Jenny whispered.

"What do you mean?"

"I can't find God either! He's gone too. He's the one who carried me through the funeral. Everyone kept saying how strong I was, but it wasn't my strength that I was relying on, it was God's. Now when I pray, it seems to bounce right off the ceiling. It would have been easier if I'd died too." Jenny swiped at her eyes with the tail of her shirt.

Tia stood to help Jenny into the living room and began hand-ing her tissues while Libby scurried through the kitchen to prepare supper. Food was her cure for most of the world's ills.

Tia sat with Jenny until the emotional storm subsided. Then she led Jenny to the table, said a brief prayer of thanks and, much as she would a child, told her to eat.

The threesome remained silent until their plates were empty. Having been friends as long as they had, their silence was both comfortable and comforting.

No one spoke until Libby had cleared away the dishes and placed a pot of tea and three delicate china cups on the table. Tea with cream and sugar had been a ritual with them since they were little girls. Libby's mother had prepared tea parties to solve all serious problems—from the division of toys to having crushes on the same boy. Now, when the teapot came out, the conversation would start.

Libby poured the tea and then doled out the sugar and cream in exact amounts that came with a near lifetime of practice. Jenny liked more sugar and cream; Tia, less. Just as it had always been in the many years they had known each other, Tia was the first to speak.

"If anything we've said or done has upset you . . ."

Jenny's head snapped up angrily. "You? Of course not. But I am hurt. My husband did die at my feet on this kitchen floor!"

"You know very well that's not what I meant, Jenny. Don't go there anymore. Reliving that day only hurts you again and again."

"But you don't know how it is!" Jenny blurted. "I can't get it out of my mind. The paramedics, the sounds, the blood—"

"Probably not," Tia agreed mildly, interrupting Jenny's outburst. "I haven't been fortunate enough to find a man I love and who loves me in the way you and Lee shared. I can't imagine the loneliness and loss you must be experiencing. But I did lose a sister, and I can speak from that experience."

Tia was referring to a car accident that had occurred when she and her twin Sheila were in high school. Fraternal twins, Tia and Sheila were as unlike as night and day. Sheila was a round-faced blonde whose common sense always took second place to her desire for fun. While Tia had remained close to Jenny and Libby, Sheila had chosen to run with a wilder, more "interesting" crowd. That choice had ultimately led to her death in a car crash with a boy her parents had forbidden her to see.

"My parents kept rehashing Sheila's accident for years. Mom had a nervous breakdown, and Dad nearly lost his business. It wasn't until they started reaching out to others with similar problems that they began to live any sort of happy life again. Now the support groups they run give their lives meaning."

"Oh, Tia, I didn't mean . . ." Jenny was immediately contrite. "I guess I'm so swallowed up in my own grief that I'd forgotten—"

"My point exactly!" Tia covered Jenny's hand with her own. "I'm not asking for sympathy. What I am trying to tell you is that I have been through another version of what you are experiencing. I know that healing after a loss as devastating as yours is a process. It happens one step at a time."

She gave a lopsided grin, then continued. "Sometimes it happens a half step at a time or one step forward and two back. For every person healing takes a different path and length of time. But it can happen. It will happen. But, in the meantime, it's OK to grieve. It would be weird and awful if you didn't."

"But don't hang on to the grief," Libby interjected.

Tia nodded her agreement. "You've been living in your pajamas, eating like a bird, and not answering your phone. Your plants are dead, your yard is a jungle, and I see dust around here that's older than Egypt. It's time to open your fists, Jenny, and let some of that sadness you've been clutching seep out. Don't allow it to permeate every pore and fiber of your body. Let it go!"

Jenny turned to look at Libby, who was watching them with gentle, sympathetic eyes. "Is it true, Libby? Is that what I've been doing?"

Libby paused as though she had something difficult to say. "We don't want you to quit missing Lee. But you have been obsessing over your loss to the exclusion of everyone and everything else.

"Even though it hurts, Jenny, please start living again. Start reaching out. The kids in your Sunday school class at church really miss you. So do the ladies who have to settle for me as their Bible study leader until you come back. I miss you! Tia misses you! If you don't do it for yourself, do it for us."

"Just a little at a time," Tia broke in. "Start fixing your hair in something other than that tired old ponytail. Throw on jeans when you get up, don't stay in your pj's all day. Try a little lipstick. Eat! You'll feel better. I'll guarantee it."

"Lipstick will hardly bring Lee back," Jenny said indignantly.

"Did I say it would? Nothing will bring Lee back. All we are concerned about now is you."

"We just want what's best for you," Libby pleaded.

"What's best for me? Lee is what's best for me!" Jenny rose from her seat and began to pace. Her hands flailed as she spoke. "How dare he leave me like this! We had our lives all planned. Next year we were going to try to have a baby. I've wanted one since the day we were married, but Lee kept saying the time wasn't right, that we didn't have enough saved to start a family. And now I'll never have his child." Jenny dropped to the couch and wept bitterly.

"He abandoned you, didn't he?" Tia said softly.

"Yes! I mean no. Oh, I don't know what I mean." Jenny took the tissue Libby handed her and blew her nose. "Lee didn't want to die."

"Of course not. But that doesn't mean that you can't be angry that he did. If you remember, I was furious with my sister for months after the funeral. I kept second-guessing her decisions— to hang out with that boy, to get in his car, to disobey my parents. But I was angry at death, not at Sheila. Once I finally realized that, it was easier to let go."

"It's insane to be angry at a dead man for dying!" Jenny moaned. "It's . . . sick!"

"It's real," Tia countered. "Be angry. You deserve it."

"Not at Lee," Jenny whispered.

"You don't have to deny you're angry that Lee is dead. Crummy stuff happens. Just don't let your emotions make you implode. You may not be ready yet, but pretty soon it will be time to move on."

"But I don't want to!"

"Your options are limited," Tia said bluntly, her compassionate expression softening the harsh truth of her words. "You can get on with your life or you can spend it in this shrine you've made to Lee. Jenny, you haven't even moved his hockey skates and stick from the back entry where he dropped them just before the aneurysm! What do you feel every time you walk by them? Not warm fuzzy memories, I'll bet."

"It was the last time I saw him . . ."

"See him up here," Libby said vehemently as she pressed her forefinger to her temple. "In your mind, in your memories. Hang on to the good stuff, honey; otherwise the bad will drag you down with it."

"I can't . . ."

"You can!" Libby's voice was surprisingly strong and passionate, a sign of just how deeply she felt her own words. "You have your faith. Even though it might not feel like it right now, you have someone to help you through this. Lean on God, Jenny."

"I thought I could once, but I don't feel like he's there for me now."

"God isn't about feelings, Jenny. He's about fact. Just because you *feel* he isn't here for you doesn't make it so."

Jenny scraped her hands through her hair. Her shoulders drooped and she stared at the floor. When she spoke, it was as though from a long distance, through a tunnel to the darkness she was experiencing.

"It's weird, you know—how I feel. Surreal. Like I'm living someone else's life and I'll wake up and walk into my own again soon. I can't get my footing anymore. Life seems so pointless and irrelevant. I see people sitting on their porches reading the newspaper or taking walks. I wonder how they can do it. How can they go on living when my life and Lee's have stopped?" Tears leaked down her cheeks. "How could this have happened? Bad luck? Punishment? For what?"

"You did cut the hair on my favorite doll."

Libby's bizarre non sequitur halted Jenny's tears. "What did you say?"

"Miss Fanny. The beautiful Southern plantation doll my grandparents brought back from Georgia. You remember. You cut off all her hair to glue it onto some picture you'd drawn. Miss Fanny in a buzz cut! Grandma nearly had a stroke! Don't you remember? I couldn't play with you for an entire week."

Both Tia and Jenny stared at Libby as if she'd lost her mind.

"Well, it's true, isn't it?"

"Of course it is, but what does it have to do with—"

"Absolutely nothing!" Libby crowed. "And that's the point. From now on, every time you feel yourself getting down, do something. Think of Miss Fanny's decimated hair or of the time you bet Tia she couldn't eat a mosquito, and when she tried, she threw up all over you. And if you can't laugh, don't cry. Pray. Keep moving. It's not always easy at my house either, Jenny.

"It's nothing like your situation," Libby continued, "but my parents are getting older and I see them changing in ways I don't like. I can't do anything about it except laugh or cry, accept it or fight a fight I can't win. So I make jokes. We laugh when it takes us twenty minutes to find Dad's glasses or Mom's dentures. Is it funny? Not really, but we do the best we can with what we have."

"Oh, Libby," Jenny began. "I am so sorry. You are absolutely right. I've been selfish, self-absorbed, ungrateful . . ."

"You don't have to get carried away," Tia muttered. "You do tend to go overboard in every direction, you know."

Jenny took a swipe at her eyes. "Listen, I feel like cleaning up. Maybe I'll fix my hair and file my nails. Now that you two have totally rattled my self-pitying cage, I need to recover."

"You'll be all right?" Libby wondered.

Jenny smiled with a hint of genuine animation. "Sure. I'm even thinking of doing a little buzz cut on my hair. If I remember correctly, I thought Miss Fanny looked lovely."

She shooed her unlikely angels out the door and closed it behind them. At least God, if he were still around, had a sense of humor.

A sound of something being pushed across the concrete side-walk outside her back door drew Jenny to the window. The dog was still there, the dish empty. He was pushing it determinedly toward her steps.

Seconds? Was that what he had in mind? Jenny smiled widely, hardly noticing that her smiling muscles felt stiff from disuse. Poor old Spot, as Jenny had already mentally named him, was coming back for more.

This time Spot did not shrink away. Instead, his tail, a moth-eaten-looking flag of dirty fur, began a wide fanning motion at the sight of her at the open back door. Much to Jenny's surprise, the dog picked the lip of the dish up with his teeth and skewered her with his plaintive eyes.

"What a beggar you are!" she chuckled, delighted by the dog's clever trick. "If this is going to continue, I'd better buy you some dog food. I'm not sure a diet of bread and gravy is good for you." She snapped her fingers. "I do have some food that Libby brought over. I know she meant it for me, but I'm sure she wouldn't mind my sharing it with a friend. Hold on."

Jenny stepped back into the kitchen for a rubber bowl covered with foil. Libby had said it was roast beef and a few potatoes. Spot might like that.

Indeed he might, Jenny realized as she turned around to find the dog standing in the doorway, bowl still in his mouth, politely waiting for the seconds he'd been promised. When she neared, he put the bowl down at her feet.

"Wait a minute, buddy! I didn't invite you in here. You probably have fleas and doggy parasites I don't care to think about."

But his eyes were so expectant and so trusting that Jenny found herself leading the way to the garage. She emptied the food into the bowl the dog had claimed and then, finding a beat-up old sleeping bag she'd been meaning to toss, laid it on the floor near the dish.

Spot wolfed down the second helping, took a drink from a five-gallon pail of rainwater Jenny had collected for the houseplants, and dropped exhaustedly onto the makeshift bed. Jenny leaned down and stroked the only spot on his body that was not utterly filthy—the top of his head. The dog closed his eyes in a gesture of total trust and fell asleep.

She tiptoed out of the garage and gently closed the door. Spot would be safe and warm for tonight. Tomorrow she would decide what to do with him. The Humane Society, she supposed, but they always had far too many strays as it was. Maybe if she took him to a groomer first and got him cleaned up, he'd have a better chance at adoption.

Thinking of veterinarians, poodle parlors, and those trusting brown eyes made Jenny fall asleep faster than she had in months.

CHAPTER THREE

The dahlia was accidentally smuggled into France,
and once there, out of the private garden of Josephine,
Napoleon's wife, making it a flower of dubious heritage.

"Are you ready?" Libby arrived at Jenny's back door wearing a
blue flower-sprigged sundress and matching flats.

"I feel overdressed to go to Tia's store."

"But it's her Spring Fling celebration. If she's not satisfied with
the number of customers, we'll have to pretend to be shoppers to
generate enthusiasm. Of course, there's never anything for her
worry about. We both know that. People come from a hundred
miles in every direction to her store. Tia carries on as if she doesn't
have a marketing degree or tons of experience. Sometimes I
wonder why a well-educated businesswoman like her wants to
hang out with dull me. I feel very lucky that Tia cares so much
about our friendship."

Tia had worked in a small gift shop through high school and
the summers between college classes. When she graduated, she
had purchased the store and gradually turned it into what it was
today.

"Tia is pretty awesome," Jenny murmured. Then she added regretfully, "And I haven't been a very good friend to anyone lately."

Except to Spot, who seemed to have adopted Jenny even more quickly than she had adopted him. He'd raced into the yard this morning when she opened the garage door, did his doggy business, and hurried back inside to the sleeping bag.

Jenny had rushed to the store this morning to buy dog food and was glad she'd made it back before Libby's arrival. Her new canine friend was something she didn't care to explain right now. Her friends thought she was going off the deep end as it was. Befriending a flea-bitten scraggler with doggy breath would not rate high on their list of logical next moves.

"I'm glad you agreed to come today. It will mean a lot to Tia. Besides, you look wonderful. Great dress."

Jenny stroked the front of the pale aqua silk shift she wore. "Thanks. But I looked in the mirror. I look like a pencil."

Libby laughed. "One more reason to start cooking again."

Jenny sighed as she slipped into the passenger seat of Libby's late-nineties Cadillac. "I'm having a hard time finding reasons for much of anything these days." To change the subject, she inquired, "How do you like your car?"

Libby grimaced. "I wanted something new and sporty—just once, but Dad insisted that I buy this. He can't see the allure of a flashy sport-utility vehicle or a convertible. Besides, I think he and Mom are afraid I might get a car that's difficult for them to get into or is too small for them."

Kindhearted Libby rarely complained about her responsibilities concerning her parents even though it put a major crimp in her social life. "So," she said with an artificial brightness that signaled they'd discussed her situation long enough, "I think you should start cooking by making one of your divine pies. Banana cream, maybe, or a fresh-baked apple. Yum."

"Lee's sister Dorothy called this morning," Jenny said. "She's coming over tomorrow or the next day. Maybe I can muster up the energy to bake something then."

"Really? I haven't heard you mention Dorothy much lately— or ever, actually."

"Lee's sister and I were not very close, and I've never figured out why. I was startled when she called."

"You and Dorothy didn't have problems, did you?"

"No. In fact, I've often felt that she desperately wanted to be friends, but it just never happened."

"It will be good for the two of you to visit then," Libby concluded. "This loss might draw the two of you together."

"Maybe. Dorothy's had a hard time too." Jenny frowned. She'd always been puzzled by her sister-in-law's aloofness. "I think there is something else going on with her. I haven't put my finger on it yet, but even before Lee died I had a sense that something was wrong."

"What do you mean?"

"I can't even say. It's just a hunch I've had. A growing uneasiness in her that's begun to rub off on me even though I've seen so little of her." Jenny grimaced. "Woman's intuition, I guess."

"You know what they say about intuition," Libby commented mildly. "It's based on things you've subconsciously observed but never really put together in your conscious mind. That means that whatever you're feeling probably has a basis in fact."

Libby didn't say it aloud, but she hoped that Dorothy didn't have more troublesome issues. Jenny was as fragile as a soap bubble floating through air. One more bump and she might pop.

"Here we are!" Libby announced brightly as she pulled into the parking lot of Tia's main store. The store was a renovated Victorian home surrounded by a wrought-iron fence in front and a hedge of rosebushes at the back. Whimsical topiaries lined the cobblestone walk to the double-doored entrance and vast open porch, which flanked three sides of the house. Wicker chairs and couches plumped with lush, brightly colored pillows invited sitting. One of Tia's clerks was ladling out fresh-squeezed lemonade and encouraging customers to partake of the cucumber sandwiches, miniscule lemon tarts, and scones with clotted cream and strawberry jam. It was all very feminine and inviting.

"I love your porch furniture!" Libby gasped, knowing that was exactly what Tia would have her say.

"It's for sale," the clerk said, loud enough for the lunching ladies to hear. "Isn't it grand?"

"All of it?" a customer echoed. "Even those rocking chairs?"

"Oh, yes. And we have an entire catalog of accessory pieces. Would you care to look at it?"

Libby and Jenny filled their own glasses with lemonade and helped themselves to food while Tia's clerk hurried for the brochures. Then they moved to the far end of the porch so they could talk.

"Do you remember that Tia was the child who sold the most Girl Scout cookies in fourth grade, and she didn't even belong to Girl Scouts!" Libby recalled with a smile. "It's no wonder she's still in sales."

"You got the credit for the cookies," Jenny reminded Libby.

"But I gave Tia the prize. There's no way I would have gone door to door every night, convincing people that their lives wouldn't be the same without a box of chocolate mints or Samoas. Tia would willingly try to sell ice to an Eskimo." Libby took a deep sip of her lemonade. "Let's finish our food so we can go inside and find her."

As expected, Tia was holding court near the cash register. Bouquets of flowers surrounded her, enhancing the fairy-queen look she'd cultivated for the day, dressed in pale teal chiffon and a huge straw hat with a cascade of silk flowers.

"Look at you!" Jenny said. "Things must be going well."

"Swimmingly, my dear." Tia gestured toward the flowers. "Can you believe this? From distributors and satisfied customers! And delivered by the most delicious-looking man. Someone from that

place you mentioned—How Does Your Garden Grow? I wish
I could have kept the deliveryman. He would have been so deco-
rative over in the Western and primitives department. Tight
jeans, boots, muscled chest."

"You've had too much caffeine," Libby commented quietly.
"Wear a little off and show us what you've done with the store
lately."

Tia made a face at her friends and slipped into tour-guide
mode. The store was a maze of rooms both small and large, each
with a different theme—candles, flowers, lush laces and tapes-
tries, stationery, finest quality pens and sealing wax, artwork,
children's gifts, calligraphy, wedding invitations and accessories,
hand-knit sweaters and appliquéd clothing—all displayed in
antique armoires, chests, and tables that were also for sale. On
the second floor, each room was copiously decorated—from the
master bedroom to the nursery to the Victorian bathroom
complete with a huge claw-footed tub.

The third floor was pure whimsy. Part playroom, part fairy-
land, it gave the feeling that one had climbed into a magical tree
house where wind chimes tinkled thanks to strategically placed
fans and small girls in frilly white dresses handed out bonbons.

"You outdid yourself this time," Jenny murmured. "Fabulous."

"Things are practically flying off the shelves," Libby said in awe.

"You like it?" Tia asked hopefully.

"Amazing. Since we aren't needed as pseudoshoppers, may we
go in the back, take off our shoes, and eat some of that turtle
cheesecake I know you keep in your freezer? You know, the stuff
you think you've been hiding from me in that container labeled
'soy burgers'?"

Tia's eyes narrowed. "Libby, how do you know about that
cheesecake?"

Libby grinned back at Tia as she steered Jenny toward the
storeroom. "I never believed you for a minute when you said you
ate only 'wholesome' foods these days. You can't fool me. Now

you can quit acting so self-righteous about your diet while Jenny and I are gorging ourselves on your stash of chocolate."

Libby looked back over her shoulder as she moved away. "Besides, aren't you the one who once told me that chocolate was one of the four basic food groups? There are no secrets among the Best Friends Forever gals. We'll leave a slice for you."

Jenny felt a bone-weary exhaustion when she arrived home. Her foray into Tia's store was the longest outing she'd had other than the one to the attorney's office concerning the estate.

It was surreal to see people working in their yards, kids riding bikes and tossing balls, the woman across the street picking flowers. Another neighbor was washing a car. Everyone was behaving as if nothing untoward had happened, as if a life had not been ripped from their midst.

The wave of depression building over her was dissipated by a welcome *woof!* as Jenny reached her front top step. Spot was there, looking filthier and dirtier than ever, his tail wagging broadly and the inevitable supper dish close by. He'd begun carrying it everywhere he went as though it were his guarantee of another meal. Jenny found that both sad and sweet.

She leaned down to touch the top of his head. "You can't be depositing fleas on my porch steps all day long. And you have no dog tags. There's a leash law in this town." She glanced at some healing scars on his flank. "But I'll bet you've learned that the hard way. What am I going to do with you, fellow?"

"Love me," his liquid eyes responded. And for the first time since Lee died, Jenny decided to take a challenge.

. . . .

At noon the next day Jenny stared into the bowels of her refrigerator and shook her head. Her friends had really cleaned it out. She was down to a box of baking soda, a can of pineapple juice, and various condiments. The cupboards weren't much better. Cold cereal, rice cakes, packaged noodles, and some weird saffron rice packet she couldn't remember buying. A trip to the store was no longer optional.

She'd taken Spot to the vet this morning for an examination and shots and then to the dog groomer for a good scrub and clipping. Spot had moaned with fear and trepidation, cowering close to Jenny. She hadn't dared leave him, even for a moment, to run to a nearby convenience store for bread and milk.

He did look better now, however, so her diligence had paid off. There was an attractive dog beneath the grime and burrs. Even Spot seemed to think so. He'd been studying his reflection in the full-length mirror in the foyer ever since they'd returned home. Either he'd never seen a dog who looked quite like the one in the mirror and was making sure it came no closer or he liked the silky fan of his tail and freshly washed fur. What's more, with his new appearance, Spot had decided that it was his right to follow Jenny inside the house instead of returning to the humble bed in the garage. Grateful for his silent yet comforting company, she had not dissuaded him.

"Life goes on," Jenny muttered, thinking what a callous phrase that was.

Why did people work so hard when life was pointless and irrelevant? How could her life have changed so much and so many others remained untouched?

The injustice made her livid.

For Libby and Tia's benefit she'd tried to keep her negative emotions at bay, but they pressed hard on her heart. And once Jenny unleashed them, they were a Pandora's box of unpleasant thoughts. Though Jenny spent a busy afternoon cleaning out the garage and preparing a sleeping area for Spot, her mind would not release the anguish of her thoughts.

It wasn't until a delivery truck pulled into her driveway and an athletic-looking man jumped out and began to unload huge

sacks and stack them near her mailbox that all her pent-up rage
came spewing out.

"What on earth do you think you're doing?" Jenny demanded.
She stood in the driveway with her hands on her hips and high
color in her cheeks. "I won't be able to back my car out of the
garage if you pile that stuff there. And what is it anyway? I
haven't ordered anything."

An indefinable emotion registered in the attractive driver's
eyes. "Are you Jenny Matthews?"

"Yes, but—"

"And did you call How Does Your Garden Grow?"

"Of course, but I didn't order anything. What are you trying to
dump on me?" Irrationally upset, Jenny didn't want anyone telling her what to think or to do right now. And this good-looking,
scruffily dressed man was delivering something she did not
want. Worse yet, he was obviously expecting her to be grateful
for it. What's more, he couldn't seem to take his eyes off her. Lee
would not have approved.

"This is fertilizer. You know, manure. The boss," a smile curled
his lips, "seemed to think you'd need it."

"Why is he trying to sell me something even before he's looked
at the lawn?"

"Maybe he's already driven by the house," the man suggested.
"And the fertilizer is a gift. 'No charge,' he said."

Jenny eyed him suspiciously, looking at him more closely. His
nails were underscored with black dirt, and his slim-fitting jeans
had seen better days. He wore his hair in a ponytail, and dark
Oakley sunglasses obscured the top half of his face. The rugged
look fit him. She surprised herself by thinking that. Lee had been
a suit man himself.

She dragged herself mentally back to the situation at hand. "A
gift? I hardly think so. Manure is at the bottom of my wish list.
You'd better return those bags to your truck."

A pained grimace twisted the lower half of his handsome face.

"But I just unloaded them and my back's already aching. If you had to sling fifty-pound sacks of this stuff all day long, yours would hurt too."

"If you want to tell your boss I refused his gift and come back tomorrow to load up, I don't care. Just make sure I can get my car out of the driveway."

"Yes, ma'am!" He worked with renewed vigor. He certainly didn't look as though he were in pain, Jenny observed. Indeed, his back rippled with strong sinewy muscles beneath the perspiration-stained white T-shirt.

Rolling her eyes, Jenny turned to her car inside the garage. She was halfway to the nearest market before she realized that for the first time in over three months, there had been something on her mind other than Lee for more than a moment.

The respite, however, was brief. Lee's tie, a gift from Jenny, the one he'd taken off on his last trip home from work, had been folded several times and poked into the empty ashtray of the car. It had been one of his favorites, a conservative navy-and-red print with a hint of yellow. Her hands tightened on the steering wheel. She'd been reluctant to move it, even though seeing it inevitably brought an ache to her heart.

Would it be this way forever? Would everything and everyone remind her of her loss?

Why did God allow a good man like Lee to die?

The trip through the grocery store was excruciating. Lee's favorite cereal, the bins of candy with their small silver shovels ready to fill little striped bags, a dozen kinds of bagels from which to choose—all reminders that they had always shopped together. Lee was always buying things they didn't need—pickled pigs' feet, deli potato salad, olives, anything in an attractive or brightly colored tin. When Jenny accused him of liking to spend money a bit too much, he'd give her his best little-boy look and throw a package of tenderloins into the cart.

Jenny was eager to escape by the time she arrived at the baked-goods section and the little coffee stand nearby. She was startled to hear someone call out her name.

"Libby? Oh, hello, Mrs. Morrison, how are you today?"

Libby's mother bobbed her head and smiled sweetly. She was forgetful and hard-of-hearing, but Libby still faithfully brought her mother here twice a week to have a fresh cruller and a pot of tea. It couldn't be easy to be an only child watching your parents on that inevitable downhill slide of old age.

"Join us?" Libby invited. "Mom is meeting a friend here today, and Tia said she'd come by if she could get away from the store. I guess a big order arrived yesterday, and she's been working with that all morning."

"Sure." Jenny sank heavily into one of the wrought-iron chairs. "I feel like I've been in a triathlon just maneuvering through these aisles."

Mrs. Morrison put an age-spotted hand on Jenny's. "How are you doing, my dear?"

Jenny knew exactly what the older woman meant. How is it to be a widow? Are you recovering? Are you still grieving? It was what everyone wanted to know about her these days and hesitated to put into words.

"Going day by day, minute by minute," Jenny said mechanically. Second by second was more like it.

"There is no other way in life, is there?"

Jenny cast a pleading look at Libby.

"Jenny is redoing her lawn, Mom," Libby deftly interjected. "She's having it relandscaped."

"But it was lovely before," Mrs. Morrison said.

"It was, wasn't it? Lee did all the work. Sometimes I think he was better than the professionals. He was so meticulous that he never overlooked a thing. Every night he'd bring in a different flower for me. . . ."

Puzzled, Libby stared at her friend, but before she could respond, Tia breezed in on a scent of lavender and violets.

"Sorry if I smell like I fell into a vat at the perfumery. I've been unpacking potpourri and scented candles for the shop."

Tia flung herself dramatically into a chair as though it were a Victorian fainting couch and simpered to the waitress, "Peppermint tea, please. Something soothing."

"Jenny was just telling us about Lee's talent in the garden," Mrs. Morrison said. "I never knew he was so skilled."

Tia glanced quizzically at Libby, who shrugged.

"He was a wonderful cook, too," Jenny continued in a bright tone that sounded as false as a three-dollar bill.

Tia cocked her dark head toward Jenny, but Libby patted her mother's hand and stood up before Tia could speak.

"Mom," Libby said, "there's Mrs. Nielsen."

Mrs. Morrison made a great show of collecting her belongings and excusing herself to meet her friend. Jenny was left mid-sentence describing Lee's cooking prowess.

When Mrs. Morrison and her friend were settled at another table, Libby returned to her friends. She was wearing a puzzled expression that matched the one on Tia's features. "I didn't know Lee was such a good cook—," Libby began.

"Let's have chocolate éclairs today instead of bagels," Tia interjected.

"Other than those waffles he always made such a production over, I can't remember—"

"Tia? Having an éclair?" Jenny was eager to change the subject even though she'd been the one to bring it up. "Am I hearing things correctly?"

"My skirt feels a little loose, OK?" Tia retorted. "One can't look her best if she's gaunt and emaciated, can she?"

"I still don't quite understand what you meant about Lee," Libby persisted, intent on her own line of conversation. "Remember how you complained that he would vanish until supper was ready and then again until the dishes were done?"

Tia shot Libby an annoyed glance and whipped a compact and mirror out of her purse. "I don't look too thin, do I?"

Jenny's head swiveled as she looked from one friend to another and back again, as if confused by this stereo set of contradicting conversations.

"And that he'd never swept a floor in his life?" Libby recalled as she shook her head. "I remember the time you decided not to sweep the kitchen floor until he noticed it was dirty. How many days was it? Nearly two weeks, right? Ho, ho, were you upset!"

"One of the clerks from the store is on some sort of unhealthy diet. She only eats bananas and grapefruit. Or is it turkey and cottage cheese . . ."

"Tia," Libby blurted, exasperation in her voice, "why do you keep talking about dieting?"

"And," Tia said through gritted teeth, her expressive eyes rolling in Jenny's direction, "why do you keep telling Jenny what a lousy housekeeper Lee was?"

"But he was—" Libby started to defend herself and then realized why Tia was trying to change the subject to stop her. "I didn't mean he was bad or anything, Jenny. Maybe just not as sterling as you said—"

"Lee was a perfectly wonderful man," Jenny said hotly. "And I know exactly what both of you were doing. You were running Lee down, and Tia was trying to change the subject because she agrees but doesn't want to hurt my feelings!"

Libby's normally serene features were agitated. "I didn't mean . . . Tia, why didn't you just stick a napkin—no, an entire coffee mug—into my mouth to shut me up?"

"What a minute!" Tia interjected. "Libby, you didn't say anything that wasn't true. You never intended to hurt Jenny's feelings. And Jenny . . . the operative word here is *man*. Libby wasn't intentionally dissing Lee. He was a man, and none of them are perfect. Neither are women. It's like the Bible says in

1 John: 'If we say we have no sin, we are only fooling ourselves and refusing to accept the truth.'

"Ever since Lee's death, you've been inching him higher and higher onto this pedestal until no other human could ever match him. Today he's alpha cook and gardener. Last month he was superjock and brilliant as Einstein.

"You've always thought Lee was the best of the best, sweetie," Tia continued gently. "Lucky guy, to have a woman who loved him as much as you did. But whether you realize it or not, you've been making Lee into something he was not—a paragon."

"He was an exceptional man," Jenny protested weakly. Tears were ready to fall onto her flushed cheeks.

"Have you forgotten all the times he was late for dinner and didn't call? Or the way he never seemed to have cash in his pocket when it was time to pay for something? Or that he insisted that he was 'training' the garbage to walk itself to the Dumpster when he forgot about doing it for days on end?"

A faint smile graced Jenny's lips. That line about training the garbage had always made her laugh. It had usually gotten Lee off the hook as well.

"I know what you are saying, but I don't want to hear it. All I have left of Lee are memories. Why can't you leave them alone?"

"Be realistic, Jen. Libby and I would do anything for you. One of the hardest is telling you truth you don't want to hear."

"Well, I don't have to listen to negative things about my husband!"

"Then start acting as if you live in the present instead of in the past! Even if you don't feel like it, choose to go out for dinner or a movie. Look for something good in every day. Don't rely on the past for your happiness. It wasn't all that great sometimes, whether you remember it now or not."

Libby glanced around the small coffee-stand area. "Tia, maybe this isn't the best place to be discussing this."

"There is no best place," Tia rejoined. "And now that you've brought it up, Libby, I refuse to stand by any longer and see my dearest friend in the entire world shrivel up and die!"

Libby spluttered indignantly as Jenny began to gather her things. "I have to leave now. I have groceries to pay for, and Libby's mother will be needing her daughter soon. I don't want her to see me like this." Without a good-bye, Jenny turned to leave.

Then something more occurred to Jenny, and she spun back toward her friends. "I know what you're trying to do. I know you worry about me. Believe it or not, I can even understand why you think you need to make me see Lee in a different light. But my head isn't messed up about Lee. I loved him and he died. It's God. He could have prevented Lee's death—if he were here, if he were real. I've spent my life putting faith in 'things not seen.' Maybe the reality is that there is nothing to see. That God isn't there after all and never was! Who knows? Who knows anything anymore?"

"Are we still Best Friends Forever?" Tia asked timidly.

Even as upset as she was, Jenny had to smile. Anything Tia or Libby did for her was always out of love. That love might be misguided sometimes, but never insincere. "BFF. You bet. But you are both lousy actresses. Neither of you could hide your true feelings no matter how hard you tried. And as much as I don't like it when you let it all hang out, that's better than tiptoeing around my feelings."

Jenny stoically held her tears in check until she had finished her shopping. She was drowning, Jenny realized, in sorrow and confusion. She had been deluding herself, trying to build a life on the past instead of the present.

Where were her hope and her faith? Why couldn't she build her new life on that? Or was faith just a cruel trick played on the naive? She'd been so sure that faith had carried her through Lee's funeral and the subsequent days. But it had fled now, leaving only an aching void behind.

Jenny drove home mindlessly. It would have been better if she'd died too, she thought. But whoever or whatever was playing this cruel trick on her meant for her to suffer, and she didn't see an end to it anytime soon.

Spot's giddy welcome when she opened the garage door made her smile in spite of herself. Tongue lolling out one side of his mouth, ears alert, he stood on his hind legs and hopped backward as she walked up the sidewalk. He would have done back flips, Jenny was sure, if he'd known he could. Petting him calmed her. His hot, doggy breath on her cheek cheered her considerably and blew away some of the cobwebs in her mind.

It didn't even occur to Jenny until her second trip into the house with groceries that not only had the pile of fertilizer bags grown, but bags of grass seed and a fountain had joined them.

The innocent stacks made Jenny see red.

She found the man in her backyard, stacking paving stone. Jenny beaded in on her target.

Her frustration came frothing out again. "Listen, I realize that you are just doing your job, but it's not a job I requested! Granted, this yard may need all this barnyard gold to make it green again, but until I talk to someone in charge and make my own decisions as to how much I will spend, I don't want you piling this stuff on my property. I didn't order grass seed, a fountain, paving stones, or a redwood forest, for that matter. I don't want to see any more! And if you have any idea of ignoring my request, please tell me right now what part of *no* you don't understand!"

"But there's no charge . . ." The man looked annoyingly amused and not at all intimidated as Jenny had hoped he would.

"Doesn't anyone listen anymore? I don't want this here! I didn't order it and I don't want to pay for it. Please!"

This was fast growing into a worst-case scenario, Jenny realized, as tears threatened to stream down her cheeks in front of this rugged stranger. But rather than hightailing it and running off, as she would have done in this situation, he took the groceries from her arms and tilted his head toward the house. Half blind with tears, Jenny fumbled to open the door.

He followed as she stumbled toward the kitchen, his boots clicking on the ceramic tile. While she reached for a box of tissues, he emptied the grocery bags' contents onto the counter and placed them in a tidy row. Then, after a quick look at Jenny's puffy eyes, he took the kettle from the stove, filled it with water, and put it on to heat.

"You don't need to do this," Jenny began, but she was speaking to someone who had decided not to hear. "Stop it! Are you crazy?"

"Got any hot chocolate?"

She was so startled, she answered without thinking. "Cupboard to the right of the sink. But I don't want . . . if you'd just leave . . . oh!" Frustration overwhelmed her, and she finally quit trying to reach this thickheaded deliveryman and gave up in a puddle of tears.

"Good. Marshmallows, too, I see."

And much to Jenny's amazement, the man made her a large mug of cocoa, swimming with marshmallows and a glob of cream from the pressurized can she'd just purchased.

"Now soda crackers." He looked at her expectantly.

"Corner cupboard, bottom shelf." She couldn't help herself. Jenny had never seen anyone take over her home this way except, of course, her two best friends.

He put several crackers beside her cup and said, "Eat up. Drink up. Cocoa for the tears, crackers for the stomach. My mother guarantees it, and her remedy hasn't failed yet." He cracked a small smile, and Jenny got a glimpse of even white teeth.

Then, before she could say anything—either out of gratitude or irritation—he walked out of the kitchen. Moments later she heard the truck roar to life and the crunching of its wheels on her driveway.

Jenny blinked, not even sure this odd circumstance had really happened. Her only proof was a tidy line of groceries on her counter, a mug of chocolate, and a stack of soda crackers. But her tears had stopped, and she was no longer angry about the pile of fertilizer bags on the lawn. Now she was filled only with bone-weary exhaustion and a faint thread of curiosity about the uppity deliveryman from How Does Your Garden Grow? And even that was not enough to keep her from crawling into her usual nest on the living-room couch, pulling a stack of quilts over her head, and falling into a blessed, dreamless sleep. She didn't even notice that Spot claimed the end of the couch by her feet or that he rested his silky head lovingly on her thigh.

Jenny didn't wake until the doorbell, which she'd been dreaming was a chime from a church bell tower, finally annoyed her into consciousness. She kicked away the tangle of blankets, wakening Spot and sending him scurrying as she stumbled toward the front door. To her surprise, it was locked—something she couldn't remember doing.

Then it came to her. The deliveryman, the hot chocolate and crackers—it hadn't been a dream. He'd locked the door behind himself!

It was Libby on the other side, her pretty face wreathed in worry. Farther down the drive, Tia paced the sidewalk like a sleek dark jungle cat.

"You are here!" Relief was evident in Libby's voice. "We called and called, but you didn't answer."

"I was sleeping." *With enough blankets over my head to muffle a monster truck race,* Jenny thought. "Come in."

"We've been so worried. Tia and I were too hard on you today. Please accept our apologies. We had no right to tell you how you should feel or what you should do about it. Grieving is a process. Everyone needs to go through it at his or her own pace. It wasn't fair of us to try to 'jumpstart' you like that. We can't know how you are hurting or what it will take for you to heal." Libby's gentle eyes were regretful. "We were selfish. We just want our Jenny back."

"You'll get her back someday, I hope. And the sooner the better. But you are right. It's my job to work through this. I agree that I haven't been doing a very good job, but hang in there with me, will you?"

Libby embraced Jenny. The tears in her own eyes mirrored those in Jenny's. Then Tia bellowed from the end of the drive. "What on earth is all this stuff doing here? Are you planning to fertilize mainland China?"

Even Jenny had to laugh. "I called a landscape consulting place, and stuff has been arriving ever since. I haven't even seen the landscape architect yet, but his poor deliveryman has gotten the sharp edge of my tongue."

"Ohhh, poor baby. I'll bet he went away bleeding," Tia said sarcastically.

"Actually, I cried and he made me hot chocolate and gave me soda crackers. It's not a bad combination to serve at a pity party. I fell asleep and didn't wake up until I heard you come."

"And where was Cocoa Man all this time?" Tia asked suspiciously.

"Gone. And he locked the door behind him."

"Have you checked the silverware drawer yet?"

"Oh, Tia, do you have to be so suspicious? It's a reputable company."

"That doesn't mean a thing. I hope you didn't exchange your gold earrings for room service."

"Be quiet, Tia," Libby said, speaking more firmly than usual. "Maybe Jenny enjoyed having someone other than us fuss over her."

"Someone with more testosterone, you mean?"

Libby threw her hands in the air in mock surrender. "I give up! You are a cynic to the core. Love will never find you because it knows it will be examined within an inch of its life. Dissected like a fetal pig, poked with pins and little flags saying *heart, soul, ulterior motives, greed.*"

"And I'll be right," Tia said complacently. "While you silly gooses—or is it geeses?—muddle along, following your hearts instead of your brains."

"Now then," Tia said, changing mental tracks with alacrity, "is anyone as hungry as I am? If so, we have sweet and sour pork, egg rolls, shrimp fried rice, and some charmingly inaccurate fortune cookies to share. Are you up to it, Jenny?"

Unexpectedly, Tia let out a bloodcurdling scream. "What was that? Something hairy just brushed against my leg!"

"That's my new dog," Jenny said.

"Since when did you get a dog? And he's big!" Tia's expressive face showed a hilarious range of emotion.

"And sweet." Libby was on the floor, nose to nose with Spot, getting her face washed.

"Don't do that," Tia ordered. "He'll give you worms or something."

"The vet put him on deworming medication. Besides, I read somewhere that a dog's mouth is cleaner than a human's. Do you think it's true?"

Tia threw her hands in the air. "I give up! We can't get you out of this house. You barely eat because you so seldom buy groceries. Your skin is as white as Casper the Friendly Ghost's, and yet you have time to find a dog and take it to the veterinarian?"

"It was an accident, really."

"People usually have those in cars, Jenny."

"He was scared and alone—like me. It just seemed appropriate, that's all."

"Well, I think it's a fine idea and Tia does too. Don't you, Tia?" Libby's words brooked no argument.

"Dandy. Right up there with the pile of fertilizer on your lawn." Tia paused. "Now that I've come to love your new pet, will you wash your hands and join us for dinner?"

To her surprise and that of her friends', Jenny said, "Yes, I will." If Spot could be so grateful for a meal that he carried his bowl almost everywhere he went, then she could be equally gracious.

"It smells good!" Jenny marveled as they set out delicate white fluted plates, chopsticks, and tiny blue-and-white teacups without handles.

"One small step for Jenny, one large step for mankind," Tia intoned as she dished up the plates.

Libby bowed her head for grace. "Dear Lord, praise to you for all the gifts you have given us—friendship, food, and fellowship among them. You know Jenny's heart, Lord. We pray for her emotional healing and for a life that makes sense once again. We don't know what you know, but help us to trust your promise that 'all things work together for good for those who love God.' Amen."

Tia added her own resounding "Amen!"

Neither woman noticed that Jenny did not do the same.

"Fortune cookie?" Libby asked as she dealt them out around the table littered with the remains of their meal.

"Sure." Tia reached across the table and grabbed two. "I love these things."

"Aren't you going to have one, Jenny?" Libby inquired. "I bought a whole package."

"I don't think so." Jenny stared into the bottom of her teacup.

"Are you fading out on us, Jen?"

"No. Maybe. I guess so." She sighed. "Lee and I used to have Chinese takeout at least twice a month."

"Uh-oh," Tia muttered. "Are we taking a trip down memory lane?"

"I know I promised not to dwell on the past, but sometimes it just crops up, the things we shared . . ."

Suddenly Libby stood up and pushed herself away from the

table. Her gentle face firmed with resolve. "I have to apologize in advance for what I'm going to say, because I promised myself I'd never, ever, say it. I believe trying to rush a person through grief is like trying to hurry a woman through pregnancy or menopause. It can't be done. But I also think that there comes a time in either circumstance when a woman needs a little help to move forward.

"I don't have a pitocin drip, estrogen patches, or miraculous pills for stopping the ache of loss, but I do have some thoughts on the subject."

Tia and Jenny stared at their friend. This eruption was as out of character for Libby as tap dancing was for a turtle.

"The way I see it, you have two choices, Jenny. Either you stagnate in this widow mode you're in now, or else you make something of these totally rotten circumstances that have been forced upon you."

"But—," Jenny began.

"No *ifs*, *ands*, or *buts*," Libby countered. "The way I see it, you need to move out of your memories and into your life! Don't get stuck where you are. Come back to us, Jenny. Come back to God."

Tears streamed down Libby's cheeks as she and Jenny clung wordlessly to each other. Tia silently cleared the table and got their coats.

No words were exchanged as the three embraced at the front door because it felt as though every word in the universe had already been put to use.

CHAPTER FOUR

The marigold, that
goes to be wi' the sun
and with him rises weeping.

—SHAKESPEARE

Jenny averted her eyes as she drove by the gas station and car wash three blocks from her house, going instead to a similar facility over a mile away. "Idiot," she muttered, but she didn't take her foot off the gas pedal as she drove by the familiar red, white, and blue building she and Lee had frequented.

She'd changed not only gas stations but also grocery stores, mechanics, bookstores, and dentists since Lee's death four months ago, weeding out one by one each thing that reminded her of the time she and Lee had spent together. She wanted to avoid those mental and emotional triggers that left her in tears at the most inopportune times and the well-meaning, sympathetic questions she was so often asked.

Lee had always taken "car duty," as he'd called it. Since Lee's death, George had washed Jenny's car on the days he did his own. Today, Jenny had decided it was time to do it herself.

Her pocket heavy with quarters, she stared at the soap-wash-rinse-wax options available to her. The machine rejected her first three quarters, and four more cars had formed a line behind her and were idling their engines, waiting for a turn at the power hoses.

"Need help?" A lanky man with a shock of brown hair and a walk that reminded Jenny of the jointed skeletons sold as Halloween decorations ambled up to her.

"It's silly, but my money doesn't seem to work."

"That's the way inflation is these days," the fellow quipped, showing nice teeth and a pleasant smile. "Let me try." The coins clicked into the slot, a light flashed, and he grabbed a hose. "Want me to soap it up for you?"

Jenny shook her head. This was to be her outing, the day's great adventure. "No, I'll do it. I need the experience." The fellow looked at her quizzically and walked back to his car. Jenny could feel his eyes on her as she clumsily managed to get the grime off the largest surfaces of the vehicle. Mud still clung to the underside of the trim and wheel casings when her money ran out, but Jenny got into the car and drove through the blower anyway.

She was still vacuuming the inside of the car when the lanky man reappeared. "I'll bet you don't need any experience with that," he commented.

Jenny looked up with a smile. "No, this is one tool I've used a time or two."

"Almost done?"

"Yes." Jenny hung up the hose and stood back to admire her work, nearly bumping into him as he stood behind her. "Oh! Excuse me." For the first time, she really paid attention to the fellow. He was rather nice looking in a beanpole sort of way, with pleasant, good-natured-looking features. What was he doing following her around the car wash anyway?

The answer was soon in coming.

"That's a pretty good coffee shop over there." He tipped his head in the direction of a colorful little diner.

Finally, Jenny's rusty antenna began to work. "I'm sure it is," she stammered, "but I've got to—"

"Join me for a cup of coffee?"

"Oh, I couldn't." Awkwardness and embarrassment seeped from every pore of her being. How many years had it been since a man had flirted with her? Made a pass?

She saw disappointment in his pale blue eyes and realized how abrupt she'd sounded. "I have a meeting. I'm sorry. Really."

Jenny wasted no time slipping into the car and driving to Tia's store, the only legitimate "meeting" place of which she could think.

"So you came here to *meet* me? I'm not sure that keeps you out of the little-white-lies category, Jen." Tia was sitting over a pile of catalogs sprouting sticky tabs and a legal pad filled with lists of special orders for the store. "Why didn't you just hang around and have coffee with the fellow? That diner has great food. I would have ordered a sweet roll or something if I were you."

"Tia!"

"It's not as ridiculous as it sounds, you know. You are an attractive single woman. Why wouldn't someone be interested in you?"

"I'm married . . ." Jenny's voice trailed away. "Or not."

"That's your problem. You still think of yourself as married. At least you finally took off your wedding ring."

"The diamond was loose," Jenny said defensively. "I'm having it repaired."

"And then putting it into a safety-deposit box, I hope."

"Tia! How can you be so callous?" Jenny rubbed at her forehead.

Tia ignored the question, concentrating on Jenny instead. "Are you having another headache?"

"Yes. Or maybe it's the same one that never quite goes away." Jenny closed her eyes and leaned back in the chair.

"Have you seen a doctor?"

"Yes, but the prescription he gave me doesn't help much. Maybe it's a virus." Jenny scraped her hand through her hair and winced, as if even her touch made her head hurt. "The doctor said I'll feel better once I deal with things."

"And what things are they?" Tia adopted the demeanor of a bulldog or an attorney during a deposition.

"What I should do with my life," Jenny said bitterly. "How I can manage now that I'm a widow and half of me is dead. Little things like that."

"And what to do when a man takes an interest in you?"

"That too, I guess. I certainly got a headache over it."

"Give yourself time. Libby and I have been pressing you too hard. We've made decisions for you and pushed you without allowing you to have input into the equation. I'm sorry for that, Jenny." Tia brushed away a stray strand of blonde hair from Jenny's cheek. "Your friends are novices at this, too. I wish there were someone better than Libby and me to talk to."

Tia looked up as the door chime rang, announcing that someone had entered the store. "Well, well. Ask and you shall receive. Here's Ellen Watson."

The woman who had entered was familiar to Jenny. They attended the same church, although different services. Ellen was only a few years older than Jenny, and her husband had died not many months before Lee.

"Tia, Jenny!" Ellen made a beeline for the two of them. "I'm so glad I've run into you."

"You are?" Tia asked.

"Not you, Tia," Ellen said, a smile softening her words. "But I have been hoping to see Jenny. She's been on my mind for days."

Ellen reached out to touch Jenny's wrist. "I think we need to talk. I know how hard it is to be a new widow. People try so hard to help us, but unless they've walked in our shoes they can't truly understand."

Jenny opened her mouth and closed it again, unable to speak.

"There's fresh coffee in the break room," Tia said. "No one is in there, if you'd like to visit."

Ellen looked to Jenny, who gave a nearly imperceptible nod. Talk? What could anyone say? Still, she followed Ellen into the cozy clutter of empty boxes, chipped coffee cups, and inviting cushioned chairs.

Long-legged and slender, Ellen dropped into a chair and curled her legs beneath her. She skewered Jenny with her gaze. "How are you?"

Jenny licked her lips and averted her eyes. Many people had asked her the same question, but no one until Ellen seemed to know the answer.

"OK. I'm taking it day by day. . . ."

"Come off it, Jenny! It's me. I've been there."

Jenny felt tears stinging behind her eyes. "I'm so lonely, Ellen!"

"And so scared?"

Jenny nodded numbly.

"And wondering how you could feel whole one day and a fragment of a human being the next?"

Jenny blew her nose with a piece of packing tissue she found on the table by her chair. "I don't know why my heart just doesn't stop. I never dreamed anything could hurt so much and still function."

"I know, I know." Ellen didn't try to lecture or to cajole Jenny out of her feelings. Instead, she seemed to submerge herself in the other woman's pain and silently shoulder some of the crushing load.

Silent tears streamed down Ellen's cheeks as Jenny wept.

Finally spent, Jenny looked at the other woman with a wavering smile. "I didn't know I had that many tears left in me."

"Believe me," Ellen said compassionately, "we are a virtual well that never runs dry. I know. I thought I'd come to the bottom a dozen times, and there were always more tears there. It's OK, though. Water is cleansing. Sometimes crying can be a shower for the soul."

Ellen dug in her purse and removed a small book. "I hope you'll read this. Another widow gave it to me after my husband died. It's about grief. It tells you that you aren't crazy just because you and half your friends have decided you are. There are stages in grief, and you aren't going to be able to skip a one before you can go on. Don't be afraid to cry or to be angry or to attempt to bargain with God. It's part of the process. Knowing this helped me to recognize my feelings for what they were—stages—and not places where I had to get stuck."

She scribbled a phone number on the back of one of her deposit slips. "Take this and call me anytime you feel like talking. And I do mean anytime. Day or night. If you get my voice mail, leave a message, and I'll get back to you. Promise me you'll do it?"

Jenny nodded dumbly.

"I mean this, Jenny. Don't hesitate. I know how long the nights can be. They're still that way for me. You'd be doing me a favor if you called."

"Thank you. I don't know what to say. . . ."

"Don't say anything. Just do it." Ellen pressed the phone number into Jenny's palm and squeezed it shut. "I'll be waiting to hear from you." Then, without even stopping to browse through the store, she left.

Jenny stared at the phone number in her palm while Tia made an odd clicking noise with her tongue.

"I knew it!" Tia finally crowed. "I knew he'd send help."

"What are you talking about?"

"God, of course. You say you can't find him these days, but he's still got his eye on you. Why else would Ellen have come in here just as she did, give you her number, and leave again? He sent her!"

Jenny gave her friend a doubtful look. "Be realistic, Tia. Lots of people come through your store. God doesn't send them all!"

"Oh, ye of little faith," Tia intoned. "You just watch. God is working. I believe that with all my heart."

"Fine," Jenny said wearily. "And I believe I should be working, too—on my yard. Before the neighbors ask me to move."

Tia stared after her friend until Jenny disappeared into her car. "Please, God," she whispered. "Help Jenny before we lose her altogether."

....

"Now what?" Jenny snapped as she pulled into the driveway to find it stacked high with branches, leaves, and a large cart full of grass clippings. She hoped George Hardy hadn't taken it upon himself to help her despite her refusal of his offer.

But it wasn't George who sauntered around the corner of her house in tight-fitting jeans, a denim shirt rolled at the elbows, and a red bandanna protruding out of one hip pocket. It was that man again, the one from How Does Your Garden Grow? He pulled the kerchief from his pocket and mopped the sweat from his brow as he squinted toward the driveway and Jenny.

"You again," Jenny said ungraciously.

"Yup. You let this place turn into a jungle." He stuffed the bandanna back into place and hung the thumbs of both hands on his hip pockets. Then he simply looked at her, waiting for a response.

"I've had a lot on my mind."

"Must have."

"Gardening was my husband's love, not mine."

"I can tell."

"But it is looking better since you've come."

"I know."

Jenny threw up her hands in surrender. The fellow was as rooted in her yard as the daisies, which, if left unsupervised, would probably attempt a takeover of the entire neighborhood. "Since you're here, would you like some coffee?" Jenny offered.

"Yes, ma'am."

Inside the house, Jenny poured only one mug of coffee; then looking outside at the sun and remembering the smell of freshly cut grass, she sighed and reached for another cup. "If you can't lick 'em, join 'em," she muttered.

When she returned to the yard, the fellow was seated in the gazebo on an ornate lawn chair meant more for looks than comfort, his long legs stretched out in front of him. He was lean and athletic-looking, Jenny noted as she carried the cups across the yard. So different from Lee, who had been compact and solid. Lee had never sauntered like a saddle-hardened cowboy, as this gardener did with such ease.

It took a moment to dawn on Jenny that it was the first time she'd thought of Lee without a pang in her heart.

"Thanks, Jenny. I mean, ma'am." He reached for the cup, but Jenny held back.

"Jenny? Do we know each other from somewhere?"

"Just a slip of the tongue." He reached again for the mug and was again disappointed.

"Who are you?" she demanded. "Your face looks vaguely familiar—like someone I might have known once. Like someone I haven't seen for a very long time. I can't put my finger on it. . . ."

"Is grade school far enough back for you?" He lunged for the cup and grabbed it before Jenny could withdraw it again.

Suddenly the handsome face morphed into something from her past—a brown-haired, brown-eyed imp with a quirky I'm-up-to-something smile. "Poor Pastor Adams!" she blurted.

Mike Adams choked on his sip of coffee, coughing, and spit it onto the ground. "I haven't seen you for twenty years, and all you can do is feel sorry for my father?"

"You were terrible," Jenny said as a smile grew across her features. She sank into the chair across from Mike, still holding her own mug in her hands. "We all thought the poor man would have a nervous breakdown right in front of the Sunday school class one day because of you." She shook her head with amazement. "So you actually didn't kill yourself before you grew up."

"I wasn't that bad." His coughing had subsided, but there was still a raspy sound to his voice.

"Only boy I ever knew who climbed into the bell tower and hung out the windows until the fire department came."

"Dad overreacted. I knew how to get down." An errant lock of hair tumbled into one eye, and Jenny could see the little boy she'd known then in the grown man's face now. How had she missed it before?

"If I remember correctly, you had a pretty hard time in junior high getting down from the city water tower after you and your friends sprayed it with graffiti."

"A minor problem."

"A broken ankle? Minor? You were on crutches for ages!"

"And it was the best time in my dad's life. He knew where I was or at least that he could catch up with me." A frown marred his tanned features. "Was I so awful as a child?"

"Pretty awful. At least to a little coward like me. You were more daring and more troublesome than anyone else I'd ever met." Jenny couldn't help smiling at the amazement she'd often felt at Mike Adams's daring do. "All the little boys thought you were awesome, if I remember correctly."

"And the little girls?" His voice was husky.

"We all knew you were crazy."

Mike sat back and laughed. "Touché. So did my family. It's not easy being the child of the preacher man, you know. Too many expectations." A troubled shadow whispered across his features, and Jenny sensed that his passion ran deep and strong about that subject. What's more, she instinctively knew that there was pain associated with the topic. Being no stranger to that herself these days, she could identify it instantly in others. Then, just as quickly, his eyes twinkled with the naughtiness that Jenny remembered, and the hurt and resentment in them vanished. "And too many opportunities to shatter them."

Jenny leaned back in her chair and let the sun wash over her frail body. The fingertips of light felt like a healing massage, and the laughter over young Michael had broken open some closed space inside her. She sighed deeply and felt at peace.

He didn't say anything for a long time, more comfortable in the silence than most could be. When Jenny opened her eyes, she found him studying her with an enigmatic expression on his features.

"A penny for your thoughts," she said.

"Oh, they don't come that cheaply. How about a nickel for yours?" He leaned back expectantly, crossed his arms over his chest, and appeared to have arrived for the very purpose of listening to every one of Jenny's musings.

"Mine? They aren't worth anything. My thoughts are like a hamster running on a wheel in its cage—always turning and never getting anywhere. My only goal is to start thinking forward instead of backward, into the past."

"The recent past, I presume."

"You know about my husband, then?"

Mike gave a brief tip of his head. His eyes were steady and compassionate. "You've had a hard time." It was a statement, not a question.

"When Lee died, my dreams died with him." Mike did not speak, and Jenny continued, more to herself than to the man across from her. "Camping trips, filling a pew at church with our family, growing old together."

It surprised Jenny that Mike didn't jump into her soliloquy to give advice, as Tia and Libby and practically everyone else she knew were wont to do. Encouraged by the unexpected silence, Jenny continued. "Everyone thinks I should be 'snapping out of it' by now. I feel like I'm just starting to realize how my life's been changed. My brain's been numb, and everyone's impatience with me only makes things harder."

Still no response, but Jenny sensed Mike listening with his entire body and mind.

"I know it upsets my friends to see me so vague and sad, but I can't work through this at their pace—only mine!"

And without knowing really how or why she did it, Jenny found herself pouring out her deepest, most private thoughts to the silent gardener, the former bad boy, the first person she'd found who actually listened to her fears and her heart-ache.

A horn honking in the driveway across the street brought Jenny back to the world around her. She gasped at the time when she looked at her wristwatch. "I've kept you here an hour and a half! Can that be possible?"

"That's not so long, in the scheme of things," Mike said with a relaxed smile. He appeared ready to stay for the entire day.

"But I've kept you from your work and nearly talked your ear off about—" she flushed—"too many personal things. And I never asked you a thing about your life!"

"Not much to tell."

"But your parents . . ."

"Guess I'd better get back to work, though," he said abruptly. "Hate to have the boss fire me."

With Jenny apologizing profusely, Mike sauntered back to his work. He put out a hand, brushed it lightly across her wrist, and murmured, "Don't be sorry for needing to talk. And don't let anyone tell you that you have to be done mourning on a sched-ule. It will be done when it's done and not before."

He turned his back to Jenny then and went to work, leaving her to find her way to the house feeling confused, yet clearer in her thoughts than she had been in months.

What a very unusual man little Mikey Adams had turned out to be.

Mike relished the soft dirt between his fingers and the warm, earthy scent that arose as he worked in Jenny's flower bed. He never felt closer to God than he did with his hands in the soil and the sun warming his back. It seemed such a privilege to work with God's creation. He smiled slightly at the thought.

Ten years ago, if someone had told him he'd spend his time digging in the dirt and using the time for prayer and praise, he would have laughed in his or her face. Yet now it felt as good and as right as anything in his life ever had—except perhaps these recent days of renewing his acquaintance with Jenny Owens Matthews.

Even as a child, he'd sensed something in Jenny's solid, earnest personality and blonde Scandinavian looks that appealed to him. She was kind to the core. She loved single-mindedly and with devotion, whether someone deserved it or not. And she was loyal to a fault. That was obvious. Tia and Libby were as close to her now as they'd been in grade school. The Best Friends Forever Club, that was them. It was odd that he still remembered, but he'd envied it then, that strong bond of friendship the three girls had had when he'd had no friends at all.

In fact, there were times when friendships—any friendships— had nearly eaten him alive with jealousy and resentment because he'd had none of his own. Mike had blamed his father for that, for demanding so much of him and of his behavior that there was no way he could live up to all that was expected of him.

"Set a standard, Michael," Father had always said. "You're the pastor's son. You have the opportunity to show other young people what it is like to know the Lord."

But he hadn't seen it that way, Mike mused. He'd seen his father's demands as harsh and unbending, too full of rules and too little fun. So he'd done the exact opposite of what his father had asked. He'd set a standard, all right—a standard for bad behavior and rebellion. It had set up a complex and unhappy relationship between them, which lingered to this day. His father still didn't understand him, Mike thought, even though he'd never loved him any less despite the frustration, humiliation, and general embarrassment his son had caused him.

So much for his misspent youth, Mike decided as his thoughts returned to Jenny, Libby, and Tia.

Why had he connected with these three now, after so many years and so much water under the bridge? He stuck a hand spade deep into the soil and turned the earth over. He didn't know what was going on, but one thing he had learned was to allow God to spin out his plans in his own time and way.

"God is never late," Mike muttered to himself. "Then, on the other hand, he's seldom early either."

Indeed, God was a master at the "wait and see/have faith in me" style of living. Mike sighed, dug deep to turn the soil, and watched a long, fat earthworm squirm up from the soil. Carefully he picked it up and put it out of harm's way.

. . . .

"It was so nice of you to have me over," Dorothy was saying, but she didn't look as though things felt all that nice. She turned her cup around and around in nervous hands and picked at the pie Jenny had made.

"We never did see enough of each other," Jenny commented gently. "Perhaps now is the time for our friendship to bloom."

Dorothy looked at Jenny with alarm. "Do you think so? That you and I could be friends?"

"I don't see why not. It's been far too long in coming. We both loved Lee. Why shouldn't we love each other?"

"When you put it that way . . ." Dorothy looked sad. "I've always wanted to be close to you, Jenny. You're so bright and full of life."

Jenny smiled faintly. "That's a description I haven't heard about myself in a long, long time. But thank you."

"It's true."

"Then why didn't we have this discussion years ago?" Jenny was genuinely puzzled. She'd always felt Lee's sister wanted little to do with her. She'd attributed it to Dorothy's busy teaching schedule and the many charitable organizations in which she was involved. Still, it had always hurt. Jenny had always wanted a sister, and the nearest she had to one after marriage didn't seem the least bit interested in her.

"I have an appointment with my attorney this afternoon. I've been neglecting Lee's estate. Dreading, more accurately. But today is the day I face it. One more hurdle to cross."

An indescribable look flickered on Dorothy's features. Was it panic? Fear? Surely not.

Real pain passed over Dorothy's features. "I'd better go. I have a Red Cross meeting in half an hour. Thank you so much for the wonderful pie. I'm sorry I couldn't stay longer."

"It's OK." Jenny could sense that her sister-in-law was uneasy and eager to get away.

After Dorothy had gone, Jenny cleared the table. Dorothy had eaten hardly any of the pie. Something was very wrong, and Jenny had no idea what it was. It felt as though Lee's sister knew something she wasn't willing to share. Was it about Lee? What could it be?

"Ready?" Carla Anthony asked, eyeing Jenny with concern as her client slid into the car. "You look like you are about to pass out in a fit of nerves."

"I thought you were my attorney, not my physician."

"It hardly takes medical school to see you're as white as a sheet. We can call the bank and tell them we'll be late if you need time to compose yourself."

"No, it's fine. I just get a little wobbly whenever I have to do something that seems so final."

"You've been avoiding the necessary paperwork too long. Tia

told me her bookkeeper has been paying your bills ever since Lee's death. Although it's not a problem for a professional to do this, it's time for you to take charge now. You can't have *Lee or Jenny Matthews* on your checks and savings accounts forever. From what you've led me to believe, Lee's estate is very straight-forward since you owned everything jointly. It's easy to change the names on any CDs and bonds. Besides, mortgage rates have dropped substantially in the past few months. It will definitely be worth it to check into refinancing the house."

"Lee always did these things. . . ."

"And now you will. It's been four months since he died. Let's get these formalities taken care of so you can move on."

"Thanks, Carla, for a kick in the pants when I need it. I know you're only here today to hold my hand."

"I called Ed Kirk, the president of your bank, to say we'd be in. He seemed relieved. After all, no one can push the day of reckoning off forever."

Carla swung into the first available parking spot.

Jenny walked woodenly beside her to the bank door, talking more to herself than to her attorney. "Lee was always studying the markets and searching for new investments. He talked about stocks and bonds and commodities like other people talk about the weather. You know we'd held off having children until Lee felt we were financially secure. . . ." Jenny's voice caught in her throat. "It was going to be this year. . . ."

Just inside the bank doors, a receptionist looked up from her desk. "Mrs. Matthews! Hello."

"Hi, Lois. How are you?"

"Same as ever, but I do have a message for you. Mr. Kirk said it might be more comfortable for you and Ms. Anthony to use his office while you look through your safety-deposit box."

"We might as well get on with it." Jenny signed in, gave the key to the woman who minded the vault, and waited for her to open the box.

Ed Kirk was pouring over some papers when they entered. He was a balding man who sported a stomach that could no longer be sucked flat and hound dog–like jowls, which quivered a bit when he smiled.

He jumped up with more agility than one might expect from a man in his physical condition and came around the desk to greet them. "Jenny! So good to see you. How are you?"

"Going day by day," Jenny murmured the pat answer she'd learned to give to everyone who asked that question.

"Good, good." Mr. Kirk appeared slightly ill at ease. After greeting Jenny's attorney, he showed them to a long conference table surrounded by padded chairs. "I thought you might like more privacy. If you'll excuse me, I'll leave you alone to look in the safety-deposit box. I'll be in the conference room next door if you should need anything."

"Very helpful," Carla commented after Kirk pulled the door shut behind him.

Jenny wasn't listening. She was staring into the open metal box.

"Where is everything?" she asked, perplexed.

Carla leaned over her shoulder. "What do you mean?"

"The certificates of deposit we purchased. The bonds my parents have been giving me as gifts since I was a child. And our collection of gold coins!" She picked up a sheet of paper covered with Lee's chicken-scratch handwriting.

Carla lifted the sheet from Jenny's flaccid fingers and scanned it. "This appears to be a list of your assets and their value on the dates they were cashed in."

"Cashed in?" Jenny puzzled. "They couldn't be cashed in. Lee was very specific about waiting until the CDs and bonds were mature. They were our dream home money and what we would need when we started having children. Lee set up a special account for future college funds!"

"Uh-huh. It appears on the inventory. It was cashed last."

"But where did he put it? Where did it go?" Jenny felt totally adrift. Lee had always handled the finances. He was so nitpicky about everything that Jenny rarely questioned him about their savings and investments.

"That's a very good question, Jenny. My first job will be to find out." Carla frowned.

Jenny stared at her, alarmed. "What?"

Carla shook her head. "Nothing really. I was just wondering if this empty box has anything to do with Mr. Kirk's solicitousness."

Jenny leaped to her feet. "Maybe he knows what's going on. Lee could have transferred money to another bank or had a money order cut or . . ."

Carla took a deep breath. "Maybe. I think we'd better ask Ed Kirk back into his office."

When he arrived, Carla held up Lee's inventory of the former contents of the lockbox. "Have you any idea what this is about?"

"I'm not sure it's my place to—" Mr. Kirk glanced at Jenny.

"Mr. Kirk, if you can shed any light on where the contents of my box are, I would greatly appreciate it." The strange currents in the air between her lawyer and banker alarmed Jenny. "What is going on?"

Mr. Kirk linked his hands behind his back and began to pace. His brow furrowed all the way back to the point at which his receding hairline joined the first, thin wisps of covered scalp. "Frankly, I'm not quite sure. As you know, we in the bank aren't privy to what customers keep in their deposit boxes. We did notice a trend about three years ago, however, that began a series of systematic withdrawals from your savings accounts. After those were depleted . . ."

"Depleted?" Jenny felt a cold sweat wash over her.

"Yes. Then Lee cashed in each certificate of deposit as it came due. When they were gone—at least those issued by our bank—he did the same with the bonds, taking whatever their face value was that day."

"Jenny, what name or names were on those CDs?" Carla asked.

"Lee's—and mine, of course. Lee or Jenny Matthews."

"So he could turn them in without your signature?"

"I suppose. But what did it matter? The money was ours. . . ." Her voice trailed away as she realized what her attorney was thinking.

"And the bonds?"

"I added his name when we were married. Jenny or Lee Matthews."

"So it's gone, then?" Carla said to Mr. Kirk.

"From this bank, anyway." He flushed a pale maroon color that did nothing to enhance his plain appearance. "And there is another problem."

Jenny heard a whimper and was shocked to realize it had come from her own lips.

"A balloon payment on a rather large loan is about to come due." Kirk wrote a number on a sheet of paper and pushed it to Carla. Her eyes widened in obvious shock, but she quickly composed herself. "And the house loan, did you carry it here?"

"Yes. Both mortgages." Ed Kirk was looking more miserable by the moment. "Your signature is right there. . . ."

"I signed whatever Lee asked of me." Jenny sounded stunned. "But two mortgages? We had our house almost paid off!"

"At one time, yes. But Lee refinanced once and then took out the second mortgage a few months ago. Surely you knew?" Kirk looked dumbfounded now.

"Lee took care of all the business," Jenny said weakly. "If he asked me to sign something, I just did." She looked at the banker with eyes swimming with tears. "I trusted him, you see."

"But after his death?"

"I couldn't get my teeth brushed, let alone do my business. Tia and my parents decided that it would be best for Tia's book-keeper to pay my bills until I got back on my feet. Dad opened an account for me after the funeral. He told me he'd keep money in my account until the estate was closed and I could pay him back. No one even considered that there wouldn't be any money!"

"Jenny, is it possible that Lee had accounts at other financial institutions? That he was playing with commodities or the stock market?"

"I don't know," she whispered. "I don't know." The man she'd loved and trusted was morphing into a complete stranger.

Carla straightened. "Mr. Kirk, we'll have to do some investigating. On Jenny's behalf, I'd like to have copies of whatever paper trail there is to this money and to the loan and mortgages."

"I'll phone your office when it's ready." Mr. Kirk stood up to help Jenny from her chair. She felt weak and boneless, sapped of whatever mysterious pulse kept humans alive. Surely she should die, her heart just stop, from feeling this way.

But she didn't. Carla drove Jenny's car home and then, from the kitchen, called a taxi. While she waited, she made Jenny a cup of tea and found a few stale cookies in the cupboard.

"You look like your blood sugar has bottomed out." Carla slipped into the chair across from her. "And Lee may have found a way to make an even larger nest egg for you. I have a private investigator who is excellent at these sorts of things. Let's give him a couple of days to check things out."

As if she hadn't heard a thing Carla was saying, Jenny murmured, "But he loved me, and I trusted him."

"I know he did, Jenny, but Lee didn't plan on dying quite yet. Once we figure out what his game plan was, maybe we can all breathe easier. OK?"

Things are far from OK, Jenny thought, but she nodded her head anyway. Staring out the window at Carla's receding taxi, she noticed that Mike had been here today. A basket of impatiens hung from an ornate scrolled stake just near the birdbath, right where she could see it. It was beautiful. Deep pink and lush with blooms, it draped ripely and richly from the edges of its container. Exhausted, confused, fearful from those moments at the bank but touched by the gift of beauty in her yard, Jenny lay down and wept.

She awoke from her nap feeling as though an elephant were standing on her chest. For a moment she couldn't remember why she'd fallen asleep crying. Then it all came back to her in a rush.

What had Lee been doing? What had he been thinking of? Was he crazy? Agitated and unable to expend the negative energy, Jenny cleared the week's collection of clothing off her seldom-used treadmill and climbed on. Punching buttons until she was going at a speed of over four miles an hour, Jenny ran.

She ran until she saw beads of sweat falling from her forehead to the digital panel in front of her. She ran until the soles of her tennis shoes felt warm. She ran until she couldn't run anymore.

Shaky-legged, she made her way to the bathroom and turned the shower on full force. She stood there, willing the sharp bullets of water to wash away the confusion and anger she was experiencing. She stood there until the water heater began to give out and the water started to cool. Then she wrapped herself in towels and lay down on the bed.

Anger was not a familiar or comfortable emotion for Jenny. She had always been a "good girl." She'd been taught well: "If you can't say anything nice, don't say anything at all." But unfamiliar thoughts and words were bubbling inside her like acid. What would God have to say about that?

CHAPTER FIVE

The narcissus bulbs are poisonous,
and there was a time that people believed
their fragrance could cause coma.
It is a flower both lovely and sinister,
a flower with a double life.

Sleep would not come.

Jenny paced the living-room floor until 4 A.M. praying, crying, and even yelling— at Lee, at God, at herself. How could she have been so stupid? Never once had she asked Lee what he was doing with their savings, always assuming that he was a financial wizard and she a simpleton with money, numbers, and figures. Why? Because he had told her so! That was why. It was nothing overt, nothing she considered demeaning. At first, when new money had come into the household, Jenny had enthusiastically asked if it could be used to pay down on the house or invested for the baby she longed to have.

Each time, Lee would sit her down, give her a kiss on the forehead, and say, "You have me to take care of you, sweet Jenny. Don't worry your pretty little head about this. I'm taking care of everything."

Well, he'd certainly done that. "Everything" was missing.

Jenny's attorney, Carla, had been in a big hurry to get back to her office yesterday afternoon to make calls to the private investigator who would help them untangle this mystery. Jenny hadn't felt able to face her friends, knowing that they would read the distress on her features and demand to know what was going on. Jenny wanted to know herself before she tried to explain it to anyone else.

Exhausted, she sprawled on the couch with her feet tangled in an afghan. Loyal Spot lay by her side to watch over her. As she lay there, she berated herself for not paying attention to Lee's investments. She'd been the clever one in school, adept at numbers and accounting. Lee, though he had been less skilled in those areas back then, had always exuded confidence and somehow had convinced her that he should be the one to "look out for the family." It had felt good at the time to be so sheltered and protected, so pampered and loved.

But now Jenny wondered if it were actually pampering or something more sinister—like manipulation and control.

She refused to let that thought go further.

Jenny allowed her answering machine to take her calls most of the day, but when she heard her attorney's voice, she picked up the receiver. "I'm here, Carla."

"Ned—my P.I.—and I have been going over some things. Would you mind if we came over?"

"Now?" Jenny was still in her robe. She hadn't even combed her hair. The day had completely gotten away from her.

"Now."

Because Carla seemed disinclined to take no for an answer, Jenny agreed. "Give me twenty minutes to dash through the shower and put on fresh clothes."

"Fine. See you then."

And Carla was as prompt as her word. Jenny was still zipping her jeans as she hurried to the door. "Come in. As long as you don't mind that I drip dry." Her hair was a mass of damp gold ringlets around her face and shoulders. Without makeup and still glowing from the heat of the shower, Jenny looked fifteen years old.

"Jenny, this is Ned Bradley, private investigator. He and I have worked together on a number of cases, mostly divorce. He's a real pro, and I want you to know I trust him explicitly. Whatever information he's ever given me has been well researched and reliable."

He looked a good deal like her father, with kindly eyes and a sort of rumpled and accessible demeanor that radiated trustworthiness. "Nice to meet you, Jenny." Ned thrust out a huge paw of a hand to engulf Jenny's cool and tiny one.

"He goes to my church, Jenny," Carla said. "Please believe me when I say Ned is a good Christian man who would never, ever want to hurt another person."

Jenny looked at Carla in puzzlement. "Why should I assume he would?"

"May we sit down?"

Jenny, now thoroughly puzzled, led them to the living room. They both declined coffee and sat down on the couch, looking at her with what Jenny could only call "pitying" eyes. "Stop that!" she wanted to scream.

Carla cleared her throat. "This is preliminary, we know, but Ned has followed the paper trail of your money, and it's a short one."

"What does that mean?" Jenny asked. "Short? How? Did Lee switch banks or investment firms?"

"Your money went directly from the bank to the casino, Jenny."

"Casino? What on earth are you talking about? Lee never went to casinos!" This wasn't registering in her mind.

"Are you sure?"

"He would have told me. . . ."

"Like he told you about cashing bonds and CDs? About closing out savings accounts and taking a second mortgage on the house?"

This couldn't be happening. It was too bizarre to be an event in Jenny's well-ordered, secure life. Carla and Ned were wrong. As was the bank . . .

That thought shook Jenny to her core. Ned and Carla were one thing. Bank records were quite another. "You must be mistaken," she pleaded. "Gambling? Lee? That's laughable!"

Ned sighed and reached for the large manila envelope he'd carried into the house. "Casinos always have cameras focused on the playing tables to make sure no cheating occurs. Deer Lake Casino keeps their tapes on file month by month and the oldest tapes are reused first. Another month and these would have been taped over."

He pulled out a series of black-and-white, eight-by-ten photos of a blackjack table and handed them to Jenny. On the first shot, there were five men at the table, all hunched over in intense concentration, peering at their cards. In the next photo, two of the men had left and a woman had joined the group. Three photos later, there was only one man left at the table. It was, without a doubt, Lee.

"He was well known there and at several other casinos," Ned said softly. "He was on a first-name basis with the dealers, which he seemed to enjoy. Several said he acted like a big shot, giving the dealers, especially the female ones, large tips. He sat only at the tables that had a minimum bid of twenty-five dollars and never bet less than a hundred a turn. Some of the dealers said that he'd often fall into a trancelike state, as if drug-induced, and never move. They also said that he was very careful to watch the clock. If things weren't going well, he could pull himself away from the table. But if he were winning, he'd take out his cell phone to call "the little woman." Are you familiar with any calls like that?"

Jenny felt herself turning to stone. They sounded sadly familiar. She remembered many nights when Lee had called saying he
had an important client to take out for dinner. The background
was always noisy, and Lee would tell her he was in the lobby of
some hotel where a banquet or wedding reception was taking
place. The scenario was always the same. A number of times
she'd asked about the restaurant, but Lee was vague, always
saying it was a place chosen by his client.

And she remembered something else. Those nights she had
inevitably fallen asleep alone. When she quizzed Lee in the
morning about the time he had come home, he was predictably
vague. Only once had she awakened when he crawled into bed.
She had not spoken but opened one eye to view the clock. It had
been 6 A.M.

"Jenny?" Carla was shaking Jenny's shoulder, trying to snap
her back to the conversation at hand.

"Yes," Jenny murmured, "I do."

How could she have been so trusting? so foolish? so naive?
Lee, a gambler? It sounded ludicrous, even now, but she knew
why she had overlooked the signs. Because she loved him with
every fiber of her being. Because she was positive that he would
never ever do anything to hurt her. He was too moral, too good,
too . . . New descriptions now seemed more appropriate.
Sneaky? Addicted? Sick? These were strange, unfamiliar adjec-
tives for the man she had loved so unconditionally. For the man
she thought had loved her.

But it was right there on Kodak paper in glossy black and
white. Lee's other life. The one he loved more than he'd loved
her.

But he'd vowed before God to love, honor, and cherish her—
just as she had promised him. The words were still indelibly
imprinted on her memory because she had planned to follow
them for a lifetime.

I take you, Lee, to be my husband from this day forward,

To join with you and share all that is to come,
And I promise to be faithful to you until death parts us.

Was this how it was done? Did being faithful include lying until even Lee probably didn't know truth from fiction? If this was love—gambling away their home, their savings, their life together—then Jenny didn't want any more love.

Carla, seeing Jenny's distress, stood up and went to the kitchen. She came back with a cup of steaming tea and a bag of chocolate chips to offer to Jenny.

Both Ned and Jenny stared at her blankly. Carla gave a small shrug. "Chocolate is my drug of choice. Chips were all she had in the kitchen. When in a pinch, make do."

It was enough to make both Ned and Jenny laugh. Jenny reached for the bag, took a handful of chips, and tossed them into her mouth. When she had washed them down with her tea, a slight bit of color returned to her face. "Is there any chance you are wrong? That Lee put the money somewhere else?"

Ned's eyes were sad. "I suppose there's always a chance. We'll follow up on everything, but I'd say in this case, the chance is about one percent. I'm sorry."

"According to Ned," Carla said, "Lee had been losing big in the months before he died. He'd expressed to several of the dealers that he was holding tight until he won it all back."

"It's all gone then? Everything?"

"Do you have anything listed in your name alone?"

"No. Lee asked me to change everything over, and I did." Her voice caught on a sob. "Because I trusted him."

"How about insurance?" Ned asked.

"We had some. And I don't remember Lee's ever having asked me to sign any papers like that."

"Then perhaps that's your saving grace. Do you have the policies here?"

Jenny nodded. "In my closet. I think Lee must have forgotten I had them."

"Will you let me see them?"

Jenny nodded and slowly made her way up the stairs. With each footstep she felt her heart sink lower. She had been betrayed by the man she loved. Not for another woman—it could have been even worse, she supposed—but still, for another love, a siren whose call was louder, more seductive and alluring than Jenny herself. Gambling. Lying. The sweetness of winning a game of deceit Jenny didn't even realize she was engaged in.

Wondering why her heart just didn't give out, stop under the strain of her torment and misery, she dug for the insurance policies in an old shoe box. What if Lee had known where she'd put these? Would they have disappeared too?

Back downstairs, Carla poured over the documents while Ned and Jenny waited. Half the bag of chocolate chips was gone by the time Carla looked up and announced, "It's small, but it's something."

"What do you mean?"

"Lee didn't have great insurance, but at least it's enough to get you into an apartment and keep you there for a while."

"An apartment? But I have this house."

"*Had* this house, Jenny. It's mortgaged to the hilt. You may have to consider selling it to pay off the mortgages and hope there's some left over to pay off the credit cards."

"Credit cards? I carried the only one we had."

Carla looked sad. "I'm afraid not. Lee had several cards—all maxed out."

"But the bills?"

"They came to a post-office box he opened. He'd used his middle name as his first name and given no other address than the box, so it's full of bills, harassing letters from bill collectors, and more recently, some notifications of legal proceedings."

"But they aren't my bills!"

"But you were his wife. That makes them your bills. We want

to keep your credit record clear if we can. I'll deal with the collection houses. When they hear the circumstances, maybe we can cut a deal."

"But my house!"

"I'm just trying to show you one plan of action. We'll explore all our options. Your bank has a financial planning service available. I talked to Mr. Kirk about it, and he says it's excellent. So gather your household expenses and a couple years of your income tax returns and make a list of your property—cars, vacation homes, whatever. They'll help you fill out a financial statement."

Jenny felt she was being buried under the avalanche of Carla's words, and the blizzard just kept coming.

"And," Carla continued, "I know this is difficult to think about right now, but you will need to find a job."

"But Lee said he didn't want his wife to work outside the home!"

"Lee isn't the master of your life anymore, Jenny. You are. You need to take charge. The fact is, you are nearly broke. You need a job in order to survive."

"But surely there is some money left somewhere!"

Ned cleared his throat. "He wasn't doing it at the time he died, Jenny, but Lee had been kiting checks—paying bills from an empty account and trying to win back the money before the check was processed and returned."

Every time she thought she'd heard it all, there was more. The man she'd loved forever was a stranger, a pretender, two people in one body, a rogue disguised as a husband.

"What else?" she finally asked weakly. Was he a cat burglar too? A con man? A kidnapper? Nothing would surprise her now.

"Isn't that enough?" Carla asked gently. "Can I call someone to stay with you tonight? I don't think you should be alone."

Jenny, knowing that tonight she would have been alone in a crowd of thousands, shook her head.

"How about Libby Morrison? I know you two are close."

"No. Libby stays close to home if she can. Her parents are pretty fragile."

"Anyone else then?"

Jenny gave her Tia's phone number.

While Carla made the call and Ned paced the floor, Jenny sat staring at the carpet she and Lee had picked out together. As she perched there, a coldness grew within her until she felt as though she were frozen to the spot and might remain so until she melted completely with defeat and despair.

When Lee died, loneliness and confusion had overwhelmed her. Now something new had been added to the deadly brew—fear. Life as she'd known it was over. No money, no man, no home, no job, no life at all. Just when she'd thought things couldn't get any worse, they had. Where was God in all of this? Was he testing her? Why? She'd been taught to believe in a loving God. Was it all a lie? Maybe he was only a vengeful God. Or perhaps he didn't exist at all and chaos and anarchy had ruled the world all along and she'd been too gullible to see it.

Jenny didn't move when the doorbell rang later or when Tia came bursting in and was pulled aside by Carla. Jenny didn't listen as the two women whispered in the corner, and she didn't say good-bye when Ned and Carla departed. Nor did she resist when Tia lowered her to the couch and covered her with the comforter from her bed and made a place for herself in the recliner nearby. If sleep came, Jenny didn't know it, for her mind was already numb with apprehension, disappointment, and an emptiness that extended into forever.

"Coffee, sweetie?" were the first words Jenny heard when she opened her eyes.

Libby was standing there with a mug and a plate that contained a flaky croissant and a daub of strawberry jam.

Jenny struggled to sit up. The living room looked as though a slumber party had occurred during the night. She automatically took the food and drink Libby thrust into her hands and held them as though she had no idea what to do with them.

"Carla filled us in so you don't have to explain anything. She also asked that you not be left alone for a while so, whether you like it or not, we've moved in."

"What about your parents, Libby, and your store, Tia?"

"We'll manage."

"I can't let you—" The doorbell broke into her statement.

It was Mike Adams dressed as usual in decrepit work clothes. Today he wore a red bandanna over his forehead tied at the back biker-style.

"I found a leak in the watering system outside and I was wondering . . ."

"You are exactly the person we wanted to see!" Libby grabbed his hand and pulled him inside.

As soon as he saw Jenny rumpled and staring vacantly into the mug held loosely in her hands, he asked, "What's happened?"

Libby drew him aside and, much as Carla had done for Tia the night before, filled him in on yesterday's news. As she spoke, Mike clenched and unclenched his hands until he was white-knuckled with fury.

"She needs company today but Tia and I both have commitments. If you're here anyway, would you mind . . . or maybe I shouldn't ask. Your boss might not approve."

"Of course he would. He's not an idiot." Mike pulled off the leather gloves he was wearing and kicked off his dirt-stained shoes at the mat near the door. "I'll be here all day. It's no problem. Just scram." Mike sat down in the recliner in which Tia had spent the night.

Their strange guardian angel in place, Tia and Libby took their leave, vowing to return as soon as possible.

Mike knew he wasn't welcome by the look on Jenny's face, but he'd learned to ignore problems greater than that. She was obviously angry with her friends for trying to coddle her, but she looked in dire need of some cosseting. The pounds she'd lost had come off not only her body but also her face. Her cheekbones were more angular, defining her beauty in a new and intriguing way. Her skin, pale and perfect as porcelain, didn't look as if it had ever seen the light of day. Odd that grief could bring out such loveliness.

It occurred to Mike that Lee had been a fool for lying, gambling, and whatever other forms of cheating he had engaged in when he had all a man could ever want right under his own roof. Why were men—himself included—so greedy and selfish that, rather than treasure what they already had, they always thought they needed more? He'd fallen into similar traps over the years before he and the Lord had come to terms. Sometimes he literally ached with regret over the women he'd had and hurt, the times he'd chosen self-gratification or the "quick fix" over the high road. "Just human." "Boys will be boys." Excuses, all of them. Only God could show someone what it was to be a real man.

What was that cliché he'd seen written on posters lately? Something about its not being important to have what you want but rather to want what you have.

Lee'd had it all and thrown it away. He must have been a very sick man, driven by demons that no one knew compelled him. It was very sad, a toxic sadness that spread its ripples in vast, unending rings like a stone tossed into a pool of water. How long would Lee's ripples affect Jenny's life?

Mike didn't speak. Neither did Jenny. The old schoolhouse clock Jenny had discovered at a garage sale and refinished to its original beauty ticked loudly in the silence. Jenny slept. Mike dozed. The clock passed noon, then one.

At one-thirty Mike went into the kitchen and Jenny awoke to the sound of dishes clinking and the microwave humming. Then he returned to the living room with two huge bowls of steaming soup and large chunks ripped from a loaf of French bread.

Before she was done eating, Mike took his own bowl to the kitchen and returned with the largest pieces of German chocolate cake Jenny had ever seen.

A weak little laugh bubbled out of her. "What are you trying to do? Fatten me up for slaughter?"

"Libby is a great cook."

"And an even better friend," Jenny added. "She and Tia have put up with a lot lately."

"Isn't that what friends are for? Taking turns at putting up with a lot?"

"I guess." Somehow she found this inane conversation comforting. "Are you my friend too?"

"It appears so."

"Thanks. I need as many as I can get."

"Apparently."

"They told you everything?"

"Most of it."

"How could I have been so stupid? so dumb? so blind?"

"Love. Far as I can tell, it makes everyone stupid."

He'd behaved very stupidly over what he'd thought was love a number of times in his life. Only since he'd found God did he realize that he'd not yet experienced true love—the kind God wanted for him. Thankfully, God didn't give up on sinners, or Mike would already have been history as far as the heavenly world was concerned.

Every time he took a tumble these days, Mike went right to the Bible to the passages about Simon Peter. There was a man who took royal tumbles from grace and was always picked up again by God's divine hand. Simon Peter's rocky path was always a comfort to Mike.

His enigmatic answer made her curious. "Have you ever been married, Mike?"

"No." Then, sensing questions coming that he didn't want to answer, Mike abruptly changed the subject. "Your lawyer called.

She thinks she might have found you a decent apartment in a new low-income housing project."

Jenny looked around her beautiful, sunny living room and felt a surge of empowering righteous anger. "No."

"Stuff happens. You are more than where you live, you know."

"Not much right now. I feel like a bag of rags that have been through the wash one too many times, but I can still fight to save my home. I've not only lost my husband but even the person I thought he was! I've lost my past because what I lived was all a lie. I will not lose my home too. If there is any way at all to fight this, I will." She looked at Mike as if to dare him to argue.

"Awright, attagirl!"

"You mean you don't think I'm crazy?"

"You'd be crazy not to fight. This is a great place." He grinned. "The house isn't much, but the yard is fantastic."

Jenny studied the man across from her. His skin was deeply tanned from his life out-of-doors and his build rangy and athletic, a by-product of his work. He appeared so earthy, so natural, so attractive that it made Jenny uncomfortable. She'd never really considered looking at other men when Lee was alive and now, even though Lee was not the man she'd thought he was, it felt like a hideous betrayal. She averted her eyes.

"What? You don't think the yard is great? What do you want, woman? The Hanging Gardens of Babylon?"

Jenny laughed.

She was almost disappointed when Tia arrived from work three hours early. Where Mike was silent and comfortable as a pillow into which she could sink, Tia was one of those little wooden foot massagers that, although soothing, was also prone to clatter.

"You look better!" Tia said. "Mike, you are a genius. No wonder you're such a good gardener. You truly do have a way with living things."

"Thank you, Tia. I've always wanted to be compared to a philodendron," Jenny retorted.

"And her sense of humor is coming back too." Tia turned to Mike. "What are you doing tomorrow? Dorothy and Ellen both volunteered to come over, but just in case something doesn't work out, maybe you could—"

"Wait a minute!" Jenny protested. "I don't need a string of baby-sitters hovering over me."

"Allow us to do this for our sakes, Jen," Tia said softly. "We were very frightened yesterday. Let us see that you're feeling better. Please?"

Jenny flung her hands in the air. "Paranoia is rampant around here. First I trusted everyone and everything. Now no one believes anyone about anything."

"So you'll humor us?"

"I find very little humor in being babied this way," Jenny muttered, annoyed but relenting.

"Quick, get out of here before she changes her mind," Tia told Mike. "I'll call you if we get into a pinch. And thank you for—"

"My pleasure." And he was gone.

"This is silly," Jenny began.

"This is serious," Tia corrected. "You need us right now, and you're going to get us. In fact, you could even come to live with me."

"No."

"No?" Tia sounded stunned.

"This is my life, and I will learn to deal with it. Besides, I have no intention of leaving this house. It's my home, and I won't be forced out by someone else's bad judgment. I realized something while Mike was here. I was hoodwinked by Lee because I didn't take charge of my own life. I let him run it. I plan to never make that mistake again."

"Wow," Tia breathed. "Mike must have really put some powerful thoughts in your head."

"No. He barely spoke. He allowed me to have my own power-ful thoughts, totally unassisted." Jenny paused. "If you aren't too tired from work, we could go upstairs and start packing Lee's things for Goodwill and the Salvation Army. No use letting them go to waste any longer. Come, Spot," she said to the ever faithful, ever present dog. "Do you want an old shoe to chew on? There are some big ones upstairs."

Puzzled but impressed, Tia followed Jenny up the stairs to banish Lee Matthews from the house.

....

Lee's sister arrived the next morning just as Jenny finished haul-ing the last of Lee's things to the basement. If it were possible, Dorothy looked even more miserable than she had the last time they'd spoken. She'd missed combing a section of her hair, and her makeup was less than expertly applied. Dorothy also looked as if she hadn't had a good night's sleep in a week. The dark circles beneath her eyes were edging toward her cheeks.

Dorothy, who was unusually meticulous in her personal appear-ance, was uncharacteristically thrown together today. She wore a long gathered skirt in need of an iron and a blouse with a stain on the pocket. Since Lee's death, Dorothy had begun stopping by to drop off a casserole, fresh flowers, or a clipping from the news-paper she thought might interest Jenny. She rarely stayed any longer than it took to deliver her gift, but it was more than Jenny had seen Dorothy in the entire year before Lee's death.

"Dot, are you OK?"

"We need to talk, Jenny. Do you have time right now?" The woman rung her hands and looked miserable.

"Of course. Come inside."

Spot's tail thumped happily at the sight of a guest. He was a social dog, and Jenny had come to the conclusion that had Spot been human, he would have been a dandy host.

"I didn't know you had a dog."

Jenny frowned. Surely Dorothy had seen him before. He was always underfoot. Or her sister-in-law had been too distracted to notice.

"He's a love, that's for sure," Jenny said lightly. "I can't believe I didn't have a pet before now, considering how much I enjoy him. Libby says I spoil him, and Tia is trying to get me to buy him an elaborate dog house." She scratched him behind the ear, and he gazed at her with adoring eyes. "Unconditional love is hard to come by, and he offers it."

When Jenny turned to look at her sister-in-law, Dorothy was crying.

"What? Did I say something? I didn't mean to . . ." Jenny was genuinely alarmed.

"It's not you," Dorothy sniffled. "It's me. Oh, Jenny, I've been so unfair to you!"

Jenny guided her to a comfortable chair and sat down across from her. "You've never been unfair. I don't think you have an unfair bone in your body. You are a wonderful teacher with students who love you. Kids know fair when they see it."

Jenny looked at her sister-in-law lovingly, realizing that this was as painful a time for Dorothy as it was for her. Dot had lost a brother, after all. "You are a very honest, straightforward person. I've always respected you for that."

Instead of making Dorothy feel better, Jenny's words seemed to do more damage. As the woman sobbed, Jenny hurried to collect a box of tissues. When the flood of tears finally ceased, a damp, soggy pile of them lay on the living-room carpet.

"Now that you've got that out of your system, can you tell me what's wrong?" Jenny gently held Dorothy's hand. "Maybe I can help you."

It seemed odd to have the tables so completely turned between Dorothy and herself. Lee's sister was always brisk and self-sufficient, whirling in and out of their lives without really making connection. Lee had never encouraged visits, and Dorothy had always seemed disinclined to do so. It was a family thing, Jenny had decided long ago, something between Lee and his sister.

"You won't want to help me when you hear what I've done."

"Dorothy, even though we've not been as close as I might have liked, I care deeply about you. Nothing can change that."

"Then you don't know about my brother."

A chill settled around Jenny at Dorothy's odd tone. "What about him?"

"Jenny, ever since I've known you I've wanted to tell you about my brother, but I didn't dare. I didn't want Lee angry with me. If he was angry, I thought I might never be able to help him. So I kept quiet. Now that he's gone, it's just killing me that I never spoke up. Jenny, Lee was a . . . a . . ."

"A gambler?"

Dorothy looked at her askance. "You knew?"

"Not until I started to settle his estate. He gambled away everything we had." Jenny's voice trembled in spite of herself.

"Oh no," Dorothy groaned, doubling over as if in physical pain. She began rocking back and forth like a lonely child trying to console herself. "I didn't think it would get this far. I should have . . . but I didn't dare . . . oh, I'll never forgive myself."

"Tell me now, Dorothy." Jenny's heart felt like a great bloody wound.

Dorothy closed her eyes to gather her wits about her. "It actually started in his teens. Lee began playing poker with some older boys on our block. My parents never knew. I found out because I was dating one of the boys, and he told me that he was concerned about Lee because he took the game far too seriously.

"Because I didn't understand the addictive personality or the difficulty of breaking a gambling addiction, I thought it was a phase that would pass. In fact, I thought it had done so, until his

freshman college roommate called to tell me Lee was in some
financial trouble over his gambling."

"College? He was doing it in college?" Who was this man she'd
loved?

"Then he quit. At least that's what he said. He was ecstatic. He
was getting married to the girl he'd loved his entire life—you."

Jenny wanted to weep but held back her tears. It was Dorothy's pain they were discussing now.

"Lee told me that loving you had cured him of his addiction.
He said that he felt like a whole man with you, that you were
all he needed." Dorothy looked at Jenny pleadingly. "It was the
truth, Jenny, for a long, long time. Then he started to gamble
again. I knew it was happening again the first time he came to
borrow money from me. I told him no. He got upset and said
he'd find it another way."

"Our savings. The second mortgage on the house."

"If only I'd said something then!" Dorothy moaned. "Between
us perhaps we could have gotten him into treatment. Of course,
he always said his gambling wasn't a problem, that it was enter-
tainment, and that he could quit any time he chose. Oh, Jenny,
I am so sorry!"

Jenny studied her own hands, marveling at how calm she was.
This did not change the facts. Lee was still dead. The money was
still gone. "I never understood your attitude toward me, Dorothy.
It was so . . . hands off."

Dorothy's already pale skin blanched even further. "I didn't
want to lose my brother. Maybe I needed him too much. I've
always wanted Lee's approval. He was so much smarter and
popular than I was that I never wanted to do anything to make
him upset with me. I didn't think I could bear it."

Dorothy wiped the tears from her cheeks and continued. "I
wanted Lee in my life at any cost, Jenny. And the cost was you
and your marriage. Lee made me promise years ago to never tell
our parents or you. It nearly killed me, but I'd given my word.

I had to stay away from you, Jenny. I couldn't love you like I wanted to or it would have all come spilling out. Now I know that is exactly what I should have done, but at the time, I thought I was doing what was best for Lee."

Dorothy looked so stricken that Jenny couldn't help but reach out for her and gather the weeping woman into her arms. They sat together rocking back and forth for a long while.

"It was a sickness, Dorothy, a cancer in his life. You didn't know. How could you? Lee lived much of his life in secret to protect himself."

"Well, it spread," Dorothy said angrily. "Lee couldn't face our parents with it, so he just spent less time with them. And he didn't want to face me because I did know, so he avoided me more and more. He would have been very angry with me if I'd tried to get too close to you, Jenny. It would have scared him. His gambling tainted our entire family."

Dorothy took a deep, teary breath. "And what was so wrong with me that I thought I couldn't live without his approval? I spent my adult life proving to Lee that I could keep his secret, and what good did it do either of us? None."

They wept together then, true sisters for the first time in all the years they'd known one another.

Finally Jenny pulled away and brushed a stray lock of hair from Dorothy's forehead. "You did your best. So did I. What happened to Lee was not our fault. There is nowhere to place blame except on sin. 'When Adam sinned, sin entered the entire human race. Adam's sin brought death, so death spread to everyone, for everyone sinned.'"

"Can you forgive me?"

Jenny almost smiled. "Forgive you? Of course I forgive you, Dorothy. We forgive as we've been forgiven. And I love you. Maybe now we can become the sisters we were meant to be."

As Dorothy wept, Spot jumped onto the footstool beside her and began to lick the tears from her face. It was something he'd done instinctively for Jenny, and the first time it had happened it had been such a surprise that Jenny had burst into laughter. It was not long until Dorothy did the same.

....

Jenny bathed—a long, slow soak that washed away some of the dirtiness she'd felt during Dorothy's visit. When she was done, she watched the water swirl down the drain, imagining that with it went some of Lee's lies and deception.

It was odd, she mused, that one Matthews sibling had been taken from her and another returned to her. She and Dorothy would be friends now, Jenny knew. She harbored no resentment toward Dorothy for keeping Lee's dirty little secret. Dorothy was no more guilty than Jenny herself—for loving someone too much, for trusting too much, for believing another human being could be without flaw. Had Jenny, in some strange way, put Lee between herself and God?

She was barely dressed when the doorbell rang. "Now what?" she muttered. She was going to have a long talk with Tia and Libby about the string of visitors they had not so subtly arranged to drop by when they had other things to do. At least they hadn't hired the gardener to come and pretend to water her indoor plants for the afternoon.

Her irritation lifted when she saw Ellen Watson, her friend from church, at the door.

"Bad time?" Ellen asked as she eyed Jenny's wet hair. "Necessary ablutions?"

"Soaking away frustration," Jenny admitted. Ellen knew much of her story and what she didn't know did not seem to matter. As widows, they seemed able to communicate on a level Jenny's other friends could not.

"You're looking better," Ellen observed. "That deer-in-the-headlights expression seems to have softened somewhat."

"I can't think of a nicer compliment," Jenny murmured wryly. "Iced tea?"

"Love some." Ellen followed her into the kitchen and made herself at home at the stenciled wooden table. "How are you?"

"OK, I guess. I'm still upright and putting one foot in front of the other."

"Robots do that."

Jenny looked at Ellen speculatively. "What do you want me to say?"

"Whatever you'd like—not just what everyone wants to hear." Ellen stirred sugar into her tea and took a long sip. "You're talking to someone who's been there, Jenny. Nothing you say will surprise or scare me."

"I certainly don't plan to scare you!" Jenny protested, puzzled.

"Oh? Then why do you hold back things that you think might scare your other friends?"

Jenny stared at the woman across from her. She was well groomed, with flawless and subtle makeup, Eddie Bauer–catalog casual clothes, and wings of gray at the temples of her short dark hair. "Who says I'm doing that?"

"Me." Ellen looked perfectly calm, sitting there like an older, wiser sister about to tell her younger sibling the facts of life.

"I don't understand," Jenny said, but something stirred deep inside her and hinted that indeed, on another level, she might.

"I just want to tell you that I'm here for you, Jenny, when the uncomfortable thoughts and questions come. I realize that this is premature, but I want you to know that you have someone you can talk to when the time comes. I wish I'd had someone like me."

"I'm sorry, Ellen, but I really don't understand . . ."

"I know you don't know me very well," Ellen continued calmly, "but we are sisters in faith. Over the next months you are going to begin to have some very disquieting thoughts. I just want you to know that they are perfectly normal and that you have a friend who is willing to talk with you about them."

"Do you mean . . . ?"

"You didn't die just because Lee did," Ellen said frankly. "In moments you went from a loving personal relationship with Lee to living in a void. Now, when you need it most, he's not here to hold you, to comfort you. What is it studies say? That we need four hugs to survive and thirteen to thrive? I've probably got the numbers wrong, but I do know we need human touch to thrive. Babies in orphanages can't survive without human contact. Widows are expected to, however."

"Ellen, Lee just died! I'm not thinking about . . ." Jenny stared at her friend.

"I know. But later you might wish for someone to hug you, and I don't want you to feel guilty about it like I did. I felt like I was being unfaithful or decadent. I retreated even further from the people who cared about me. I felt ashamed."

"What did you do?" Ellen's frank words had startled her, but Jenny felt the truth in them, and curiosity overcame her.

"With the help of a counselor, I learned that I was not alone with these feelings. Single Christian women aren't weird or sinful because they have natural human feelings and desires. Once I quit beating myself up over this and rebuilt some of my self-esteem, I felt better."

"But . . ."

"All I'm here to say is that God doesn't make junk. He's more aware of who we are than we ourselves are. And He loves us." Ellen grinned playfully. "And I say hooray for that."

She looked around the room. Jenny was aware of the cobwebs in the corners and a film of dust thick enough to write in on the end table. "Now that I've said that and you know that I'm here to talk with about any feelings a new widow could possibly have, I'm in the mood to do some cleaning. How do you feel about entrusting a rank amateur with your dust cloth?"

"You don't have to. . . ." Jenny was still reeling from Ellen's frankness but experiencing a lightness of spirit just knowing that she had discovered such a loyal and unshockable friend.

"I know I don't. That's why I won't clean unless you help me. If you're anything like I was, I couldn't concentrate on anything after my husband's death, but I could run a mop. I must have washed and waxed my bathroom floor a dozen times."

"You do bathrooms?" Jenny asked with a weak smile. "Why didn't you say so earlier? I'll get a bucket. No, I'll get two." She signaled Ellen to follow her as she led the way to the nearest powder room.

CHAPTER SIX

Saffron, the autumn crocus,
was considered as valuable as jewels
for its medicinal properties.

Proverbs 17:22 says "A cheerful heart is good medicine."

"No, no, a thousand times no!" Jenny crossed her arms over her chest and thrust out her lower jaw defiantly. "I'll chain myself to the bed or the yard lamp before I will allow you to kidnap me again!"

Tia and Libby had literally dragged her to a singles get-together that had turned out to be their most disastrous move yet to get Jenny out of the house.

"I will not go out with you tonight. I will not go bowling with the church group on Saturday. What's more, I will never ever, *ever* go anywhere that you think there might be single men again. It's June. Let me sit in the yard and enjoy the flowers. At least at home, I can spray for pests!"

"Just because you've had a couple bad experiences you want to give up," Tia accused as she collected the dishes from the dinner table and handed them to Libby to wash. "So one guy fell in love at first sight and another turned into a human octopus as soon as you were alone with him. What's the big deal?"

"The big deal is that one was a stalker, the other a pervert."

"Such strong words. Wouldn't *infatuated* and *vigorous* better describe them?"

"Tia, for once, listen to what I have to say. No! I don't want to meet men, and I don't want to date. I'm up to my ears in legal and financial problems, and I can't even decide if I should love my dead husband or despair the day we married." She stuck her hand in the pocket of her jeans and found an antacid to put in her mouth.

"I told Carla I wouldn't move. She and my banker are doing everything they can to consolidate the bills and get my payments down to something I can manage, but without a job, I'm sunk."

"You haven't had time to look for a job," Libby pointed out. "It's not as if you've been rejected by every company in town!"

"True, but I'm less confident than I used to be," Jenny retorted in understatement. "After all, I've discovered that the life I'd lived was a lie. Lee was two people—the one I knew and the one who gambled everything away. Which was the real man? The more I think of it, the more I believe that the secret Lee was the real one."

"There's no way you could know that," Tia said.

"Isn't there? I didn't tell you because I knew you'd try to stop me, but I've driven to those casinos and talked with the pit bosses and dealers."

"You didn't!" Tia and Libby were shocked. Jenny was showing them a new, feistier side than they'd seen in a long while.

"I did. And they knew a person other than the one with whom I lived. The Lee who was a big tipper and a grandiose talker. He acted as though he lived to gamble. In fact, he told one of the dealers he'd like to be a professional gambler one day."

"Huh?" Tia scrunched her nose into an expression of distaste. "Are you sure somebody wasn't pulling your leg?"

"And the Lee that went gambling," Jenny said softly, "left his wedding ring behind."

Stunned silence filled the room.

"You mean he pretended he wasn't married?" Sweet, sheltered Libby was horrified.

"He told people he was single." Jenny's jaw firmed with resolve. "He knew there was no chance my friends or I would ever enter that world, so I suppose he felt perfectly safe in saying those things."

"He didn't . . ." Tia began.

"Step out on me? No. The private investigator checked it out. Lee's mistress was a blackjack table." Jenny leaned back on the couch and sighed. "He lived like he was never going to die, never have me find out or never be accountable to anyone."

Tia and Libby remained helplessly silent. What was there to say?

Suddenly Jenny stood up. Her voice was calm and steady. "I'd like to thank you both for everything you've done and all the time you've spent with me, but I need to get used to the fact that I'm alone now. I can't count on one of you every time something reminds me of Lee. I'm a big girl, and it's time I start behaving like one."

"Jenny, I don't think—"

Jenny continued as if Libby hadn't spoken. "Lee has been gone nearly six months. It's time for me to face my own issues head-on. I want you both to go home and catch up on all those things you've been putting off to baby-sit me. Lee's death and his lies are things I must come to grips with alone." Her tone brooked no argument.

"Are you sure?" Tia asked.

"Positive."

"Will you call if you need help?" Libby asked doubtfully.

"Definitely. Now go."

"Not without a prayer first." Tia reached for Jenny's left hand while Libby grabbed her right. The three stood in a tiny circle as Tia prayed. Tia's and Libby's eyes were closed tight as Tia petitioned for God's help for Jenny to sort out Lee's death.

Because her own petitions seemed to fall on oblivious ears these days, Jenny didn't even try to pray. Instead, she stood still as stone, eyes wide open, staring through the window into the yard, wondering if she should put another flower bed where she could see it from the couch.

....

Silence could be deafening, Jenny decided as she wandered from room to room looking at the photos and painting that had once pleased her. She stopped at the bookcase to stare at the titles of books she had loved and could no more. The furniture, the wallpaper, the carpets—all the things she had thought herself so clever for choosing—looked silly and overdone.

But it was her bedroom that was most painful. It looked bare without Lee's things around—his magazines, slippers, robe, and music tapes—but she needed to store it all to rid herself of the thoughts of his death and the many ways she herself had died with him.

Perhaps she was wrong to think she could do this—to be alone with her thoughts and feelings without the comfort of her friends and the distractions they provided. Jenny went back downstairs and lay down on the couch when the effort of standing seemed too much. She missed Libby's quiet comfort and Tia's benign bossiness. Of course, she still had Spot.

"Come here, fella," she cajoled. The dog catapulted himself to her side and fitted his now sturdy body into the curves of her own and sighed in contentment.

She and Spot spent a lot of time on this couch. It was her little haven inside the house—downy cushions, inviting warmth, an undemanding nest in which to hide. When everything else seemed too overwhelming, Jenny headed for the couch. She eyed the day-old newspaper, the empty yogurt container and crusty spoon, the cold coffee in a travel mug, and realized that she practically lived there, hiding from herself in a nest in the center of her own home.

When the doorbell rang, she thought long and hard about getting up to see who was there. She wouldn't have, if Spot hadn't begun to bark.

It was Mike. "I wasn't sure you'd answer the door," he said matter-of-factly. "Here's an encyclopedia of flowers that I thought you might like to look at."

Jenny accepted it gratefully. She'd watched him from the house for nearly most of this past month, but they had not spoken. It was as if they were hiding from each other in plain view.

"What's up?" he asked as she gestured him into the house and onto a chair in the living room.

"What's down is more like it. Me. I sent Tia and Libby packing, thinking it was time to get on with things. Spot and I have been in hibernation ever since."

"So I see." He eyed the dog, who had returned to the warm spot on the couch Jenny had vacated.

"Maybe you can tell me what's wrong with me," Jenny suggested as she rejoined the dog. "I know Lee is dead. I understand rationally what he did and what he was, but still . . ."

"You can't accept it?" Mike finished for her.

"Everyone tells me what the reality of my situation is, but I don't want it to be that way! I want something different, something more . . . comfortable."

"So you just keep fighting it?"

Jenny looked up sharply. "Fighting? Is that what I'm doing?"

"I think so. Fighting what is. Fighting the facts. And no matter how long or hard you fight, you aren't going to win."

"So then what am I supposed to do?" Jenny asked impatiently. It was annoying how he was able to hit the nail on the head every time they discussed her internal weather, as if he had experienced every one of her very private emotions . . . but perhaps he had.

"Accept things the way they are and get on with it."

"But I don't like . . ."

"Probably not, but what are you going to do about it anyway? You can't bring Lee back. You can't reclaim your investments. All you can do with your past is learn from it. Trust me on this. The education I've had from my past would keep dozens on the straight and narrow."

"What do you mean?"

"No matter how much I rebelled, I was still a preacher's kid saddled with a different set of expectations than those of my friends. Even if my father had never said a word, I still would have had them. I would have imposed them on myself. But because I wasn't smart enough to realize that, I fought the fact that I was a PK by attempting to prove how wild I was.

"I generated all sorts of emotions for my situation. Anger. Resentment. Bitterness. Jealousy. But like I said, fighting reality never gets you anywhere."

Mike stretched lazily, and Jenny noted just how tall he was. "Besides, acceptance of our circumstances, whatever they are, brings peace, Jenny. You've been short on peace lately, haven't you?"

"You could say that," Jenny said, her tone heavy with irony.

"You aren't comfortable with the change in your life, but things are changing anyway, whether you like it or not."

"You've got that right." Something stirred in Jenny, a niggle of hope she hadn't experienced for a long while. "And you think that if I stare reality in the face and say 'Send me your best shot,' that I'd feel better?"

"Can you feel any worse?"

The frustrated gurgling sound that emanated from Jenny made Spot prick his ears and take notice.

Mike chuckled. "Is that a no?"

Jenny grinned in spite of herself. "Logical people annoy me, did you know that? And right now you are very annoying!"

"Then come outside with me and tell me where you want the next flower bed. I suspect you'll suggest one to look at while you lie on the couch." He grinned at Jenny's startled, guilty expression. "But it won't work. When I get it in, I'll have Tia and Libby move the couch so you'll have to stand up to see it."

Jenny followed him outside into the sunshine and felt immediately better. Was she so transparent that he could sense every one of her convoluted thoughts, or did Mike read minds as a hobby? In only minutes, the sun, the fragrance of the flowers, and the soft drone of Mike's voice as he discussed the pros and cons of a bed of perennials lifted her spirits.

Unfortunately, looking reality in the eye and accepting what she saw was a gut-wrenching, painful activity. Any tranquility Jenny might have had vanished when she opened the road atlas Lee always kept by his easy chair and a casino flyer fell out. It was addressed to "Lee Matthews; member, High Rollers Club," and invited him to a free weekend stay, meals and room provided, if he would only visit their gaming tables and use the "free" coupons enclosed. Lee had already filled in the blanks of the application.

She paced the width and breadth of the house on the edge of hyperventilation, muttering to herself. "Look reality in the eye. He was an addict. An addict! Denying it doesn't make it less true. My husband was two different people. It wasn't my fault! There was nothing I could have done. . . ."

Desperate yet determined to do this battle without her friends around to soften the blows, Jenny turned to something she hadn't resorted to in a long while—her Bible.

She opened the Bible and read half the night, frantically thumbing through its pages looking for solace, for comfort, for whatever it was that she had lost with Lee.

"God, are you there? Help me!" she cried out. "Can you hear me? I'm so scared. Lee is gone and I never actually knew him. And you are silent, Lord. Speak to me? Tell me how to find my faith again. I can't go on this way. I'm afraid to live and terrified to die! That doesn't leave me many options, Lord. Show me the way."

She woke up on the couch at 7 A.M. Her body felt stiff and heavy, as if her limbs were weighted with lead. Her throat and eyes were scratchy, and her head pounded with one of the familiar headaches. She couldn't remember falling asleep. All she could remember was praying so frantically, so desperately that she heard herself screaming toward the ceiling of her living room. If God was up there, she decided, he was going to hear her this time. And he must have—because in the early hours of the morning Jenny remembered a peace blanketing her that could not be explained, a silent voice telling her it was time to quit fighting, to rest, and to trust. Then the healthy heaviness of her eyelids and weariness of her limbs pressed on her until she could no longer stay awake. Sleep was a welcome guest.

Now Jenny slowly she made her way into the shower, avoiding a look in the mirror as she passed.

Hair still lank with moisture and hanging heavily around her face, Jenny wrapped a terry-cloth robe around her and secured it with a belt. Then she sat down on the bed and held her head in her hands.

She couldn't go on like this. But what could she do? Run away? With what money? Hide? From whom—herself? Where? Lee had taken the easy way out, she decided. He had died.

The power of that thought struck her just as the doorbell rang. Trembling and drunk with exhaustion, she pulled on a sweat suit and crept down the stairs to open the door.

"What happened to you?" were Mike's first blunt words. "I've seen drowned rats that look better than you do right now."

"Nice to see you too." Jenny tried to shut the door in his face, but Mike would have none of that. He put one large booted foot in the doorway and pushed past Jenny as if she weren't even there. She'd become accustomed to his comings and goings around her place. In some ways he moved in and out of her life as much as Tia and Libby did.

She followed him into the kitchen to give him a piece of whatever mind she had left and found him making coffee.

"Sit down," he ordered.

Without a word, Mike found eggs and bacon in the refrigerator. While the bacon was frying, he put wheat bread in the toaster and poured orange juice into two tumblers.

He was wearing jeans—newer this time—and a white T-shirt under a faded denim shirt. His wallet made a squarish form in the hip pocket of his jeans. Jenny had not realized before how powerfully built he was or how graceful. He moved around the kitchen like a big jungle cat, all muscle and determination. She chewed on a piece of the toast he'd covered in butter, sugar, and cinnamon as she watched him.

"Drink this." The coffee was giving off wisps of steam and smelled rather inviting now that she had something in her stomach. She inhaled deeply before she put her lips to the cup.

"What happened last night?" Mike asked. His voice was gentler now that she had eaten and some color had returned to her cheeks.

"Why should something have happened?"

"Knock it off, Jenny. Remember me? The biggest fibber ever known to grace the presence of Wood Glen Church Sunday School. It takes one to know one."

"You were rather good at it," Jenny said in an attempt to divert his attention. "I remember the time you insisted you had swollen glands and gave half the Sunday school the mumps. Or the time you told everyone your mother was pregnant when, of course, she wasn't. Your father loved that one!"

"Don't try to distract me," Mike said with a slight smile. "If I appeared attention deficit then, I'm much more focused now."

"I spent the evening alone. Spot and me. Just like you left us."

"Then the healing has begun."

He took a straight-backed chair and pulled it close to her— closer than he'd ever been before. She could see what would become a five-o'clock shadow beneath his smoothly shaved skin and the little bronze flecks in his eyes. His lashes were thick and dark. When he studied her from beneath those half-closed lids, she felt oddly exposed, as though he were x-raying her heart. Spot's warm body next to hers and his hot breath on her arm were soothing to her tumultuous senses.

"I don't feel much like I'm healing, Mike. I'm still just like a big raw wound that gets deeper and more infected every day. I feel so weak and so faithless sometimes." She couldn't explain the previous night to him because she couldn't understand it herself—not yet, anyway.

"Feels like God went on an extended vacation and left you behind, huh?"

She was startled by his perceptiveness. "You understand."

"Yes. And like everything else in my life, I learned the hard way."

Even in her state of mind, Jenny had to smile at that. "What did you do?"

"To get back to God, you mean?"

She nodded solemnly.

"First I got mad. Swore off God forever. Decided that anyone who asked that much of a person wasn't worth the trouble. Besides, I didn't feel like he was doing anything to help me. *What kind of God would leave me in a lurch?* I thought. I decided that my dad had been deluded all those years he preached. That he'd messed up my life with unreasonable demands for a deity that, if he did exist, was totally unreasonable and completely disconnected from humanity. Then something happened that gave me some insight about God and myself."

"And that was?"

"Dad's congregation was building a new church. A huge thing with a pointed steeple that went straight up into the sky and could be seen for miles. On top of the steeple there was to be a cross, a lighted beacon for lost sinners and unbelievers." Mike grinned a little shamefacedly. "Like me."

Jenny leaned forward expectantly.

"I just happened to be hanging around the day they were raising that cross to the top of the steeple. It was huge; it must have been eight or ten feet tall. I stood next to it and felt dwarfed. My dad still has a picture of that somewhere. Then the crane started lifting it to the top of the steeple. Higher and higher it went until it reached the top. And do you know what?"

"No," Jenny breathed, rapt.

"The higher that cross got, the smaller it got until it looked like a toy in the sky." He paused and drew a breath. "That's when I realized how to get back to God."

He laughed at the puzzlement on her face before continuing. "You see, I knew that cross was huge. I'd seen it. I'd felt it with my own hands. I'd taken a photo of my dad standing by it with a big grin on his face. I knew for certain that it was gigantic, but when it moved away from me it got smaller and smaller. All of a sudden it hit me that, unlike that cross, God doesn't move. And if he hadn't moved, then it meant I had. Basically, once I figured out who was doing the moving and who wasn't, I moved back."

"How?"

"For one thing, I talked to people who understood my experience."

"I have Tia and Libby." Jenny hesitated to add, "and you."

"Sometimes to really understand something, you have to have experienced it yourself or been trained to deal with those experiences."

"You went to a counselor? Macho you?"

Mike grinned. "Even us thick-headed Neanderthals sometimes have a warm and mushy spot, you know."

"I'm sorry, that's not what I meant."

"Sure you did, but that's OK. I just happened to have an old school buddy who became a Christian counselor."

"Counseling? How would I pay for it? What would I say? 'Do you deal with a lot of wives of dead men who had split personalities and problems with compulsive gambling and lying?' I'll bet there are a lot of those lurking around. And while you are at it, can you find me a financial counselor too?"

Mike looked at her with one dark eyebrow lifted. "Hey, lady, you asked."

Jenny sighed and flung herself backward against the chair. "I did. I'm sorry. I should be thanking you, not—"

"Forget it." He glanced at his watch. "Have you heard from Tia or Libby yet?"

"What makes you think I will?" It was aggravating how right he was all the time.

He just gave her a disgusted look that reminded her of him as a small boy. Mike Adams hadn't been anyone to mess with then, and he certainly wasn't now.

"I can guarantee that one of them will be calling me soon." A phone rang in the distance. "See?"

"I should have known." He grinned. "You are blessed, Jenny, with great friends." Then he slapped the palms of his hands on the tops of his thighs and stood up. "I've got a job out of town today."

"Go. Play in the dirt. Have fun." Jenny stood up to get the phone. "And thanks again."

. . . .

She tried so hard to be brave. Mike was glad she had her faithful human watchdogs as well as Spot to care for and about her. He had three yard estimates to do and he'd put them off too long already. He didn't quite trust her, but it wasn't his place to intrude any more than he already had. Still, he worried. Jenny's vulnerability and despair—combined with fear, loneliness, and disappointment—were a poisonous combination.

He'd walked his own tightrope of failure and depression and knew what a grip it could maintain once its bloody claws were in you. His own failings were still painfully with him—he was reminded of them every day. But there was the one reminder who had turned into his most beautiful little gift, Mike mused. Luke.

Mike gave thanks every day for the hard times as well as the good ones because he'd learned that while one was going through them, it was sometimes difficult to know in the long run which would be which.

He guessed he'd have to do more praying about his patience— or lack of it—too. Though his impatience had gotten him into trouble before, he obviously hadn't learned from it. He'd lumbered right into Jenny's situation without a second thought even though rescuing damsels in distress was certainly not his forte.

He'd meddled too much already but it was difficult to stay away. He'd told himself he'd do some yard work, renew old acquaintances, and see what happened. He hadn't dared hope he would care this much about Jenny. She brought out every good and right feeling in him. He'd not expected that to happen to him—not now, maybe not ever. While one part of his mind told him to leave this situation, there were whisperings in his heart that said otherwise.

"Blast it all anyway!" he muttered as he left. What made him think his heart was right? The only woman he would accept these days was one sent expressly by God for him. Would a beautiful but sad little widow with financial problems and more spirit than experience be the one? It seemed quite unlikely.

Of course, God seemed to enjoy the unlikely. His Son was born in a manger. Christ's mother was a teenage virgin; and Joseph, her husband, a carpenter, had to make sense of his unexpectedly and uniquely pregnant wife. Yes, indeed, God cherished the unlikely and the flawed and the outcast. That meant that Mike, in spite of his fear of being hurt or disappointed, needed to keep his mind open. God's certainly was.

· ·

Dorothy arrived not long after Mike had departed clutching a bulging shopping bag.

"What's up?" Jenny greeted her at the door.

"I've been cleaning cupboards. Ritual shedding, I call it. I came across kits of every kind—counted cross-stitch, needlepoint, crewel, tatting, hardanger—everything. Some are started, others are not. I wondered if you'd be interested in any of the kits." Dorothy looked at her hopefully. "Or perhaps just sitting and working on one with me?"

"That might be nice." Jenny wasn't totally enamored of the idea, but it would be something to do.

"I need to keep busy," Dorothy admitted. "And if we could keep busy together . . ."

Jenny saw Dorothy's hopeful expression and knew how hard her sister-in-law was trying to make up for lost time, to right the wrongs she felt she'd committed, to become friends.

"I'll take a couple of those kits if you'll come up to my closet with me and try on some of my clothes. I've lost so much weight that some of them just hang on me. We used to be the same size. Maybe you can find an outfit or two."

Dorothy's eager assent sent a pang through Jenny's heart. Here was someone as lonesome and miserable as she. *The Three Musketeers,* Jenny thought. Dorothy, Spot, and Jenny. Three lonely souls bonding together for support. Then Spot gave a gentle *woof* and Jenny mentally chastised herself for the negative assessment.

Who knew what turn life would take next? Perhaps they were

the seed for a beautiful garden of friends she couldn't yet imagine. She took Dorothy's hand and led her upstairs to the bedroom closet.

"How's this?" Dorothy pivoted in front of the mirror in a tailored navy suit that looked as though it had been made expressly for her.

"Great. Take it. Now try this on." Jenny held out a white sundress.

"I can't. You've given me too much already. What will you wear?"

"What I've always worn. Jeans. T-shirts. Cargo shorts. I'm not sure why I bothered with all these clothes to begin with. I only dressed up for church functions or an evening out with Lee." Jenny threw a pair of shoes into Dorothy's box of clothes. "And please, take these. I can't stand high heels anymore!"

Dorothy looked at her strangely, as if to say, "Well, duh . . ." "Jenny, you're changing. In good ways, I mean. You're back to basics. Real. Sometimes I thought you lived your life only to please my brother. Now I see that you are learning to please yourself as well. That's good. I've always liked the real you."

"I didn't know . . . ," Jenny whispered.

"I didn't either. I see the change now, in retrospect." Dorothy chewed on her lip for a moment before continuing. "When we live with deception, sometimes we learn to deceive ourselves as well. When we live with sickness or sin, we change to accommodate the sickness or the sin.

"We know my brother was sick. Now it's time for us to get well."

Jenny didn't argue. Similar thoughts had crossed her mind, but she'd willed herself not to voice them. It was still difficult to admit how deeply the cancer of Lee's lies had eaten into their lives.

"You came at just the right time," Jenny admitted slowly. "Yesterday I started going through Lee's books. Then, because that was so difficult, I decided to clean the medicine cabinet."

"And?" Dorothy sounded surprised at the abrupt switch in subjects.

"I found something there I didn't expect. I found a bottle stuck into the far corner of the cabinet and partially obscured by other bottles. 'Take one to three per day as needed for anxiety,' the directions said. I didn't know Lee suffered from anxiety."

"You didn't know he'd squandered all your money either," Dorothy said bluntly. "He had good reason to be anxious."

"He must have been in so much pain," Jenny said softly. "If only he'd trusted us to help him. . . ."

"But he didn't. Please don't beat yourself up thinking of what might have been. They were Lee's choices, not yours. You can't help someone who doesn't think he needs help—or, worse yet, thinks you are to blame for his problems."

Jenny smiled faintly. "Look reality square in the eye, right?"

"And win the stare-down," Dorothy added.

Jenny clapped her hands together and stood up. "All this purging of clothes and emotions has made me very hungry. Libby left a coffee cake in my freezer. Why don't I make tea and see if Ellen or Libby can join us?"

Dorothy's eyes brightened, and Jenny realized just how lonely she must have been these past weeks, blaming herself for not speaking up and for facilitating her brother's problems. An unexpected surge of gratitude bled through Jenny. Here was someone who needed her—Jenny—to rely on. It felt better to give comfort than to receive it. Jenny knew instinctively that as she helped Dorothy to heal, she, too, would benefit from the balm of love.

"More coffee cake, Ellen?" Jenny asked after Dorothy and Libby had left.

"Are you kidding? We ate the entire thing except for that one little piece!" Ellen leaned back in her chair and undid the top button of her slacks. "I'm stuffed."

"OK. Then here goes." Jenny put the plate on the floor, and Spot's pink tongue darted out to finish the last piece.

"He didn't even taste it!" Ellen observed. "I, at least, chew when I pig out!" She studied Jenny for a moment before asking, "How's it going?"

"Two steps forward, one back. Some days it's two steps back and one forward. You know how it is."

"I do. That's why I'm going to bring up something that you may or may not like."

"More helpful advice?" Jenny moaned. "I've had enough already to write a book!"

"Then stick this in your chapter called 'Sensible Things You Do for Yourself' and subtitle it 'Finding Yourself Professional Help.'"

"Do you think that's really necessary?" Jenny asked, surprised. "After all, I have you, Tia, and Libby. . . ."

"And we are all so personally involved with you that we can't see the forest for the trees," Ellen said bluntly. "You need a clear-headed Christian professional who will listen to every word you say and not pass judgment or try to 'fix' you. You need someone who can help you fix yourself. That's something else I learned after my husband died. I could have gotten along without help, but seeking it out made my journey so much easier. Give yourself all the breaks you can."

Ellen reached into her pocket and pulled out a business card. "This woman did a lot for me. I think she can help you too."

Jenny studied first the card, then her friend. "You really call things like they are, don't you, Ellen? No beating around the bush for you."

Ellen grinned. "Life's too short not to celebrate it, Jenny. Time in the valleys can lead to peak experiences you never imagined. My theory is to get through those valleys as quickly and efficiently as you can so that you have plenty of time to enjoy the mountain-tops." She put her hand on Jenny's. "Will you give this a try?"

Much to her surprise, Jenny felt herself nodding.

. . . .

"So how was your counseling session today?" Libby asked brightly. "I am so glad you visited with Ellen and that she encouraged you to see someone."

"It was fine. Ellen was right. Talking helps." Jenny said. She was preparing a casserole for dinner for herself and her two friends. It had been a long time since she'd felt like cooking, so the counseling must be doing some good even if she and the gentle, soft-spoken Christian woman she met with had not yet reached the true crux of the matter.

But Jenny knew. The realization had been forming in her mind for a long time. All her anxiety and fear could be boiled down to one simple, unexpected issue: She was afraid to die.

For her entire life since the time she was eight years old, Jenny had known she was going to heaven. She'd accepted Christ as her personal Savior and trusted in his promises. Until now.

These days she didn't know what to believe. She'd lost God. She'd moved away from him in the very same way Mike had talked about himself and that cross atop the church. If God hadn't moved, then Jenny knew she'd traveled many miles in the wrong direction and she needed to get back from where she'd gone. Soon.

While Jenny's thoughts were on the meanings of life, death, and eternity, Libby's were slightly more mundane.

"Have you thought about the weekend yet?" Libby asked. "I need to get things organized at home if we're going to be gone."

Jenny realigned herself with Libby's thought processes. "To your family cabin?"

"No, our little jaunt to Mars! Of course, the cabin! Where's your mind?" Libby hesitated. "Don't answer that question. I don't think I want to know."

Jenny smiled. "Actually, believe it or not, the counseling is helping."

"I won't believe it until I see you acting like your old self every moment. Here's your opportunity. Remember all the good times we had there when we were kids? Swimming out to the pontoon and lazing in the sun? Making S'mores out of graham crackers and marshmallows? Staying up late and sleeping till noon?"

"Those were good old days," Jenny agreed. Some of the trio's best summer weekends had been spent in that old cabin.

"Then the trip is on?"

"It will be a lot of work."

"Don't you remember how delicious food tastes in mountain air? Or how cold and fresh the spring water is? And the scenery—"

"OK! We'll go! I can't stand all this pressure."

Libby stood up and whooped, kicking her legs and waving her arms as she did so.

"Now what's that all about?" Jenny asked when she could quit giggling.

"A dance of joy, of course! Oh, Jen, we're going to have so much fun. You'll see. You'll come home a new woman!"

"Good," Jenny muttered under her breath. "'Cause I'm not crazy about the old one these days."

CHAPTER SEVEN

In A.D. 493 Clovis I, King of the Franks,
was advised by his Christian wife Clotilda
to redesign his battle flag to three yellow irises,
which symbolized faith, wisdom and valor.

"You look like Meriwether Lewis on the Lewis and Clark trail," Tia commented to Libby as she trundled up the wide front steps of the Morrison's rustic log cabin in Minnesota's north woods.

It was a splendid day for early August. The leaves of maple and oak would soon be a heady riot of color. But not yet. Sunlight glanced off the glistening leaves and made them shimmer with every shade of green.

"What part of old Meriwether?" Jenny asked. She was also loaded with supplies and bedding. "Is it the beard and mustache or the leather clothing?"

"Libby has been looking a bit hirsute," Tia acknowledged. "Have you tried any depilatories lately?"

"Ho, ho, ho." Libby was not amused.

"Maybe you are right, Libby," Jenny rejoined. "I don't think it's Meriwether Lewis at all. It's Santa Claus!"

"And all this time I wished you'd get your sense of humor

back," Libby groused without rancor. "Be careful what you wish for. You might get it! You two are ganging up on me."

"You are the one who told us we'd need all this junk for a weekend up here."

"It's better to be safe than sorry," Libby parroted piously.

"Libby, that's the story of your life! Miss Cautious personified. Don't you ever wonder what it would be like to live a little?"

"Like you, Tia? Work twenty hours a day, fly off to market, come home without ever having seen anything of the city you're in but what's outside the cab window?"

"Who cares what's outside a window in the city? This is the scenery that counts! Why haven't we been up here for an entire year? Less than three hours from Minneapolis and we're in a brand-new world. It's not even noon and there is no traffic, no road rage, no people driving eighty miles an hour with a cell phone in one hand and a burger in the other—"

"Girls, girls," Jenny chastised. "You promised me a fun weekend, remember?"

"I'm having fun. Aren't you, Libby?"

"Sure. Now if I can only get this door open . . . oh my!" Libby dropped her baggage on the deck and stared at the interior of the cabin in horror. "I know we haven't been up here for a while but—"

"Let's see." Tia and Jenny pressed close to peer over Libby's shoulders.

An eruption had occurred inside—an eruption of down and feathers, of pillow and furniture stuffing, of just about everything that could be chewed by rodent teeth.

Tia screamed as a sparrow dive-bombed through the door within inches of her head. Jenny turned to say something to her, and her face went through a series of expressions—alarm, concern, shock, and then glee. As Jenny giggled and pointed at Tia, Libby's features expressed the same changes.

Puzzled, Tia asked, "What are you two laughing about? That bird nearly took my ear off!"

Libby leaned against the cabin and crumpled slowly to the deck as though her legs could no longer hold her. Jenny dropped to her knees and laughed until she cried.

"What? What! Snap out of it, both of you!"

Jenny lifted a weak arm and pointed toward Tia's shoulder. "Your . . . jacket!"

"What about it?"

"The . . . the bird!" Jenny literally howled with laughter at Tia's dawning realization. She glanced at her shoulder to see the warm spread of bird droppings sliding down her arm.

Tia gave an earsplitting shriek and tore at the jacket until it came off. Then she threw it as hard as she could into the nearby shrubs.

Jenny and Libby howled even louder as Tia went though a series of shudders and tremors of disgust. Finally Jenny lay on her back on the deck, weak and spent from laughing.

"I have never laughed so hard in my life," she finally choked. "The look on your face, Tia!"

"So glad I could entertain you," Tia said with a grimace. "How gross!"

"But how wonderful!" Libby responded.

"Wonderful? Excuse me, but that was a very expensive jacket. And now it's covered with bird poop!"

"Oh, chill out," Libby said, still chuckling. "Do you realize this is the first time I've heard Jenny laugh in ages?"

The object of her comment was still lying on the deck hiccuping and giggling and wiping tears from her eyes. "That was just too funny. Oh! My sides hurt!"

"You'll get over it," Tia said as she took Jenny's hands and jerked her to her feet. Then Tia smiled. "And although I may not sound like it at the moment, I'm delighted to have been involved in whatever makes you laugh."

"It felt good," Jenny admitted. "I thought I'd forgotten how."

"If you get that much enjoyment out of bird droppings, you

will have a heyday with the destruction mice have done," Libby predicted. "I just looked. Every drawer and cupboard is full of their nesting material. We're going to have to clean this cabin from top to bottom and set traps before I'll be able to sleep."

"Fun," Tia muttered. "That's what you said we'd have. Nobody said anything about slave labor."

By nine o'clock that evening they'd banished every bit of debris and had scrubbed the small cabin from top to bottom. Libby had even hung out the laundered curtains and had washed windows.

"I'm whipped," Tia announced. "Time to light the fire."

Before Libby could protest, Tia struck a match to the twigs and rolled newspaper she'd carefully crafted in the fireplace. The paper burned quickly, and the twigs, being very dry, soon began to crackle and pop.

"I'm not sure that's such a good idea," Libby began, but it was already too late. Smoke was curling back into the room, and black soot fell from inside the chimney. Tia screamed another bloodcurdling shriek and Jenny, who'd been nearly asleep on the couch, opened her eyes to see Tia covered with soot. Laughter bubbled up inside her again.

Libby hurried to the fireplace to sprinkle some crystals from a can onto the fire. "Dad said to use this right away to burn the soot and debris out of the chimney. We haven't had a chimney sweep up here in years."

"You do now," Jenny giggled. Tia's face was nearly as black as her hair, and her pristine white turtleneck sweater was a hideous shade of gray.

"All right, I give up! Tell me what to do next. Fall into the creek? Be mauled by a bear? Bitten by a poisonous snake? Carried off by a pterodactyl?" Tia flung herself backward onto a chair, only to have it cave in beneath her.

It felt good, Jenny thought, to be the comforter rather than the comforted. By the time she and Libby cajoled Tia through the icy outdoor shower and into her pajamas, she had finally quit muttering to herself.

"I'm hungry," Tia whined. "Did we eat today?"

"Not since lunch at two. I'll find something for a snack."

While Libby was preparing a simple meal on the camp stove, Jenny went outside to look at the stars. They were so much brighter here without the lights of a city of three million to dull them. The constellations were easy to pick out on their inky bed of sky. Jenny greedily breathed the fresh clean air and felt a peace inside herself that she hadn't had for a very long time.

It took her a moment to realize what the difference was. She actually felt God here in the perfection around her. Jenny's heart stirred and she tried to listen, to hear his voice inside her mind, to discover what wedge inside her had so distanced herself from him.

The screen door slammed and Libby came onto the porch. "Soup's on. Corn chowder, actually. With breadsticks and veggies. It's not so heavy we won't be able to sleep."

Vaguely disappointed by the interruption just when something important was forming in her mind, Jenny turned to her friend. "You were right, Libby. It was a good thing to come here. I feel . . . real . . . for the first time in ages."

Libby said nothing, but gave Jenny a hug so emotion filled that words were unnecessary. "Come inside," she said finally. "Or Tia will think we abandoned her to nature and left her to die."

Jenny giggled. "What's been bad for Tia has certainly been good for me. My sides still ache from laughing."

"Fine. Just don't mention it to Tia. She's a little touchy right now."

"The fireplace incident didn't help, coming as it did right after the bird droppings. Plus, there seems to be something wrong with the oscillating fan, so we'll be plenty warm in our beds tonight."

"Uh-oh. Like *real* campers do it?"

"As opposed to campers like Tia, who think that staying at a discount motel is roughing it? Yes, indeed."

"I do feel sorry for Tia, but it is refreshing to have someone whining more than me for a while." Jenny gave Libby a hug. "I've been having such a pity party for myself that I've not thought nearly enough about how dear you and Tia have been to me."

"Our turns will come," Libby said softly. "And you will have to be strong for us." Her face lit up. "We've always worked together for the good of the group. We've done it for years and hardly realized it was happening. Now we are just more conscious of it, that's all."

Jenny hugged Libby again. "Best Friends Forever, right?"

"You've got it, lady. And BFFs are mighty hard to shake!"

The two walked inside linked arm in arm to find Tia madly rummaging through their supplies. "I know I packed it. I just know it. It was on the top of my list, so where could it be?"

"What are you looking for?" Jenny asked as Tia grew more frantic.

"The toilet paper!"

"I told you we didn't have any up here!" Libby moaned. "You're supposed to be the organized one, or I would have brought it myself!"

"It must still be on the counter at home." Tia closed her eyes. "I can see it sitting there by the canisters. But I was positive I put it with the—" new dismay etched her features—"the distilled water to wash my hair."

"No water either?" Libby sighed. "Then we'll just have to make do."

"But the water up here is so filled with minerals. Do you know what it will do to my hair?"

"Then don't wash it," Libby said. "It's still fine for drinking. We can get lake water to prime the pump."

"And we can use old catalogs and magazines for toilet paper,"

Jenny added. "Would you like *Newsweek, Good Housekeeping,* or the *Wall Street Journal?*"

"Augh!" Tia flopped onto the couch and held her head in her hands.

Libby and Jenny looked at each other and shrugged their shoulders. Then Libby announced, "I think it's time to pray."

"For toilet paper?" Tia's voice was muffled in her hands.

"No. For all the things we do have." Libby took Jenny's hand and reached for Tia's. When they had formed a tiny circle, Libby began. "Dear Lord, thank you for the many blessings you have bestowed on us. Sometimes we forget what's good in our lives and focus only on the bad. We'd like to thank you for all those things we so often take for granted—for friends and family, for wholesome, nourishing food for both mind and spirit, for cars that run, and for the beauty of nature."

"And, Lord," Jenny prayed, "for human angels that you send to hurting people, for Libby and Tia. I'd also like to thank you for Lee. Despite his problems, I loved him and he loved me."

It was quiet for a moment before Tia spoke. "Thanks for all that you've provided to make our lives easier, like generators and toilet paper. Oh, yes, and thank you for birds."

"Amen!"

Tia raised her head and looked shamefaced. "Sorry I was such a complainer. I'll be better, I promise."

"We'll see," Libby said, her voice full of portent. She dispensed mugs of soup to each of them and the room fell silent as they ate.

It was just like being in high school again, Jenny thought as the threesome sat near the fireplace in their pajamas, wrapped in hand-crocheted afghans Libby's mother had made over the years, for the summer evening had turned cool. When Jenny had married Lee, it had changed the dynamics of their friendship a bit, but now that he was gone, they'd slipped right back into that Best Friends Forever mode they'd promised one another in childhood. Jenny felt a bit of the black void inside her filling.

"Well, I don't know about the rest of you, but I'm tuckered out," Libby announced as she took her dishes to the sink. "I'm not accustomed to staying up until 3 A.M. anymore."

"Is it that late already?" Jenny was amazed at how time had flown.

"I'm going to the bathroom," Tia announced. She stood up, wrapped her granny-patch afghan around her shoulders, and shuffled to the door in her pink bunny slippers. "Wait up for me."

There was little chance not to. Moments after Tia left the cabin, a bloodcurdling scream rent the night.

Libby and Jenny threw off their blankets and raced for the door. Tia stood on the front step beating at her head as if she'd gone mad.

"Get off! Get off! Oh, help, get it off!"

"There's nothing on your head, Tia," Libby said calmly. "What did you think it was?"

"A bat! It flew down from the eaves of the porch. Those spiny wings can get caught in your hair and tangle it up. Am I going to have to cut all my hair off?"

"Only if you want to look like a punk rocker or a professional basketball player," Libby said as Jenny bit her lip to stifle a giggle. "It may have brushed by you, but it certainly didn't land."

"That's it. I'm going in. I've had enough trouble with airborne creatures today."

"But what about your trip to the outhouse?"

"That's what old coffee cans are for. I'm not stepping foot out of this place until daylight." With determination and mustered dignity—undaunted by either bunny slippers or pajamas covered with airy white clouds on a background of blue sky—Tia marched into the security of the cabin.

Birds could certainly make clatter, Jenny thought as she opened one eye to the bright sunlight streaming across her bed. They were nature's jazz band, tuning up with squeaks, squawks, and the occasional melodious warble. She stretched from toes to fingertips with feline sensuousness. Her body tingled with energy.

Energy! Jenny hadn't experienced that in so long she'd almost forgotten how it felt. It had also been a very long time since she'd had a truly restful night's sleep.

There was another clatter in the air as well, this one coming from the kitchen. Libby had already cooked a huge pot of oatmeal filled with dates, walnuts, and sunflower seeds; sliced thick chunks of homemade whole wheat bread for toasting; and set the table with cream, brown sugar, butter, and strawberry preserves.

"You take good care of us," Jenny said and gave her friend a good-morning hug.

"I have to eat too, you know."

"Libby, ever since I've known you, you've been a caretaker. When will it be time to take care of you?" Jenny sat down at the table and curled her fingers around the pottery mug filled with coffee that Libby had poured.

"Don't spoil my fun, Jen. I like this. It makes me feel good."

"Just don't pour every bit of yourself into it. Otherwise you might be empty when it comes time for you."

"Are those words of experience?"

Jenny shrugged. "Maybe I do know now that Lee and I were never equal partners in our marriage. He ran the finances, I ran the household—and never the two did meet. It's obvious that he never consulted—or maybe even considered—me in the financial decisions. And he had no idea how much time I spent cleaning, trying new recipes, and ironing the perfect placket on his shirts. I tried to answer his needs practically before he knew he had them. I had him on a pedestal and he didn't belong there."

Jenny was relieved to see Tia shuffle into the room. This trip Tia seemed bent on providing comic relief. Her black hair looked as though it had been combed with an eggbeater. Her nose was pink, and there were blanket creases etched in her cheek. She looked exactly as she had upon waking as a nine-year-old.

"Coffee." The word came out as a guttural plea. It took a few sips of the steaming brew before Tia was able to find her voice. "I think I'm allergic to something out here."

"Besides bird and bats, you mean?"

"Very funny. Hah, hah. You should be on television." Tia poured down more coffee.

"What do you two plan to do today?" Libby asked brightly. She was wearing hiking shorts and sturdy boots.

"Not climb the Alps like you," Tia muttered.

"I'm going to have a morning nap, lunch, an afternoon nap, and then start reading the first book I've looked at in ages. I have a lot of sleep and novels to catch up on," said Jenny.

"I'm with you," Tia said. "Sounds perfect to me."

"OK, if you want to miss all of nature. While you two are lazing around like lizards in the sun, I'll be hiking." She bent to lace her boots tightly. After she'd rubbed sunblock on her face and arms, she announced, "You two can get your own lunch. I'm taking a bag of trail mix, some fruit, and a bottle of water with me."

Libby went to the galley kitchen, found the food she wanted, and tucked it into her backpack. She swung the pack across her shoulders, settled a brimmed hat on her head, and marched briskly to the cabin door. Her long legs looked muscled and sturdy peeking from beneath her shorts. She stood in the door-way and asked once more, "Are you sure neither of you wants to come with me?"

"Positive," her friends chimed in unison.

"Humph!" Libby snorted as she turned to leave the cabin. After she shut the door, Tia and Jenny could hear her burst into a loud rendition of "Michael, Row the Boat Ashore" and the crunch of her walking stick keeping time with her footsteps.

"A veritable songbird," Tia yawned. Then she leaped to her feet and peeked out the window. "She's gone. Couch potatoes rule! Do you want hot chocolate with an obscene amount of marshmallows or should we eat the chocolate bars Libby brought for S'mores?"

"Hot chocolate, but you're making it. I'm on vacation."

Humming, Tia went to the sink and picked up the pitcher that held the water for priming the pump. She began to pour water and energetically push and pull on the handle of the pump until she could hear water being lifted up the pipe. "Here it comes!" she announced cheerfully as the first droplets dribbled up from the well. And with those droplets came a tiny green salamander no bigger than Tia's finger.

It might as well have been a tyrannosaurus oozing out of the pump, the way Tia bellowed. She jumped back, holding her arms out in front of her as if to ward off an attack. By the time Jenny got to her, Tia was huddled on top of the kitchen table mewling like a kitten.

"It's just a baby!" Jenny chirped. She took a piece of cardboard and gently slid it beneath the terrified creature and carried it out the front door to the long grass.

"You frightened that poor little thing," she scolded when she returned to the cabin. "I think he was six shades paler after that noise you made."

"I scared him? Look at me! I'll never be normal again!"

"You never were normal, Tia. Nothing's going to change that." Calmly, Jenny pumped water into the teakettle, lit the gas stove, and set the kettle on the range to boil. "We're supposed to be roughing it a little bit. Now that poor baby has been sucked out of its home."

"Yeah, right." Tia crawled off the table, her eyes still darting about in her head. "Remind me to feel bad later."

The morning and early afternoon passed uneventfully. Tia ate most of the M&Ms that Libby neglected to put into the trail mix,

pitcher of iced tea. Jenny read until she was sleepy, dozed, and woke up to read again. Their moment of greatest effort involved painting each other's toenails. Both were barely dressed for the day when Libby returned from her hike midafternoon.

Tia's encounter with the lizardlike creature became fodder for many laughs as Tia recounted the story. Each time Tia mentioned the little salamander it grew in size and ferocity, until Libby pictured an alligator slithering up from her well and into the sink.

"Anyone for a swim in the lake?" Libby asked.

"Too cold," Tia complained.

"A campfire outside, then?"

"Too buggy."

"Tia, why did we come up here anyway? You refuse to leave the cabin!"

"Oh, all right. A nature walk would be all right. Something short. No making new trails or anything."

It was perfect as they made their way up the side of a small incline that overlooked the pristine blue lake. Jenny stopped as they reached the apex of the hill and threw her arms wide as if to embrace the beauty. "Have you ever seen anything as gorgeous as this? It's perfect!"

Tia nodded. "Amazing, huh? If I saw an oil painting of this at the flea market, I'd never buy it for the store. No one would believe it was real."

Jenny dropped into the grass and gazed at the pastoral beauty. "I must be feeling better," she mused. "I'm beginning to see beauty again. For a while, I'd lost the ability to do so. When Mike started reviving my yard, I felt a few twinges of appreciation for nature, but this—"

"'The Lord is my shepherd,'" Libby began. "'I have everything I need. He lets me rest in green meadows; he leads me beside peaceful streams. He renews my strength. He guides me along right paths, bringing honor to his name.'"

Tears sprang to Jenny's eyes as she recalled the Twenty-third Psalm. What comfort those words had once given her and now, here in this place, she began to understand even more fully the riches God could provide if only she would trust him. Unbeknownst to her, a little of her heart began to heal.

That evening when they were all lying about like great fat lizards themselves in oversized T-shirts, white cotton socks, and green-and-blue facial masques that looked more than a bit salamandarish, Tia brought up the subject of Mike Adams.

"I can't believe the turnaround in that guy," she marveled. "I would have voted him most likely to spend his declining years in a penitentiary. Rules were made to break as far as Mike was concerned. He was the ultimate rebel. Who'd have thought?"

"God works in mysterious ways," Jenny murmured, hoping not to be drawn into this conversation.

No luck. Tia and Libby both eyed her—an alarming concept considering one face was blue, the other lime green. Peering at her, their eyes looked like boiled eggs with colored yolks.

"Maybe God's got plans for you and Mike."

"Yeah, right."

"You said he was a Christian now, didn't you?"

"That doesn't mean we're going to be a couple, Tia. Don't be absurd."

"I think it's great," Libby interjected. "I'll bet poor Pastor Adams was pleased with the change in his son."

"Talking about change . . ." Jenny yawned so widely her friends could see the dental work in her back molars. "I want to change the subject. I'd love to chat more, but I'm sleepy."

Tia groaned at Libby's words. "Then I guess I'd better chip this 'beauty' mask off my face before it turns to concrete."

"Jenny?" Libby's voice came out of the darkness. "Are you asleep?"

"No. It's too quiet to sleep."

"City slicker," Tia mumbled. "What do you need? Traffic, fire trucks, and police sirens to serenade you?"

"I was wondering about something," Libby said, ignoring Tia. "Why is Lee's sister at your house so much lately? I thought she never came by."

Jenny bit her lip. Should she tell them?

"You aren't keeping something from us, are you?" Tia accused. She could always read people—even in the dark. That was part of what made her such an astute businesswoman.

"Dorothy knew about Lee's gambling all along."

"And she didn't tell you?" Libby sounded indignant.

"She wanted to, but Lee had asked her not to do so. She didn't come around because she felt so badly that she didn't want to face me."

"I'm sorry, Jenny, but that's a pretty poor excuse. If you'd known about Lee, you might have been able to help him!"

"And you wouldn't be in such financial trouble right now," Tia added.

"But would I have believed her?" Jenny asked. "I'm not sure. I didn't give Lee credit for simply being human. I accepted everything he said as truth. As long as I was in that mind-set I wouldn't have believed anything negative Dorothy might have said."

"You are unbelievably forgiving, Jenny. Of both Lee and Dorothy," Tia marveled.

"Frankly, I'm furious with both of them."

"Really? I didn't know you had a furious bone in your body," Libby commented. Jenny could hear her squirming to get adjusted in her sleeping bag.

"I've discovered a few," Jenny murmured with irony in her tone. "At first it frightened me. I was taught that good Christian girls didn't get angry."

"And do they?"

"Of course they do! Even Jesus got angry when he found money changers in the temple."

··126··

"'In the Temple area he saw merchants selling cattle, sheep, and doves for sacrifices; and he saw money changers behind their counters. Jesus made a whip from some ropes and chased them all out of the Temple. He drove out the sheep and oxen, scattered the money changers' coins over the floor, and turned over their tables,'" Libby quoted. "John 2:14-15."

"Exactly. He had righteous anger, anger at the injustice of it all, of turning his Father's house into a house of trade. We all should be angry at sin. Though God loves the sinner, he still hates the sin."

"So you'll just be angry at gambling?"

"I'm pretty furious with Lee too," Jenny admitted into the darkness. "But Ellen gave me a book on the stages of grief. Anger is one of the stages a person must go through to reach acceptance. If that's the way God planned it, then it must be OK. I'm admitting my anger and trusting that God knows I'm on my way to accepting what Lee had become. After all, that's what God is all about, isn't it? Acceptance and forgiveness?

"Some days I wish Lee were alive just so I could strangle him myself. Then I realize that he was a very sick, compulsive man. But he was still more than a gambler. He was a loving man who in many ways tried to do all he could. That's all any of us can do, really. No one is all good or all evil. We are all shades of gray."

It surprised even Jenny to have these words come from her lips. Lately her emotions changed with her moods until she was beginning to wonder if this roller-coaster ride would ever end. It surprised her, too, that she was talking about God as if he were taking an active part in her life these days. She hadn't felt it, but there it was. Jenny fell asleep puzzling the mystery.

....

Libby was up before the birds the next morning and had the SUV nearly loaded when Tia and Jenny finally made their appearance.

"I smell coffee but I don't see it," Tia accused.

"Out on the porch with muffins. I thought it would be fun to enjoy the early morning sun before we leave."

"Fun. Right." Tia the night owl sounded less than impressed.

But Jenny eagerly headed for the porch. Energy she thought she'd lost forever seemed practically boundless up here—away from home, from the piles of debts, from the constant triggers that reminded her of what she'd lost.

"What makes food taste so much better when it's eaten outside?" Jenny wondered aloud as she wolfed down her second muffin.

"I'm not sure," Libby answered, "but I do know I'm going to start setting the picnic table at your house when we eat there. You look wonderful. Practically robust."

"Libby, Libby, Libby," Tia chided. "Always taking care of someone else."

"And I, for one, am very grateful for her care," Jenny murmured softly.

"I have some business of my own to take care of," Tia announced as she moved down the porch steps and across the clearing to the quaint log outhouse, which Libby always referred to as "plumbing with a view."

Jenny and Libby paid no more attention until they heard a frantic hiss from across the yard a few minutes later.

"Look!" Libby gasped.

Tia was framed in the doorway of the outhouse, her dark eyes huge in her pale face. In the clearing between her and the house was a gigantic moose cow and her gangly calf.

"Help!" Tia mouthed, but Libby shook her head.

"She has to stay where she is until they leave," Libby whispered to Jenny. "A moose with a calf can be very dangerous. If the cow thinks her baby is in jeopardy, she will attack. Sit very still."

Tia seemed to get Libby's message and stepped timidly back

into the outhouse. She swung the door closed, and her friends could see one dark, frightened eye ringed in pale skin through the oversized peephole in the door.

"It's huge!" Jenny gawked at the bony knees and platterlike feet of the calf. "And cute in a ugly sort of way." The calf frolicked around its tolerant mother, who had found some tasty green morsel on which to chew. They appeared ready to spend the day.

Jenny clapped a hand to her mouth to force back a giggle. What if it did stay a few hours? She and Libby could tiptoe into the house and pass the time reading and visiting. Tia, however, . . .

The same thought must have occurred to Tia. She opened the door a crack and gestured at them to chase the pair away.

Libby shook her head slowly and firmly. No deal. Tia would stay put until mama and baby decided to leave on their own.

Jenny, comfortable in her rocker, was content to watch the pair browse through the underbrush. When the cow decided to scratch her side on the rough wood corner of the outhouse, however, Jenny could barely keep from covering her eyes. What must Tia be thinking inside the little, shaking structure, the scraping sound of hide and hair against timber echoing in her ears?

It wasn't long—in Jenny's mind at least—until the pair began to move away. The crashing and crunching of their large feet diminished as they moved out of sight.

"OK, Tia, you can come out now," Libby called.

No Tia emerged.

"Tia?" Libby cast a worried glance at Jenny, and they both stood up.

"Are you in there?" Jenny pushed open the outhouse door.

"Where else would I be?" Tia was crouched on the floor, her back against the two-holed bench. Dusty motes floated in the light through the half-moon hole on the side of the structure. Tia stood stiffly, with as much dignity as she could muster. It wasn't much.

"I was so scared! What if they'd knocked this dumb thing over? I could have been trampled or worse!"

"What could be worse than being trampled by a moose?" Jenny wondered.

Tia cast a disgusted glance at the two-holed bench. "I could have fallen into the outhouse pit!"

The image of Tia headfirst in one of the most odiferous and repugnant places one could be set all of them laughing. They laughed so hard they had to support one another as they staggered to the house in a giggly little circle. In fact, they laughed so hard that none of them could make it up the steps, and they fell into a heap on the stairs. And then they laughed some more.

"Your eye! It looked like a brown headlight shining out of that hole!"

"What did it feel like when the cow scratched herself on the building?"

"My hair practically stood on end. I could see the headlines when the place started to shake. 'Prominent Businesswoman Killed in Moose Raid on Outdoor Biffy'."

"How about 'Loose Moose Loosens Businesswoman's Mousse'?" Libby screeched with laughter at her own joke.

"The subtitle could be 'Hair-Raising Experience Raises Moose Hide While Moussed Hair Hides'," added Jenny.

Ten minutes later, when they had finally settled down, Libby reached for her friends' hands. "I think we need to pray about this."

"I lived through it," Tia said.

"Exactly. God wants us to call upon him in the good times too." Libby bowed her head. "Dear Lord, thank you for the peace, safety and joy you have brought to our weekend. We praise you for the levity too, Lord. Thank you for laughter and for the healing and recovery we've experienced here. We know your hand is in it. Amen."

"Amen!" Tia crowed.

And even Jenny could sincerely add her own soft but sincere

CHAPTER EIGHT

*Phlox: signifies sweet dreams and proposals of love;
it is the Greek word for flame.*

—WILDFLOWER FOLKLORE

Mike had been at the house while they were gone. Her yard was slowly evolving around her, taking on the form and shape of his creation, which seemed to represent her at the stages of life through which she'd been passing. The choking weeds were gone, as was the distressing disarray, which had so aptly mirrored her mental state. Now the garden was a niche of optimism and flowering greenery.

Spot, who'd been boarded at the kennel while Jenny was away, was giddily investigating every shrub and blade of grass.

It had taken her some time to notice, but even the flowers changed with the advancing season. Today there was a lush hydrangea blooming near her front step.

"Great plant," Tia commented as she dumped Jenny's things on the front step.

"Yes, I suppose it is."

"You doubt it for an instant? This yard looks a hundred—no.

"I know. Mike is amazing, but I can't continue to accept his generosity. He says he uses overstock and his employee's discount to purchase the flowers but he refuses to tell me what I owe him. 'When I'm done,' he says, but I'm going to talk to him next time I see him in the yard. Until I see a bill from him I don't want him to do any more."

Jenny's shoulders sagged. "Besides, now that I know what a financial mess Lee left me, even bargain basement purchases are too much for me."

"Don't look a gift horse in the mouth," Libby chimed in.

"Where does that stupid saying come from, anyway?" Tia challenged.

"It has something to do with horses' teeth. You can tell how old a horse is by the length of his teeth. If someone gives you a horse, you should be polite and not check its teeth for age. It's rude to question a gift, that's all."

"Libby, you know the most amazingly trivial things!"

Libby smiled sweetly. "Why, thank you, Tia. Having your admiration means everything to me."

"Knock it off, you two, and help me bring my things inside."

As soon as Jenny was through the door, she headed for the couch. "I think I could sleep all day!"

"Wilderness camping isn't enough for you?" Libby played injured.

"It's not that. It's this conversation. Tia, I know your book-keeper has been keeping my bills current, but with what? Don't tell me you've started counterfeiting for me while I was tromping off to the north woods!"

"Hardly. Your parents have sent a check here and there, and the insurance money will be coming through soon. I've been subsidizing you a little, that's all. . . ." Tia held up a restraining hand, stopping Jenny before she could protest. "Don't worry. It's not a gift. My bookkeeper knows exactly how much you owe me, and I'm taking my share off the top once your check comes."

"I didn't mean for you to get stuck paying my bills," Jenny wailed. "It was just that I was so shaken after Lee died I didn't think I'd get anything done properly by myself."

"You did the right thing," Tia responded calmly. "Your lights are still on and bill collectors aren't pounding at your door. Jenny, I'd give you the money if I had even the faintest inkling that you'd accept it, but I know you better than that. For now, let me help the one way I can. Please?"

"It's too much," Jenny whimpered. "I can't."

"Nonsense. Of course you can. The most important thing to me is your mental health," Tia assured her. "Now that you're feeling a little better, we'll just have to find a job for you."

"Doing what? Housekeeping? Running errands? Washing floors? There's big money in that, all right. Maybe I can get two jobs—something during the day and the other during nights and weekends."

"That wouldn't be productive. You don't want to grab the first job that comes along," Tia advised. "You should wait until you find something that you love to do."

Seeing Jenny's distraught expression, Tia added, "And if it's killing you that I've loaned you some money, I'd be happy to have you work it off in the store. I have someone going on maternity leave in October. If you haven't got it worked out by then, you're hired."

"Tia, I can't believe you." Tears of gratitude filled Jenny's eyes, and she buried her nose in the fur of the dog that had joined her on the couch.

"What's the fun of being successful if you can't share it? Allow me the pleasure of that, will you? Besides, wouldn't it be a hoot to have the three of us all working under one roof? We'll either move more product than ever before or chase all the customers away with our giggling. It's a win-win situation either way. Bucks or fun. Come on, Jen, don't look so sad! I'm trying to cheer you up!"

"You have! That's why I'm crying. Thank you for being so very dear to me."

"Gifts are for sharing, that's all."

Even Libby was sniffling by this time. "I don't have any extra money, Jen, but I can help you job hunt. I'll help you to find your passion."

"For my entire married life Lee was my passion. I lost myself living for him."

"Then this is the time to set out on a treasure hunt. The prize? The real you!" Libby reached for the classified section of one of the papers that had collected in Jenny's absence.

"Hmmm, let's see. Here's someone looking for a personal attendant for a handicapped adult . . . babysitters needed . . . computer operators, roofers, truck drivers, bartender, hotel security, housekeeping and front desk opportunities, janitorial . . ."

"Libby, get to another page," Tia ordered. "Jenny can't do any of that."

"I don't have a college education, Tia. Maybe that's all I can do!"

"Keep reading," Tia ordered.

"Here is an ad for an opening in a gift and card shop. All the big name stores like Wal-Mart and Kmart are advertising for cashiers. Oh! Here's a good one—Dairy Queen. You'd like that. Do you think you get to eat your mistakes?" Libby scanned the page. "The YMCA needs swimming instructors and lifeguards, and there are lots of places looking for secretaries and waitresses."

"And my mother wanted me to go to college before I got married," Jenny sighed. "Why didn't I listen then?"

Though she didn't say it, Jenny knew the answer. She'd thought she couldn't be whole without a man. Lee completed her; he made her who she was—or so she'd believed. So she'd married him.

"Don't be discouraged," Tia consoled. "We aren't done yet."

After her friends left, Jenny went into the kitchen to find something to eat. Staring disinterestedly into her pantry cupboard, Jenny's gaze fell on the stack of cookbooks she'd collected. She pulled out one called *Chocolate Decadence,* which contained only recipes using chocolate—everything from soups and Mexican food to Black Forest cake and a dozen cheesecake recipes that made her mouth water.

Making a quick decision, Jenny scanned her cupboards for ingredients and began to bake. It wasn't until the doorbell rang that she realized she'd been in the kitchen nearly four hours. A marble cheesecake, a chocolate layer cake with fudge filling and frosting, and three dozen German chocolate cookies covered her counters. She still had a turtle cheesecake in the oven and the ingredients mixed for no-bake drop cookies.

Spot, who'd spent the time alert for falling crumbs, had finally crumpled, exhausted, into a corner of the kitchen.

"Anybody home?"

It was Mike. Jenny was glad to hear his voice. She needed to talk to him about all the time he spent in her yard.

He walked into the kitchen and did a double take at the sight of all the food spread around the kitchen. "What happened? Did Hershey's take over your house as a factory?"

"Something got into me," Jenny admitted. "I used to bake all the time and I loved it, but when Lee died, I quit."

"And today you started again."

"Do you think I went overboard?"

"It depends. How many divisions of the armed forces are you entertaining this weekend?" Mike pulled out a chair and sat down at the table.

"Just you so far. Coffee?"

He eyed the feast before him. "Gallons of it."

Jenny picked at a cookie while Mike tasted one of everything she'd made. Finally she got up the nerve to say, "Mike, I have to ask you to stop coming here and working on my yard."

His handsome features registered surprise. "Why? Don't you like the way it's turning out?"

"I love it. But I can't ask you to spend any more extra time here. You've got a job to tend to, and I know that you aren't charging your full fee when you work here. I called How Does Your Garden Grow? for my balance, and it was practically nothing. I refuse to take advantage of you because we went to school together."

"Who says you are taking advantage of me?"

"It's obvious, isn't it? The hydrangea by the front step, for example. What about that?"

"It's the flower of the month," Mike said, as if that explained everything.

"You mean it was on sale?"

"I mean that I bought it recently. July's flower is the hydrangea, which represents the essence of this time of year on the calendar of flowers. June was the butterfly bush, and August is to be the pink rose." Mike dished another piece of cheesecake. "Most women like August a lot."

"Where do you come up with these things?" Jenny marveled. "And what happened to that horrible little monster child who stomped on every flower bed at the parsonage?"

Jenny's heart did a little flip-flop at the guileless, boyish grin on Mike's face. "Paying penance, I guess. I wrecked a million flowers and now I'm going to plant a million and one."

She didn't know what to make of him. He was as much a mystery today as he had been years ago.

A frantic pounding on the back door startled them both. Outside was George Hardy's granddaughter Kim. Tears streamed down Kim's cheeks, and in her cupped hands she held a butterfly.

"What's wrong, sweetie?" Jenny knelt by the child and stroked the silvery gold strands of her fine hair.

"My butterfly is sick."

Jenny peered into the not-quite-clean hands. The butterfly was more than sick. It was dead. "Honey, I'm afraid your butterfly is—"

"Very lucky," Mike interjected.

Jenny was too startled to speak as Mike beckoned the child to come closer. He studied the butterfly with the intensity of a surgeon about to attempt a rare and difficult procedure. "Yes, indeed, this is a very lucky butterfly."

"Will it get well?"

Mike appeared to puzzle over the child's question before he answered. "Yes and no."

"Huh?" The tears had stopped, but the little girl looked as confused as Jenny felt.

"The butterfly is dead. Do you know what that means?"

The child's eyes filled with tears. "Is my butterfly going to heaven?"

"That's what I meant by yes and no. The butterfly won't get well down here with us, but I'm pretty sure there are butterflies in heaven."

"So he'll get well there?"

"God keeps his eyes even on the sparrow, which isn't a very pretty or exotic bird, so I imagine he would keep a very close eye on something as pretty as your butterfly."

Jenny watched with amazement as Mike's dark head and the child's blonde mop of fairy-dust hair bent low over the butterfly.

"When will it go to heaven?"

"I think part of it might be there right now. All that's left is the shell. Do you want to help me bury it in the yard? When it was alive, its shell was important, but now that has been left behind. The important part of the butterfly has gone."

"Like when Grandma died?"

"Just like that." Mike took a napkin from the dispenser on the table, and together he and the child wrapped the butterfly and went into the backyard.

From inside the house where she waited with the dog, Jenny could see them looking for just the right spot for the paper-shrouded butterfly. When they found it, Mike dug a tiny hole, and the little girl lowered her weightless burden to the ground. The solemn ceremony was over in a matter of minutes. When Mike returned, he sauntered to the sink to wash his hands.

"Now what was that all about?" Jenny wondered.

"Heaven," Mike said calmly. "I suspect there are a lot of butter-flies in heaven—especially for those who are fond of them. We'll have to wait and see when we get there, I guess."

"Isn't it a little grim, talking about death like that with a child? Wouldn't it have been better to have distracted her and taken the thing away?"

He studied her with piercing eyes, and Jenny felt as though he were reading messages stamped on her soul. "She wasn't afraid of death. Are you?"

There was a time in her life not so very long ago when Jenny would have said no with both confidence and bravura. But ever since Lee had died, something had also died in her—the unwavering conviction that there was someone who really could triumph over death. Oh, she felt that was true some-times, but her faith was more tenuous now, more dependent on her moods and feelings than on trust in things unseen. It frightened and confused her. She'd wandered off the only path she'd ever known and finding it again seemed precari-ously difficult.

"I don't know," Jenny admitted softly. "I wasn't. Once. But I'd never confronted it—up close and personal—until Lee died. Even then I wasn't afraid, at least, not for a long time. I know God carried me through the funeral. I would never have made it without divine help."

"So what happened?"

"I don't know. I've lived in a fog, stumbling along, not know-

thinking he was out there, and not being able to find him." She sighed—a deep, wrenching sigh. "I'm still in the fog and every day that I can't find him, I worry more and more that he was never there at all. Does that make sense to you?" Jenny's upturned face was heartbreakingly hopeful.

"Sure." Mike stared at her, gauging her with his eyes. "I don't think there are many Christians who haven't lost their way a time or two—or ten."

"You?" Jenny inquired.

"Jenny, I've spend most of my life lost!" Mike said with exasperation. "That's why I consider myself an expert at this."

"But you seem so . . . together . . . now."

Mike grimaced. "I still fight with anger and resentment every day, Jenny. I didn't like my youth, and I blamed that on my father. I built a wall between us that's taken years for me to chip away." His expression grew unreadable. "I wish that it were different. That *I* were different. But . . ."

Then he shrugged, and some of the light came back into his eyes. "You do remember Simon Peter, don't you? He stumbled constantly, and still God used him in a mighty way. I'm an even more unlikely specimen than Peter. God should really have fun with me."

"I thought those things you said to Kim would have frightened or confused her, but they didn't seem to do so."

"Why should she have been afraid?"

Jenny's eyes darkened. "Putting something—or someone—you love into the ground, hoping that someday, somewhere you'll see them again. . . ." Her voice trailed away.

"Not *hoping,* Jenny. *Knowing.*"

A tear streaked down her cheek. "I don't know anymore, Mike." She scraped her slender hands through the thick tendrils of her hair. "I'm so afraid."

He studied her for a while, saying nothing. The calm silence allowed Jenny to compose herself. "I'm sorry. It's dumb."

"It's not dumb. As my long-suffering father might say, 'It's life and death.'"

"And there's the rub." Jenny gave a small, scornful sound. "I used to quote the Bible. Now I quote Shakespeare."

"I'd like to share something with you that I learned a few years back. If you don't mind, that is."

"Please. I'd like that."

"As you keep reminding me, I was a wild child. My parents were this close—" and he held his thumb and index finger a sixteenth of an inch apart—"to giving up on me. They bailed me out of jail, put me in drug rehab, covered bounced checks, tried tough love and, well, you get the drift."

"I had no idea!" Jenny stared at Mike. In her sheltered existence she'd never before known anyone who had experienced those things. No wonder he seemed so different from her, so alien and provocative.

"But they gave me one more chance when I busted up my Harley and landed in the hospital with a broken leg, a concussion, cracked ribs, and an arm in a cast the size and shape of Minnesota." He grinned ruefully. "They had me where they wanted me. Immobile. Unable to run. Trapped like a pinned-down fly."

"And what did they do to you?"

"Talked, prayed, talked, and prayed some more. I was in a coma for a while and they didn't know I could hear them, but I could. It was then, when my parents didn't even know I was listening, that I realized how real and sincere their faith was. I may be the only person around who ever accepted Christ while unconscious."

"And I have to go through that to regain my faith?" Jenny asked weakly, unsure where Mike's story was heading.

"I wouldn't recommend it. But I did take something away from that accident that I'd never realized before. Something I nearly had to die to understand." His eyes were darkly compelling, and Jenny noticed the firm thrust of his jaw. What this man was telling her came from the very depths of his soul.

"What?" she whispered, captured by her hunger for answers and for the charisma of this man.

"Until you can accept your own death, you cannot really live."

"Death is inevitable, of course, but . . ."

"No *buts* about it. You're going to die and so am I. We won't know when or how, but it will happen. And until you know for sure what's going to happen to you in the afterlife, you are going to live your life in a tentative, cautious, even miserly way. *Not* fearing death is what gives us life."

"But you didn't see Lee. . . ." Her voice caught in her throat. She could still picture him collapsed on the kitchen floor, a pool of blood forming beneath his head and blood pouring from his mouth and nose. Where was God then? The terror she'd felt the washed over her anew. She'd cried out to God, but he hadn't listened. Or, if he had, he hadn't acted. After all, Lee was dead. Very, very dead.

"You've got to come to terms with it, Jenny. With Lee's death and with your own."

It made her tremble to realize how closely he had come to hitting the mark where her faith was concerned. It was true. Death in the abstract and heaven ever after were easy enough to accept when one had been raised as Jenny had. But seeing it up close, in all its ugliness and terror, had kicked the supports from beneath her faith. Jenny was afraid to die.

"It's simple for you to say," she murmured. "You were always reckless, always living on the edge. You never feared dying."

"Only because I didn't feel I had much reason to live. I felt the invincibility of youth and the burden of being a failure."

"You? A failure?"

"You'll have to admit, I never lived up to my father's standards. More than once, a church council suggested that if he couldn't control his son, perhaps he couldn't shepherd a flock, if you understand what I mean."

"Your father nearly got fired because of you?"

"More than once." Mike looked rueful. "And my parents still say they love me. Go figure."

"Just how do you propose that I erase the tapes that still play in my mind? The ones of Lee dying and of me being unable to help him? Or the ones that whisper 'If there were a God, he would have helped Lee'?"

"We all have tapes, Jenny. Anyone who has lived has them. It's weird, but it seems we keep the bad ones and lose the good ones."

"What do you mean?"

"Which ones keep you up at night? Those of the pleasant memories and good times or the ones of Lee dying?"

The look on her face gave him his answer. "What keeps you up, Mike?"

He took a long time to answer. "Taunts. Jeers. Teachers saying I'd never amount to anything. Kids calling me a loser. People from Dad's congregation whispering about what they could do to help my parents with me. I won't even mention what the police used to say when they rousted me out of one bit of trouble or another."

"Oh, Mike, I had no idea!"

"We seldom do know what drives another person, Jen. All I know is that the tapes we have in our mind can be hurtful or helpful, depending on how we use them. You'll have to figure it out for yourself. You've got God to help you."

"Quite a conundrum if I'm not sure anymore that I believe there is a God."

"Then do as I did. Yell straight up at heaven and tell him that if he wants you to believe in him, then he'll have to give you the faith to do it with. Then sit back and see what happens."

Jenny stared at Mike as if she'd never seen him before. In many ways, she hadn't. The breadth and depth of his character was too expansive to be revealed all at once. Mike was like the garden, full of life and seeds of wisdom that bloomed in just the right season.

"I'll think about it," Jenny finally said.

"You do that. Ask for help too. You might be surprised how much you might get."

. . . .

Jenny was beginning to worry about Dorothy. She hadn't called or come to the house in nearly four days. That was odd. During the past months, Dorothy had been steady as clockwork about checking in frequently. On the way home from the grocery store Jenny swung onto Maple Street, where her sister-in-law lived.

The house where Lee's parents had once lived was now Dorothy's. It was a cozy two-story with inviting French windows and a brick walkway. The drapes were closed and the place looked uninhabited. Jenny's step quickened. Dorothy usually kept the windows and doors wide open. She knocked and pressed her ear to the door to listen for footsteps.

It was a long time before Jenny heard any sounds of life inside the house. Finally the door opened a crack.

"Dot? It's me, Jenny. Are you OK?"

"What time is it?"

"Nearly eleven. Did I wake you?"

The door swung open just enough to allow Jenny to see the dusky interior of the hallway. Dorothy was still in her pajamas and robe.

"No, I was just sitting in the living room having coffee."

"In the dark?" Jenny pushed her way past Dorothy and into the inky house. "Why don't we open a few curtains?"

She felt Dorothy stiffen but ignored the silent protest. Jenny strode from window to window, throwing open the draperies and unlatching windows to let in light and air.

"Isn't that better?" She turned to her sister-in-law, who still stood in the doorway blinking and grimacing at the bright light. "Are you trying to turn into a mole or something? Hiding away in your burrowed hole?"

Dorothy gestured toward the coffee carafe on the chest in front of the sofa. "I'll get another cup if you'll join me."

"Love to." Jenny plopped into one of the worn-out easy chairs that had been in this room ever since she'd started coming here fifteen or even twenty years ago, when they were all still in grade school. She remembered Dorothy's and Lee's father sitting in this very chair, smoking a pipe. That was in the days before pipe smoking was considered unhealthy and politically incorrect. A smile tipped Jenny's lips. It seemed so long ago, part of another age and time.

But it *was* another age and time, she reminded herself. She lived in the here and now, and at all costs she had to stay here.

Dorothy shuffled into the room with a mug. She looked into it as if wondering just how clean it was and wiped the rim with the sleeve of her chenille bathrobe. "I haven't been Susie Homemaker these days," she said. "Hope there's nothing unseemly on this cup."

"It's OK." Jenny took the mug and filled it with coffee. Then she sat back and studied her sister-in-law. "If you haven't been housecleaning, what have you been doing?"

"Self-flagellation, mostly."

"Is that a big word for sitting in the dark and beating yourself up for what happened to your brother?"

"You've got it."

"You should come to my house. We could do it together."

"I'm beating myself up over you, too. If I'd told you about Lee years earlier, maybe some of this mess could have been averted." Dorothy's tone was bitter. "But, no, I couldn't do that! My baby brother needed a caretaker, someone to hide his little secrets, to justify his bad habits, and there I was ready, willing and able!

"Not only did I allow Lee to continue with his destructive behavior, I allowed his actions to change my own life—and yours."

"I did some of that myself, you know," Jenny said as calmly as she could. As much as she hurt right now, Dorothy was suffering even more.

"Maybe, but the unwritten rules of our family started right here in this room. 'Don't discuss our problems outside the family.' 'Don't say what you feel.' 'Don't show weakness.' 'A Matthews has a reputation to uphold.' Mom and Dad were great believers in the never-let-them-see-you-sweat theory of life. Other people had problems. We didn't."

"You were one of those *Father Knows Best*–type families," Jenny admitted.

"Perfect on the outside, all messed up on the inside," Dorothy said. "I see it now. We fed off each other. My parents made me think that Lee and I were responsible for pleasing them and each other. We had this symbiotic relationship, this tendency to live through each other vicariously. If Lee did something wonderful, we were all happy. If I did something wrong, it affected not only me but all of us. Control was a big thing in our family. I see now that I allowed my brother's behavior to make me into something I wasn't—secretive, aloof, unfriendly." Tears flooded her eyes. "And I didn't allow us to become friends because of it."

"Oh, Dorothy . . ."

By now Dorothy was sobbing. "I can't tell you how many times I envied you, Tia, and Libby your friendship! I wanted so much to be a part of it, but I knew I couldn't let it happen. I might let something slip, something about Lee. . . ."

"Lee's problems weren't your fault, Dorothy. They were his. People have to taken ownership of their own mistakes."

"I'm beginning to realize that now, but at the time, I thought that if I could keep the gambling a secret, maybe somehow, someday, I could get him to stop."

"You took Lee's problems as your own. Even after Lee and I were married, you didn't stop blaming yourself."

"No. What's more, I watched him do the same thing to you. Oh, Jenny, can you ever forgive me?"

Jenny looked at the pale, broken woman across from her and

felt her heart swell with love. "I forgive you, Dorothy, even though there is nothing to forgive. We do the best we can with our lives. Sometimes it just doesn't work out like we'd planned. Hard as this is, Lee's death has given us both a fresh start. We're clean slates now. We have the opportunity not to make the same mistakes twice. We can love people and not have to control or be controlled by them." She reached out and touched her sister-in-law's tear-stained cheek. "Maybe we can make something good come from this, Dot. Then at least Lee's death wouldn't be a total tragedy."

"You think so?" A glimmer of hope flickered in Dorothy's reddened eyes.

"I don't see why not. Tia and Libby keep telling me it's possible." Jenny's eyes darkened. "I've hurt and ached and cried so much that pretty soon something good has to happen."

"I know that feeling," Dorothy sniffled.

"Why don't you get in the shower?" Jenny suggested, wiping away her own tears. "I still remember how to make an omelet. Libby always says cooking for others makes her feel better. Will you give me a chance to cook for you?"

Dorothy stood up and reached for Jenny. They hugged so hard and long that their bones should have snapped in protest. Then Dorothy left quietly to shower, and Jenny went to find just how many eggs her sister-in-law had left in the kitchen.

. . . .

"I don't care if your hair looks like it had a lube job at the garage! You are going out with us today, no matter what!"

"I just don't feel like it, Tia. You and Libby go without me. Have a good time. Tell me all about it when you get back."

"No."

Jenny was startled to hear genuine anger in Tia's voice as she spoke. "You cop out on everything we plan, and we're sick of it. We're trying to help you. Will you please let us?"

"Tia, are those tears in your eyes?" Jenny looked from Tia to Libby, and her heart grew heavy. They were such good friends. So well-intentioned and kindhearted, even though all their efforts seemed so much in vain right now. "Oh, all right. I'll go to your hen party and listen to the chatter. Give me five minutes to change."

Libby and Tia did a high five as Jenny turned to go to the bedroom. Jenny saw it but did not comment. She would do this for them if they thought it would help.

When she returned to the living room wearing a linen sundress and a straw hat with a linen band, Libby whistled. "You look maaavelous!"

"It's amazing what a hat can do for hair that looks like it came from a grease pit," Jenny retorted. "Now let's go before I chicken out."

The Emerald Grill was an upscale luncheon spot located in downtown Minneapolis between two financial centers that catered to business executives. Jenny and her linen apparel fit right in. Unfortunately, Jenny thought, nothing else about her did. She no longer related to this group of four former high school classmates, who had all, with the exception of Angelique, decided that marriage at nineteen was not for them.

Angelique rose and gave Jenny a hug. She smelled of roses. Cloying and heavy as the perfume might be, Jenny knew that it had cost Angelique big bucks to acquire it. "You look darling. I wish I were so thin." Angelique held Jenny at arm's length and scanned her from head to toe. "You must wear a size nothing!"

Before Jenny could respond, Lydia spoke. "We are so glad you came today. Tia said you weren't going out much." Lydia had always been a favorite of Jenny's—down-to-earth, practical, without a nasty bone in her body.

"So how is the house-building business?" Jenny managed as she sank into a chair at the round table, which was set with crystal, china, and silver.

"Hassles and more hassles. How did an interior decorator wanna-be turn into a building contractor anyway? If I'd been smart, I would have married a pilot and spent my time traveling like Angelique."

Maybe, or maybe not. Angelique hadn't gotten it right the first time or the second, Jenny knew. Angelique's first husband had been emotionally abusive, something none of her circle of friends had known until the unexpected shock of her divorce struck them full in the face. Unfortunately, she'd run headlong from one disastrous marriage into a second because her self-esteem was so in tatters. Though she might be dripping in success now, Angelique also knew the pain of having to accept food stamps and subsidized living. Jenny admired her all the more for her current success because of what she had endured in her past. Angelique had fought an uphill battle all the way, and she deserved a little time at the top.

"Since you brought up your business," said Nikki, a platinum blonde whom Jenny would always remember as a shy, mousy brunette, "I need some tips. We're building a new house, and Jim and I have had a real disagreement over tile. What do you find works best?"

While Lydia and Nikki commiserated over the woes of flooring and Angelique regaled Tia and Libby with her latest photo safari in the Serengeti, Jenny visited with Marty, the class valedictorian. Marty wore thick glasses that disguised her beautiful green eyes.

"Gag me with a spoon," Marty drawled, Valley-girl style. "Can you believe these are our classmates? Continent-hopping, business-owning, house-building tycoons?" She put a hand on Jenny's wrist. "It is so good to see you, honey. I can't even imagine how hard this has been."

Jenny felt herself tearing up at the kindness. "What are you doing these days?"

"Same old stuff. Research. Writing."

"And your health?"

Marty's expression tightened. "My diabetes? Brittle as crystal on a winter's day, but I'm managing. I haven't pigged out on Twinkies and cola for a long time. I know it's not good for me, but sometimes I would just love to fall on my face into a French silk pie!"

Jenny nodded. "Are you still in school?"

"Finishing my doctoral thesis. By the time you all are grand-mothers, I'll be teaching college." Marty saw the look on Jenny's face. "Oh, I'm sorry. I didn't mean . . ."

"It's OK. Just because Lee and I didn't have children doesn't mean I might not have some of my own someday."

Had she really said that? Jenny wondered. She'd never consid-ered having children with anyone but Lee—had she?

"That's the spirit!" Marty encouraged.

The waiter came then to take their orders, and the chatter focused on food for most of the meal. Jenny smiled to herself. These women might be smart, successful, and intimidating from the outside, but she had known them deep down where it mattered. They'd all had their share of problems—health, spouse, and career mishaps that drew them together as no glitzy soirees or newsworthy acquaintances could. Jenny was relieved. They were still real and somehow, reality, the nitty-gritty truth of things, had become very important to her these days.

After air kisses and good-byes were shared by all, Jenny escaped into Tia's vehicle.

"Wasn't that fun?" Tia gushed as she slid into the driver's seat. "It was just like old times."

"Not quite," Libby said dryly. "I can't remember us having that many diamonds to flash around or big names to drop. I feel like a real plain Jane in that crowd."

"You?" Jenny said weakly. "What about me? By marrying at nineteen I insulated myself from almost everything they were discussing. I don't know what kick boxing is or what the weather conditions are in the Serengeti in March. I felt like Noah coming off the ark and seeing how the world had changed."

"Don't worry about it," Tia said. "Every life takes unique turns, and we all have different things we enjoy doing, that's all."

Jenny sat very quietly, pondering Tia's words. *What was it that Jenny Matthews enjoyed?* She'd enjoyed being with her husband, doing whatever he'd wanted to do. She had loved her church, though lately, in her tumultuous state of mind, it had been an uncomfortable place to be when she went. She cherished her friends, but they had lives of their own to lead.

Who, exactly, was Jenny Matthews and how did she—not friends, husband, or family—like to spend her time?

She must have made a small noise because Libby turned to her in the backseat. "Jen? Is something wrong?"

"It just occurred to me that I've spent my entire adult life catering to the wishes of others and that I don't even know what my own interests are anymore!"

"So you finally noticed?" Tia looked at her friend in the rear-view mirror.

"You mean you knew?"

"Jenny, you disappeared bit by bit into the role of Lee's wife. First you quit aerobics class; then you decided not to sign up for the stained-glass workshop. After a while you refused to consider going to the flea market with me just for a getaway."

"It was so apparent to everyone but me?"

"No. Just to Libby and me. We are the ones who know best how talented you are, and we felt the saddest when you turned your back on your own interests."

"I don't even remember having interests," Jenny sighed. "Those years were lifetimes ago."

"You're a great artist," Libby reminded her, as if Jenny had forgotten her skill with pastels and colored pencils.

"You dabbled in watercolors for a while," Tia added. "I still have one hanging in my bedroom."

"And you used to bake for the entire football team. Remember that? They used to call you Jenny Crocker."

"I'd forgotten!" Jenny sat back in her seat and smiled fondly at the memory. "They loved my chocolate chunk peanut butter cookies best. I made two double batches at a time and never had a crumb left."

"And the cheerleaders' bake sales always consisted of your baking, which sold first, and then the boxed mixes the rest of us cooked up." Tia grimaced. "I think that's what gave me my fear of the kitchen. Total humiliation at having my food rejected."

"Thanks for the memories," Jenny said as they pulled into the driveway of her house. "I enjoyed myself."

And she had. Jenny didn't even notice the uncommon quiet of the house as she let herself inside. Spot barely looked up from his primo location—the middle of the couch. Fine watchdog he was. He'd watch as everything in the house was stolen!

Jenny's mind was whirling rapidly. She went directly to Lee's study and began digging for a catalog she'd seen while searching for clues to Lee's financial life.

She found it facedown under a pile of magazines. It was a college catalogue like any other, but Jenny poured over it as though it held the key to a great mystery. But perhaps it did— the mystery of the rest of her life.

. . . .

"I have news!" was Jenny's greeting when Mike arrived at five o'clock the next afternoon. Since Jenny had fussed about his coming during "working" hours, he'd started coming later, telling her when she protested that he could do what he wanted on his free time. And that what he wanted was to finish this job properly.

"You made an Elvis sighting?" He wore his usual shabby jeans, a white T-shirt, and a faded plaid flannel shirt open at the front and hanging outside his jeans. "Or are you the lady who found a Monet in her attic with a bunch of other pictures of flowers from the five-and-dime?"

"I'm going to college!" Jenny clapped her hands together with childlike glee. "Me!"

"Great. When do you start?"

"Right away. The university offers adult-education classes that can be taken for college credit. I've signed up for a watercolor class and a portrait-drawing class."

"Very ambitious."

"Do you think it will be too much? It's just that Marty has her doctoral thesis to finish, and there's all that talk about Angelique and the Serengeti, and Lydia with her flooring problems. . . . I thought I'd better take two classes to catch up!"

Mike tucked his head back and looked at her as if she were a slice of bread short of a sandwich. Then a dawning realization spread across his features. "I get it. You had lunch with some of our old classmates, who gave you a raging inferiority complex. To compensate, you decided to become an artist so you'd have something to talk about too."

"That's right." Jenny appeared a little awed by his quick comprehension. "Tia and Libby still don't get it." She sat down on the top step, and her sundress spread around her like a fan. Only the tips of her bare feet stuck out beyond the pale yellow cotton. Jenny wiggled them as she spoke.

"I have to take my life back. I gave it away somewhere down the line—happily, I might add, but now that Lee is gone, I have to get it back. The only thing I could think of that I could do—something that would drive thoughts of Lee out of my mind, even for a few moments—was art. Lydia and the others kept talking about 'finding their passion' and discovering what it was that engaged them. The only think I could think of was painting, drawing, and creating something from nothing."

Then Jenny faltered. "Do you think I'm crazy?"

"No," Mike said slowly, a crooked grin gentling his features. "Long overdue, maybe, but definitely not crazy."

CHAPTER NINE

*Watercress: This plant was eaten by the Romans
to "quiet deranged minds."*

—WILDFLOWER FOLKLORE

Jenny walked out of her sixth interview of the day, stopped
at a nearby ice-cream shop to purchase a double banana split
with extra toppings and nuts, and went to her car. There, she
methodically ate the ice cream until she felt a huge lump forming
in her stomach.

If there was anything more humiliating than job hunting with
a résumé that included nothing more than "housewife" and a
list of voluntary positions for various charitable causes, Jenny
didn't know what it was. Her typing was rusty, her high school
accounting too elementary, and her last paying job was a stint
as a roller-skating waitress at a retro ice-cream parlor while she
was a senior in high school. It was embarrassing to consider
that her last *real* job was more than ten years hence. And she
really needed a job.

Her phone was ringing when she walked in the door.

"Well?" Tia asked breathlessly. "How did it go?"

"About as well as the maiden voyage of the *Titanic*. Where was my brain after graduation? What was I thinking to not have gone on to college? Did I plan to let Lee support me forever?"

"Yes, you did," Tia said bluntly. "I remember the conversation quite well. I even heard him encourage you to make being his bride your career."

"How could I have been so naive?"

"You were in love, that's all. Giddy. Moonstruck."

"And stupid."

"No use crying over spilt milk," Tia said with her usual practical tone. "I told you that you can work for me any time you want to."

"Thanks, but no thanks. It's time I learned to stand on my own two feet. Taking a job from you wouldn't be much different from expecting Lee to support me forever."

"Thanks a bunch."

"You know what I mean, Tia. I have to think of something that will bolster my self-esteem."

"How did your art class go?"

Pleased warmth seeped through Jenny. "Good. Very good, in fact. Finally, I've found something that keeps my mind totally engaged for an hour or two. In fact, I did something really crazy."

"No kidding?" Tia said wryly, as if to suggest that Jenny didn't have an impulsive or crazy bone in her body.

"I was on such a high from the painting classes, I signed up for a cake decorating class through adult education."

"What do they have to do with each other?" Tia puzzled.

"Cake decorating can be an art," Jenny said defensively. "And I love to bake. It will be fun."

"Speaking of fun, Libby and I have a surprise for you."

"Oh?" Jenny had good reason to be wary of her friends' surprises. Over the years these surprises had spanned the ridiculous to the sublime—from her bra cups filled with water and frozen solid at a slumber party to real diamond earrings, hardly more than chips really, purchased with money they'd earned baby-sitting.

"Three months at Health Place! Isn't that great?"

"Isn't that the gym near your store?"

"Exactly. You can go there every day to work out and then stop by for tea on your way home. I'd love to work out with you, but you know me—I get all the exercise I need here at the store moving, unpacking, and lifting." Tia looked very pleased with herself. "Isn't it a fantastic idea? Maybe you'll meet a man there."

Jenny, whose idea of exercise was a man-free hike in the mountains or a run with the sun beating down on her shoulders, murmured, "Yeah. Great."

. . . .

"Really great." Jenny muttered the next afternoon as she surveyed the impressive Cybex equipment and vast mirrored walls of Health Place. "At least there is no danger of meeting a man here—except those old enough to be my grandfather."

Every machine was in use, and every operator looked like an escapee from a senior citizens center, which, Jenny was to discover, was exactly the case.

"We specialize in geriatric health," a fit aerobics instructor in her fifties told Jenny. "Our company feels it has positioned itself well for the swell of aging baby boomers coming down the pike. We have gyms going up all around the nation." Then she smiled beatifically at Jenny. "But we love to have younger patrons as well. They are in the minority, of course, but a mix of ages is good. I hope you like it here."

"They were how old?" Tia screeched later when Jenny told her and Libby about her visit to the gym.

"Sixties mostly. Some seventies and a few eighties. I met the sweetest little lady who said she was eighty-seven and had increased her muscle mass by nearly 300 percent since she started weight training."

"This is terrible!" Libby moaned. "Tia, why didn't you research this place more fully before we bought the membership?"

"It's not so bad," Jenny hurried to say. "The people are really lovely. And some of them can bench-press more than I can. It's impressive, really, at their ages."

"Get a grip, Jenny. The bench-pressing part was just an added perk. It was the men we were hoping you'd meet that were our first priority." Tia said as she chewed on the end of her pen in annoyance.

"Then I'm glad. You two have no business trying to set me up with men. I don't want to meet any. It would be like a dog chasing a car for me to go man-chasing right now. What on earth would I do with one if I caught him?"

"Do you think we can get our money back?" Libby asked.

"I'll try," Tia said with a sigh.

"Oh no you don't. I'm going to that gym every day. The people are lovely, and it has shown me that I need to work on my physical health. But from now on, quit trying to create a love life for me!"

"The body is God's temple," Libby reminded Tia gently. "Maybe that's what he wants Jenny to take care of right now. She's lost a lot of weight. She could stand to bulk up a bit."

"Oh, all right." Tia looked unhappily at Jenny. "But this does not mean I've given up finding social outlets for you."

"You don't have a boyfriend, Tia," Jenny pointed out mildly. "Why don't you spend your energy on yourself?"

"Hah! Who has time? Not me. Besides, you are the one who is lonely."

Jenny shrugged helplessly and gave up. They just couldn't understand. Lee, even as flawed as he was, was not interchangeable with others of the male species or so easily replaced. But how could she expect them to comprehend? They were angry for her because she had not yet come to the point of working through her own anger toward Lee. But that would take time. For Jenny, love didn't fall by the wayside easily. It had to be wrenched from her with agonizing pain, as Lee had managed to do with his deception and his double life. And even with that, there was still much of him that she would always love. No one was purely good or thoroughly evil. Humans were multidimensional beings—so complex, so fragile, so mysterious. Jenny could never hate Lee, nor could she love him as she once had. Though so much was still the same, everything had changed.

Neither Tia nor Libby had ever had a truly serious relationship with a man. Tia was too independent and driven; Libby, too committed to her elderly parents. It was an area in which they'd simply have to "agree to disagree."

....

"Are you rebuilding the engine or just giving the old buggy a tune-up?"

Jenny scooted out from beneath her car when she heard Mike's voice. "Hi, stranger! Where have you been the past few weeks?"

Mike shifted uncomfortably from one foot to the other before answering. He was wearing even more disreputable garb than usual and held a pruning shears in his hand. "I had some other business to catch up on."

"I should think so," Jenny said as she stood up and dusted the seat of her jeans. "You were spending far too much time here. I'm surprised your boss didn't fire you. I'm glad your other customers finally got some attention."

"Oh, the boss is a good guy."

"But probably not a saint. I'm glad you got back to business."

"So what are you doing?" Mike indicated the car with the tip of the shears.

"My car broke down about three days after you were here last.

When I got the bill from the garage I almost had a coronary. The price of the part was under fifteen dollars and labor was two hundred and fifty! I decided then and there that I would no longer be taken advantage of, so I signed up for a basic car maintenance class the beginning of this month. It's a good time to be inspired to learn something, with all the community education classes just beginning. So far I haven't learned much more than how to change a tire, check the oil, and add water, but I can save a bundle if I learn how to change oil, add my own window cleaner, change wiper blades, and a few other things."

Jenny studied him as he kicked the tires of her car and ran his hand along the rear fender. "Good for you," Mike said with approval. "It's nice to see you becoming an independent woman."

Those were words that would never have come from Lee's mouth, she realized. Lee had liked the fact that she depended on him 100 percent. She had never minded because she was comfortable with the verse in Colossians that said "You wives must submit to your husbands, as is fitting for those who belong to the Lord." But she was beginning to see that there was a difference between submission and dependency.

Her total dependency on Lee had weakened her. Every time a minor household emergency had come up, it had felt like a full-blown crisis to her. She'd felt helpless when the washer overflowed or a fuse had blown. She'd needed to call a repairman when the refrigerator overheated, only to learn she could have prevented the catastrophe by cleaning the pan beneath it. Lee had taken care of all these things, never once showing her how to do it herself. He had enjoyed keeping her dependent on him. Lee had unintentionally dismissed the second part of the statement in Colossians: "And you husbands must love your wives and never treat them harshly." He had never intended to be unkind by keeping her wrapped in a protective blanket of love, but now, without him, the harshness of the world showed her that he had kept her from being ready to face it.

That was why Mike's attitude intrigued her.

"What are you staring at?" He was looking at her suspiciously, his boyish good looks never more obvious.

"You must be a very secure person," she said.

"Where did that thought come from?" He raked his fingers through his hair in puzzlement. Sometime during the last few days, he'd had a haircut. The ponytail was gone, and he looked clean-cut and handsome, the last sign of his rebelliousness gone with the snip of a shears.

"My husband liked to work on the car himself. I wasn't allowed. I guess he thought it wasn't a woman's job."

"A woman's place is in the House," Mike intoned. Then he winked. "And in the Senate."

A bubble of laughter burst from her. "You are still a scamp, do you know that?"

"Thanks, I think."

"Lee didn't tease me much," Jenny said softly. "He was a very serious man."

"Nothing wrong with that."

"No. There isn't. It's just that you are so different that it startles me sometimes. I forget that all men aren't Lee."

"Pardon my cliché, but variety is the spice of life." Mike kicked at the pavement with the toe of his scuffed boot. "Jenny, do you ever *not* think of Lee?"

She considered the question carefully, wanting to give him her most honest answer. Mike was the only one in her life who actually asked questions about Lee, wondered how she was feeling about him. Everyone else was so busy trying to make her forget; only Mike allowed her the freedom to remember.

"When I'm painting or decorating a cake I forget about everything but what I'm doing. It's as though the act of creating something out of nothing engages my whole brain, leaving no time or space for random thoughts."

Now it was Jenny's turn to poke at a crumbled spot in the

concrete beneath her. "I realize that Lee was a different man from the one I thought I married. It makes me angry, sad, and regretful. I'm so confused. Does that make me a traitor?"

"How so?" Mike seemed to melt against the side of the car, his arms crossed in front of his chest, his hips angled, one leg crossed in front of the other. "Give me an example."

Jenny looked at the ground as she chose her words. When she looked up, there was sadness in her eyes. "I wonder sometimes if what Lee and I had together was real at all. Was I always living a lie?

"He wanted me to depend on him, and I did. Too much. He made everything seem so easy that I took it at face value. I should have been more aware and watched for signs of trouble. But instead I trusted him implicitly. Perhaps that was too much for him. I gave him too much responsibility for my life. I expected to derive my happiness from him. That wasn't fair of me. Only after his death did I realize that I expected him to shoulder more than he could handle."

"Those aren't the words of a traitor, Jenny, but of a bereaved wife who feels guilty for all the 'should haves' and 'could haves' in your married life. But there's nothing that can be changed now. All you can do about the past is learn from it."

A reflective expression flickered on Mike's features. "For as little as my parents thought I was listening to them, I certainly learned a lot from them. Every morning after breakfast and devotions, I was excused from the table when my mother said, 'Time to get back into the harness.'"

"Whatever did she mean by that?"

"I asked her once and she laughed. She said she remembered her grandfather's draft horses—big Belgians with feet the size of plates. Ned and Nettie were their names. Her father would harness them up and use them to pull the wagon when he picked rocks from the field. Ned and Nettie always pulled together, Mom said, each taking part of the load, working together so that one did not tire more than the other. She said she and Dad were like those draft horses and marriage was like the harness holding them together. As long as they each pulled a fair share of the load, the work got done. And it was always easier to work together than to work against each other. What's more, as long as they were in harness, they never strayed. Not too glamorous a metaphor, but it worked."

They stood silently for a long while, both considering the concept that had held Mike's parents together for so long. "I like it," Jenny said finally. "So 'getting hitched' is a pretty accurate statement after all."

Mike laughed, and Jenny noticed the even flash of his smile and the strong cords of his neck. Then, like a thunderclap, she remembered the big news she had to share with him.

"I nearly forgot! I have wonderful news. I found a job!"

Mike held out his hand to Jenny and she gave him a high five, their hands slapping in the air. "Awright! Way to go!"

"It's not that impressive," Jenny said modestly, "but it's perfect for me. One of the couples at my gym owns a bakery and catering service. The lady told me one day as we waited for treadmills to open up that arthritis was forcing her to turn away business. She decorates all their wedding cakes, and it's becoming too much for her. I told her about my class and she asked to see some of my work. I'd just frosted six Styrofoam cakes for Tia to use as displays in her store—one for her wedding supplies, another for a child's birthday party, another to be surrounded by her tea sets—that sort of thing. Mrs. Meyers loved the cakes and hired me on the spot. I am now employed part-time as a cake decorator and caterer."

The look of admiration and pride on Mike's features made Jenny feel warm and rosy. It was odd how susceptible she was to his approval. Of course, she had known him forever, she thought defensively—just as long as she had known Lee, Tia, and Libby. Why shouldn't she enjoy it?

. . . .

"I feel as though I'm sitting in the Garden of Eden before the Fall," Tia said dramatically as she sprawled on Jenny's wicker chaise lounge the following Saturday. Libby had taken one big wicker rocker and Jenny, the other. They were in the new gazebo that had appeared one day while Jenny was at work. She and Mike had fought about it earlier that evening but Mike refused to remove it, saying it was a discounted sale item that he couldn't pass up.

Jenny had learned that Mike was laid back about most everything but her yard, which by now he had adopted as his own. "Do you know where Mike lives?" she asked.

"No. Why?"

"It must be an apartment somewhere. He obviously doesn't have a yard of his own to keep up."

"So relax and enjoy," Libby advised.

"He's probably luckier than the rest of us. Every time we buy something we have to take care of it—water it, clean it, store it—just like all those things of Lee's we put into your basement. More stuff means more responsibility, and that equals more worry as far as I'm concerned," Tia said.

"Those are pretty strong words coming from someone who sells 'stuff' for a livelihood," Libby commented.

"So I'm a contradiction in terms," Tia agreed. "Sue me."

"Maybe someday those things of Lee's will just be 'stuff', but right now it's all I have left of him," Jenny murmured.

"You have memories."

Jenny winced. "Yes, but right now the hurtful ones surface first."

"Listen to the rustle of the leaves on the trees and the pouring water in the fountain," Tia advised. "There's not a thing you have to do or think about right now. Just relax."

"Uhmmm." Jenny closed her eyes. She loved the sound of

running water. It reminded her of the days she and her friends had spent holed up in their pup tent in the backyard in the drizzling rain. They had napped, swapped stories, giggled, read Nancy Drew mysteries, and waited for the sun to shine. Suddenly her eyelids flew open. "Tia, I don't have any fountains that sound like that."

"You must. We all hear it." She cocked her head and listened to the sound of pooling, splashing water.

Jenny bolted out of her chair as though a firecracker had exploded beneath her. "Oh, no! It's the flower beds next to the house! I forgot to turn off the water. Mike left a note telling me to do it at noon."

"Jenny, it's seven o'clock in the evening."

The trio shared a horrified glance that propelled them all into action at once.

The flower beds along the far side of the house looked like rice paddies, so sodden that water was sitting on top of the soil, tips of the new plants barely protruding above the water. Many of the low-growing ground-cover plants were completely submerged.

"No. No!"

Jenny grabbed the faucet and gave it a hard twist. Tia raced through the puddles to do the same with another faucet at the far end of the house.

"This is awful!" Jenny moaned. "Will it kill the plants?"

"I'm not sure that's the worst of your problems," Tia said as she waded back to where the others stood.

Libby broke the bad news. "Jen, this water has been going into the window wells. Maybe we should check your basement for damage."

Jenny blanched, her eyes on the mini-lake that had collected in her basement window. "Lee's things! They're stored on this side of the basement."

She took off running, her thongs slapping at the heels of her feet, water splashing, soft ground sucking at her every step.

Jenny was already at the bottom of the basement stairs when Libby and Tia caught up with her.

It was worse than any of them had imagined. The unstaunched flow had poured into the lower level for most of the afternoon. All the cardboard boxes Jenny had piled against the east wall of the basement were soaked, sucking up water like dry sponges.

"We'd better get these outside to dry," Tia said, grabbing a box. She turned around to find Jenny on her knees on the flooding concrete, staring at the mess with a look so forlorn that Tia dropped the box and went to her side.

"We'll get it cleaned up, don't worry. By the time Libby and I are done you won't even know—"

"Lee."

"What?" Tia leaned closer to Jenny.

"Lee. That's all that was left of him and now it's ruined."

Libby leaned to open the box Tia had been carrying. In it was a collection of Lee's hockey trophies and framed photos of the team from each year they had played together. "You stored every single thing of his down here?"

"I thought it might help," Jenny said weakly. "Everywhere I looked, I was reminded of him, and the sadness kept returning. Libby, even our wedding pictures are in those boxes! Ten years—gone!"

It was a grim threesome that surveyed the disintegrating boxes. Tia was the first to move. "We can't just stare at this stuff. Let's salvage what we can."

Unfortunately, there was very little to save.

It was midnight by the time they had moved everything into the garage, sorted through it, and determined what could be kept and what had to be destroyed.

Jenny sat on the floor with a shell-shocked look on her face. Libby handed her a cup of tea, which she took with robotlike movements. "It's all gone. Every bit of it. Gone."

"I know of a place that restores photographs. Maybe they can do something with the wedding pictures." Tia tried to sound hopeful.

"I can't afford to have them done right now."

"When the time comes, then."

"And his books! He loved them so much."

"It's all just stuff, Jenny. You have what is most important about Lee left in your memories," Libby said. "Stuff fades sooner or later anyway. Yours just faded sooner, that's all."

"Maybe this is just another signal that it's time to move on. To leave the past in the past," Tia added.

"Move on to what?" Jenny scoffed. "Are you saying this is one of God's signals? If he wants me to move, why doesn't he show me where?"

"I believe God wants you to trust him to do that. Once you do—trust him completely, that is—he will show you."

Before Lee died, Jenny would have agreed with her friend wholeheartedly. But her trust in God had faded, lost somewhere in grief and confusion. She couldn't generate the feelings of trust she'd once had.

Where are you, God? she wondered. *What are you doing?*

....

"If you turn down one more date, Libby and I will start answering your phone and accepting for you!" Tia's dark eyes flashed. Two weeks had passed since the flooded-basement fiasco, and Tia was losing patience. "I know every one of the men who've called you, and they are all very nice."

"Nice. That's true, but none are my type." Jenny defended her reasoning to refuse the men from her church who had called her for dinner or a movie.

"What type is your type?"

Jenny opened her mouth and then closed it again. Not long ago she would have answered "Lee."

Today she was not so sure. He wasn't replaceable, like a broken lightbulb or a torn shirt. Nor was he as perfect as she'd once assumed. He was flawed, sinful, deceitful—all the things the Bible says about mankind. All the things she was.

Lee was now a part of her past. Jenny sensed that her future held something—or someone—far different.

"My type is someone who is businesslike, fiscally responsible, trustworthy, faithful, and spiritual."

"Jenny, that sounds like the trustee board at church, not a man!"

"Then fix me up with them!" Jenny allowed annoyance to color her tone. She was sick and tired of her friends assuming that a nice man to date would be a cure-all for her troubles. She was independent for the first time in her life and, to her amazement, liking it. It was empowering to know that she had the ability to chart her own course on the sea of life. Instead of being a little lifeboat attached to the side of a ship, she was the ship itself, traversing rough waters and not sinking.

"We give up," Tia said. She beckoned to Libby. "Let's get out of here and go someplace where we can be of help. We'll find someone who will actually listen to our good advice."

Libby shrugged helplessly and trailed out of the kitchen behind Tia.

Jenny smiled as she closed the door behind them. She knew they wouldn't be gone long. By tomorrow evening they'd have another "cheer up Jenny" scheme in place. Jenny almost hoped that something not-too-dreadful would happen to another acquaintance just to get her do-gooder friends off her back for a while.

It wasn't Tia or Libby, but Ellen, who showed up at her door later that evening.

"Come in, stranger," Jenny greeted her, glad to see the elegant-looking woman standing on her front step. "Don't you look nice?"

Ellen was wearing a slim red sheath dress that contrasted dramatically with her dark hair. Jenny thought perhaps she saw a little gray in the stylish coiffure, but it only enhanced Ellen's appearance.

Ellen came in, kicked off her black heels, and dropped her stylish little shrug into a careless pile next to them. "I'm exhausted. Could I possibly get a cup of tea and hide out here for a while?"

"Sure." Jenny paused on her way to the kitchen. "Hide out? From what?"

"Too much attention," Ellen said cryptically. "Get the tea and I'll explain."

When Jenny returned with the teapot and a display of crackers and biscuits on a plate, Ellen was staring out the front window into the darkening street.

"I've hated nights since I became a widow," Ellen murmured without turning. "My husband died at night. Every night I spend alone seems endless."

"I thought you were complaining about too much attention," Jenny responded. She set the tea on a small table and poured two cups.

"I know. I contradict myself." Ellen sighed and settled into the big chair Lee used to inhabit. It didn't bother Jenny to see her there. In fact, she rather liked the contrast of Ellen's scarlet dress against the upholstery. Then she reined in her wandering thoughts and turned to her friend.

"Do you need to talk?"

"How are you handling the loneliness, Jenny?"

That was the last question Jenny had expected Ellen to ask.

"All right, I guess. I have a lot of background noise in the house—music, television—I even play books on tape while I cook or clean. Anything to engage my mind and keep me from dwelling on things that distress me. I never turn all the lights off in the house, and I drink gallons of warm milk and cinnamon before I go to bed so I will sleep. I'm not able to read much yet because my concentration is so poor, but I have hopes. . . ."

"Then you are doing better than I am," Ellen confided.

"I am?" Jenny was dumbfounded.

"I don't want to stay home alone, so I accept every invitation I can. I've joined a dozen organizations, a volunteer rape crisis hotline, and a dating club."

Ellen chuckled at Jenny's shocked expression. "A Christian dating service, but a dating service nonetheless. I had my latest escort drop me off here so I wouldn't have to walk into my own home alone. Pitiful, huh?"

"Would you like to stay here tonight?" Jenny asked, stricken.

"No. I just needed someone to talk to, someone who might understand."

"Oh, I can do that, all right," Jenny murmured. Then she blushed. "Some nights I sleep in the twin bed in the guest room because it doesn't seem so large and lonely."

"Then you do know what I mean!" Ellen looked relieved. "Sometimes I think I'm losing my mind."

"Two steps forward, one back. I think you told me that once."

"Then I'm in my two-steps-back phase. I'm not a wimp, Jenny, but being a widow is tough, even for a strong woman. Sometimes I want my husband back so badly I ache in every fiber of my being."

Jenny nodded. She'd suffered the same unrelenting, incurable pain. She screwed her face into a thoughtful expression. "I know. I visit that place daily."

"And how do you escape it?" Ellen asked.

Jenny considered her answer. "I don't really know. Sometimes, even though I have my doubts that God is listening to my whining anymore, I pray. Sometimes I force myself to list all the good things in my life I can think of. Sometimes I mentally plant a garden or remodel a room in the house. I'm trying so hard to not look back."

"That's the key, isn't it? Not looking back. Jenny, do you hear yourself? Do you realize how far you've come?" Ellen's eyes brightened. "My dear, you have just made my day!"

"I have?"

"You have!" The tension in Ellen's face had been replaced by something far more peaceful. "And you just said the very thing I needed to hear."

"Which was?" Jenny felt as if this were a little surreal. She didn't know what she could possibly have said to create such a transformation in her friend.

"You've quit looking back!" Ellen said. "That's the trap I've been falling into lately and didn't even realize it! Why couldn't I figure that out for myself?" She pretended to knock herself on the forehead with the heel of her hand. "I was buying into it all and not even aware of it. Seeing you reminded me that our lives are entirely different now, whether we like it or not. My counselor warned me about this, about times when it would seem like I'd forgotten all the painful lessons I'd learned. But talking to you reminded me that all we can do is look forward. And the best way to do that is . . ."

". . . by not looking back!" Jenny joined Ellen in completing the sentence.

Ellen finished her tea, her features far more peaceful than they'd been when she arrived. Her dark eyes were glowing as she held Jenny's hands at the door and thanked her. "I remember the first time we talked. You said I helped you. Now you've helped me. Thank you."

"I wish I could take more credit," Jenny said, with a weak smile. "You seemed to figure it all out by yourself."

Ellen gave a quick glance heavenward. "Oh no, not by myself. Sometimes God gives us a catalyst to jump-start us, I guess. Thanks for being mine."

God. Jump starts. Catalysts. What did it all mean? Jenny wondered. If Ellen was so sure God was there working out her life, then was it possible he was working through Jenny's own doubt and confusion as well? They were miserable tools for an almighty God, Jenny decided. But he had used strange tools before—everything from blindness and disease to the belly of a whale.

Somehow that thought made her smile. Jenny could have sworn she'd spent a lot of time herself lately in the metaphorical belly of a whale. The one good thing she could say about her life was that at least it didn't smell like fish.

. . . .

A thump against the back of the house the next afternoon told Jenny that Mike was outside working in the yard. Spot had decided that Mike lived out there just as Jenny lived inside the house, and he hadn't even moved a muscle when he heard Mike's old truck clatter into the driveway. In fact, the dog had become so fat and relaxed that he even snored sometimes. Jenny allowed him to sleep on her bed just for the warmth of his body and the rumbly sound he made when he was chasing cats in his sleep.

Jenny scratched Spot's ears and worried about Mike as the sounds continued outside. Mike had worked so hard for her. At first it had been difficult even to notice the changes in the garden, let alone in herself. But as the weeks had passed, Jenny had seen many improvements in the yard, and she had found a calmness within herself that had been missing for a very long time. It had come when she'd started her mornings with devotionals and prayer, a habit she had forgone in the first months after Lee's death. Now she was able to see with new eyes the gift Mike had given her.

"What are you doing out there?" she yelled through the screen door as he dragged a concrete birdbath to another corner of the yard.

"Filling this corner. It looks pretty barren compared to the rest of the yard." He allowed the pedestal to settle into the earth and wiped his forehead with the back of his hand. "Heavy monster, too."

"Come in and have some lemonade. I made it for Tia and Libby, but they haven't stopped by yet." She pushed open the door and invited him inside.

"I'm dirty," he warned as he kicked off his boots to reveal snowy white work socks.

"Everything is washable. I'm in this weird phase lately that Libby calls 'ritual cleansing.' Out with the old, in with the new. And from now on, if it can't be washed in the dishwasher, the washing machine, or under a hose, I don't want it. I'm no longer Susie Homemaker."

"What brought that change about?" Mike settled down at the table. It flitted through Jenny's mind that he looked as if he belonged there.

"My priorities have changed, I guess. Things don't matter; people do—something to that effect. I've been struggling to regain my footing where God is concerned," she admitted. "He and I had a falling out."

"You fell; he didn't," Mike concluded.

"I guess so. But I still can't understand the *whys*. Why did Lee have to die? Why did it happen at a low point in his life? Why me?"

"Jenny, are you still afraid of dying?"

"Of course not!" Then she paused. "Maybe just a little . . . I feel like everything has been kicked out from under me and there is nothing I can trust 100 percent." *Even God*, she added to herself.

Mike was silent so long that Jenny grew uncomfortable. "Mike?" she finally ventured.

"I've said it before and I'll say it again. Until you come to grips with Lee's death—and your own—and that fear is banished, you can't really live, Jenny."

"My death?" she tried to sound lighthearted. "I'm not planning to go anywhere."

"Neither was Lee."

Jenny felt a cold chill go all the way to her center.

"I don't want to talk about this, Mike."

"I know you don't. I didn't either, but when I finally got around to it, to listening to my father, I felt better."

"Conversations about death will never make me feel better."

"But conversations about life will."

"You are contradicting yourself."

"Death is part of life. 'When Adam sinned, sin entered the entire human race. Adam's sin brought death, so death spread to everyone, for everyone sinned.' Not one of us is going to escape it."

Jenny felt like childishly covering her ears and making noises to block out Mike's voice.

"Have you known anyone who is so afraid of dying that they forget to live? Someone who doesn't travel on an airplane because it might go down? Or travels to New York City because he is afraid of crime? Or spends her life bleaching clothes and sanitizing counters so no germs can get to her? Maybe you know someone who never leaves the house during flu season or won't share a bag of popcorn—"

"What on earth does all that have to do with anything?"

"They aren't living, Jenny. They aren't appreciating this amazing world we live in because they won't travel. They cocoon themselves in their perceived idea of 'safety' from flu bugs, crime, or accidents so they won't die. But we're all going to die, whether we wash our hands before every meal or not. That leaves us only one thing to do."

"Now what?" she said peevishly.

"Accept death. Embrace it."

"Embrace death? Do you mean something like 'Wheee! I'm dying!'"

"I'm not crazy. You just think I am. Consider what I've said for a moment. God promises us an afterlife far better than anything we can imagine. If we accept his gift—the death and resurrection of his Son—then we can live without fear. Both living and dying will be adventures planned for us by God." Mike winked and added, "He's the ultimate tour guide."

Jenny didn't know what to say. Mike had managed to spear through the core of her fear and confusion right to the heart of the matter. She had lost her faith, and she wanted it back.

"Leave it in the hands of your tour guide, Jenny. God will get you there."

Before she could speak, Mike snapped his fingers. "I almost forgot." He stood and went to the screen door. He reappeared with a tiny basket filled with pansies.

"How pretty!" Jenny exclaimed.

"Would you like to know what pansies symbolize?"

"Of course." Jenny fingered a velvety, jewel-toned petal.

"Reaching deep inside for thoughtful answers."

"Did you plan this?" she asked suspiciously.

Mike laughed, and the smile lines at the sides of his eyes creased appealingly. "No, I wouldn't have been so clever."

He leaned toward Jenny and brushed his knuckles against her cheek. "Think about it, Jen. Good night."

And he was gone.

CHAPTER TEN

According to the symbolism of the sunflower,
being the best is transitory
but being happy is forever.

There was no sleeping for Jenny that night after her conversation
with Mike. The pansies on her bedside stand reminded her of
their talk every time she opened her eyes to peer at the illumi-
nated digital clock. At 3 A.M. she got out of bed and went to the
kitchen to warm some milk.

She dug for notepaper while her milk was heating and settled
at the table with the steaming mug. The yard was turning into
such a serene place that Jenny often found herself making notes
of her ideas for the yard to run by Mike. She wanted projects she
could do herself for little or no cost and knew that whatever she
could think of he would know how to implement.

As she sketched her ideas and sipped the milk, Jenny thought
about Mike. She couldn't continue to haunt him for favors and
accept his free labor any longer, no matter how many times he
insisted it was fine with his employer. Jenny chewed on the tip
of her pencil. By the look of his clothes and the disreputable

rattletrap he drove, it was obvious that he needed to spend his time working at a job that paid him in something more than lemonade and Libby's cookies.

"I hope you understand that this is for your own good," she murmured aloud as she flicked through the yellow pages with the eraser end of her pencil. Jenny jotted down the phone number of How Does Your Garden Grow? She would call there in the morning, tell whoever was in charge what a fine worker Mike Adams was, but that she no longer needed him at her place. Their business wasn't making anything from her as it was, according to Mike, since he was using overstocked plants. They should be glad to see her disappear from their list of clients. That decision made, Jenny yawned and went to bed.

"Aren't you afraid of hurting Mike's feelings?" Libby asked over morning coffee when Jenny told her what she had decided. "He's worked very hard here. Maybe he'll think he's not good enough for you."

"He knows that's not true. I've been telling him to tend to his own income for a long time. Besides, I did a great deal of bragging about him to the lady to whom I spoke. Maybe he'll get a raise."

"It certainly looks like he needs one. Why would anyone that smart choose to muck around in the dirt? He could have been any kind of businessman. But a gardener? There is no accounting for taste."

After Libby's departure, Jenny took her coffee mug to the front porch to bask in the early sun. She tipped her face to the warm, healing rays and soaked them in until she could feel her muscles soften. So engrossed was she in this relaxation exercise that she didn't even hear a guest drive to the house or walk up the wide front steps.

The visitor was leaning against the porch railing, arms crossed, looking amused when she opened her eyes.

He was dressed in chinos and a chocolaty brown polo shirt that did something wonderful to his eyes. He wore deep brown loafers the color of his shirt, and there was not a hair out of place on his head—a man straight out of *GQ*. For a moment, Jenny thought she was dreaming. *Why was this gorgeous man standing there watching her doze?*

Then recognition dawned. "Mike! What are you doing here?" She sat up and scrubbed at her eyes. "And why do you look that way?"

"What way?" He jingled his car keys in his right hand. Jenny looked beyond him to a brand-new platinum V-8 Jeep Grand Cherokee.

"Where is your junker?"

"Which question do you want me to answer first?" The smile lines deepened.

"What are you doing here? And did you rob a bank?"

He chuckled. "No. I haven't even visited an ATM machine. And I'm here because you called me."

"I don't even know your phone number." Jenny uncoiled and went to stand in front of him.

"You said you wanted to fire one of my landscapers."

"Yes, but—"

"By the way, thanks for saying you thought I deserved a raise. I'll have to take that up with myself soon."

"Huh?" Jenny's nose wrinkled in bemusement.

"I'm the owner of How Does Your Garden Grow?, Jenny, and one of its landscape architects. I do like the idea of a raise. Thank you for suggesting it. My secretary thought it was a real hoot."

"But you always looked so—"

"Scruffy? Dirty? Sorry. I was helping unload a semi when your call came in. When I heard your name, I decided to make the visit myself. My *real* lawncare people wear shirts with the company logo on them. It feels good to occasionally get down and grub in the dirt, so I decided I'd do your job myself. I didn't mean to trick you, but I knew you'd probably send me away if you thought I was doing charity work for an old friend."

"But isn't that what you've been doing?" Jenny asked, unsure if she should be angry or flattered.

"No. I was doing it as much for myself as for you. I got into this business because I have a knack for making things grow and a love of digging in the soil. As my business expanded, I found less and less time to do what I liked best—be outside in the sun with the plants. You were my opportunity. Besides, you have to remember the iris."

He gave her a single graceful stem with a flower so velvety blue and purple that it hardly looked real.

"And what does this mean?" Jenny asked, relenting.

"Creativity will bear fruits of contentment. In this case, for both of us."

"Don't be so self-effacing. You tricked me!"

"Do you mind? Really?"

He wore the boyish, chastened look that she had seen many times before—always when Mike's father had discovered his son's latest disobedience.

"Michael," she said with a heartfelt sigh, "you teach me patience."

He roared with laughter. "You remember that? After all these years?" Mike shook his head. "My father said that every time I screwed up. I must have made that man into a saint a hundred times over! Does that mean you'll let me finish what I started?"

She threw her hands in the air. "You never listen anyway. Should I expect anything different now?"

"Not if you're smart." He lifted a cardboard tube from the floor by his feet. "I've finished the plans for your yard—weeks ago, in fact. That's what I've been working from all this time. Want to take a look?"

"No. I can't afford you and I can't trust you. Those weren't overstocks you've been bringing. You've been giving me your best items and not charging me. You know I can't afford to pay you right now. . . ."

"Jenny, allow me this. I've been having more fun with your yard than you have. You've let me do everything I've wanted, and you've got to admit, it's turned out well. If you'll let me finish and agree to have the work photographed, I'd like to enter a competition that's held each year among landscape architects. Usually I set up a faux garden somewhere at the greenhouse. It would be far better for me to use a real yard. What do you say?"

"You aren't making this up, are you?" she asked suspiciously.

"Not a bit of it. In fact, I'll show you the magazine that announced last year's winners. How's that?" He looked pleadingly at her, like a little boy terrified of having his brand-new bike whisked away. "Please?"

"Oh, for pity's sake! Go ahead! Build a pagoda if you must. But I'll pay you back somehow, someday."

"Deal." Mike grinned. "I'll have the pagoda delivered tomorrow."

With Jenny muttering something about Mike being incorrigible, they spread his designs out on the kitchen table, holding the corners down with two mugs of hot chocolate, a plate of cookies, and a floral centerpiece. Mike pointed out each idea with an enthusiasm that amused Jenny. He was like a little boy showing off a prize. How lucky he was to have found himself and a career he loved. If only she could do the same for herself.

"Mike, I've been meaning to ask you . . ."

"Yeah?" His fingers were stepping out the number of plants he'd added for a rosebush hedge.

"How is your father?"

His hand stilled over the paper, and he took a long time to answer. "Fine."

Jenny blinked, startled at his clipped tone. "I didn't mean to pry."

"I know. Dad is fine."

"Do I deduce from the tone of your voice that you don't want to talk about your father?"

"Not tonight. There's still some pain between us, Jenny. There is a thing or two about my past that Dad has had a hard time coming to grips with."

And that, Jenny knew, was the end of that subject for the evening.

. . . .

"You are kidding!" Libby clapped her hands to her cheeks to dramatize her astonishment. "Naughty Mikey? A successful businessman?" The trio was sitting around Jenny's kitchen table on a bright fall Saturday, drinking tea and sampling Libby's latest attempt at the perfect breakfast Danish. Since Lee's death, they had begun sharing breakfasts once or twice a week.

Spot circled the table, going from woman to woman, begging for food by laying his chin on someone's thigh and looking into his target's face with dark, plaintive eyes.

"With five lawn-and-garden stores around the state," Tia murmured, obviously awed by the achievement. "Wow."

"That will teach me never to judge a book by its cover," Jenny admitted.

"Or a man by his clothes. I'll bet Mike cleans up really well," Tia added thoughtfully.

"Oh, no you don't," Jenny protested, already knowing what she was about to say. "Don't you dare suggest we see more of each other socially. We are friends, and I want it to stay that way."

"Party pooper," Tia groused.

Jenny had to admit, however that she was growing more and more curious about Mike. He'd learned life's lessons the hard way, just as she had. Her wounds were just fresher. His reticence about his father was one symptom of unresolved grief.

But what did she—a new widow who'd been left in financial chaos and confusion—know? She had nothing to offer another person except friendship when she felt so empty herself. It was obvious that Mike felt the same way. He had never confided to her anything personal about himself or his family. It was as though they didn't exist, except for the occasional pithy quote from his father.

Jenny was grateful that Mike had never shown a hint of interest in her other than friendship. His hands-off policy was rigid to the point of sterile—the very thing Jenny needed in order to trust him.

Therefore, it was rather mind-blowing when Mike arrived a few minutes later, in his disreputable truck, with a young boy in tow.

The boy was dark, with some of the same intensity that Jenny remembered so clearly from her own childhood with Mike. He was slim and agile as he darted to the back of the truck and began to unload bags of peat moss, as if he'd done it dozens of times before.

"Who is that?" Tia's dark brows furrowed so deeply that they practically met it the middle.

"Do you think it's who and what I think it is?" Libby moved to the kitchen window for a closer look.

"Did Mike ever mention that he had children, Jenny?" Tia stared over Libby's shoulder at the boy whose actions and body language were the mirror image of Mike's.

"No. He never says a word about family."

"He's married and has children!" Libby wailed, her disappointment palpable. "And we thought that maybe someday . . . in a year or two . . . you and he would . . . oh! Why'd he have to go and do that?"

Jenny, surprised at her own disappointment, had not realized that she had actually cared whether or not Mike might be available to her.

"I had no idea," Jenny murmured.

"So you were thinking about him after all—even just a little bit?" Tia asked.

"Even if I were, it obviously wouldn't matter," Jenny retorted sharply, suddenly annoyed that her friends were trying to put words in her mouth.

"But you are finally noticing that the world did not end when Lee died. That's progress, Jenny. You've taken a big step back into life."

Jenny shrugged. "Maybe you are right. I don't know if I've turned some mysterious emotional corner, or if the reality of the financial mess Lee left me has shown me that he wasn't perfect and has allowed me to move on."

"You've got him in perspective now, Jen, that's all. Your years with Lee are very important chapters in your life, but they aren't the only ones to be written. God has plans for you. He said so in Jeremiah: 'For I know the plans I have for you,' says the Lord. 'They are plans for good and not for disaster, to give you a future and a hope.' And God just doesn't lie."

Jenny sighed and turned from the window. "My immediate future includes aerobics," she announced. "Now, if you two will excuse me, I have thirty minutes until class begins."

God doesn't lie, Jenny mused as she changed into shorts and a T-shirt for her morning workout. She'd grown to enjoy her time at the gym and the lovely people who frequented it. She'd never had as much grandparenting as she'd had since she'd started coming here. Everyone knew her story and made every effort to be kind.

Mrs. Meyers, the woman for whom Jenny was decorating cakes, walked into the dressing room as Jenny was tying her shoes.

Jenny was one of the few who wore real workout clothes here. Most of the ladies dressed in the shiny, brightly colored two-piece jogging suits so popular with this age group. And they all

had their hair salon-styled and sprayed and their makeup pains-
takingly in place. For most, the gym was the social event of the
day. The coffee shop was always busy, but the sauna and steam
room were Jenny's exclusive domain.

"How are you today?" Jenny asked.

"Good for an old woman like me." Mrs. Meyers was warm,
funny, and had a quick wit.

"Age is an attitude."

"And it's my attitude that old age is a bummer." Jenny
suppressed a grin. Mrs. Meyers tried to keep current on whatever
new vocabulary came her way from her customers at the bakery.
She especially enjoyed the teenagers who stopped after school
for snacks.

"Arthritis acting up again?"

"Worse than ever. My doctor says I have to get off my feet and
quit using my hands so much."

"That's not so easy," Jenny commiserated. The bakery was
practically a child to the elderly woman. Mrs. Meyers wouldn't
leave it in the hands of just anyone.

"I know. Say a prayer for me, will you, dear? There's an answer
out there, I know. I just have to find it."

After she'd returned home from the gym, Jenny sat at the table
holding her coffee cup in both hands and thought of all that had
transpired in her life lately.

She'd resented Tia and Libby's unrelenting pressure to "rejoin
the world" and yet somehow, when she hadn't been paying
attention, the process had begun. The painful reality of Lee's all-
too-human flaws, the quiet yet steady daily presence of Mike in
her yard, the single-stemmed flower he so often gave her—the
tulip, which represented turning adversity into victory; the
Welsh poppy, which was to "release optimism"; and one day, a
single mushroom, which, according to Mike, signified "surviving
darkness." There was also the unflagging support of her friends

who had moved her through a wall of denial and pain without her conscious awareness.

Jenny now sensed a plan unfolding, a plan too complex and too wise to be coincidence. Who else could it be, influencing her life so profoundly and so subtly, but God? Through all her doubt, denial, and disbelief, he had begun to stitch a new tapestry for her life.

"Oh, ye of little faith . . ." Jenny murmured to herself. "Shape up!" She went to stand in the window and watch the man and child loading tools. As Mike closed up the truck, he said a few words to the boy. The child spun around and headed for Jenny's door.

She had it open before he had a chance to ring the bell.

"Hi, there," she said. "What's your name?"

"Luke Adams." Suddenly he looked shy and began stubbing his toe into the concrete step, a habit Jenny always associated with Mike. "My dad said to tell you that we'd come back later. He has a bunch of stuff to do today, but he'll be free tomorrow night."

Even though there was no doubt in her mind that Luke belonged to Mike, it still felt odd to hear him called "Dad." That was mostly, Jenny realized, because if Mike was "Dad," then there was likely a "mom" in the family too. Mike's careful hands-off brand of politeness now made sense. He was an honorable man. That was apparent. And a secretive one.

What other surprises did he have in store?

Then she realized that Luke was still there, staring at her in puzzlement. "Are you OK, lady?"

"Oh yes. Just fine. I was daydreaming, and my thoughts wandered, I guess."

Luke processed that and accepted it without question. Then he surprised her with a complete switch of topics of conversation. "Do you like horses?"

"I suppose I do. It's been a very long time since I've been around any."

"Do you want to come to the horse show this Saturday? I'm showing my horse in halter and Western pleasure classes." Luke looked sincerely hopeful, as if he'd be disappointed if this total stranger did not say yes.

"My dad says you are really lonesome. He says you stay in your house a lot. That must be boring. I thought maybe you'd like to come and watch me. Everybody else is busy on Saturday and can't come, so I thought maybe you . . ."

Jenny marveled at the thoughtfulness of this child and wondered if his father had put him up to it. But as she'd been told before, she shouldn't "look a gift horse in the mouth."

"Thank you very much. I'd like to see you and your horse."

"You would? Really?" The boy had obviously expected to be turned down. "Great! It's in the 4-H arena at the fairgrounds. We start at two. It's mostly parents there, so you don't have to come early to get a good spot. You do know where the fairgrounds are, don't you?" Luke sounded as though he were talking to someone without all her faculties.

"I can find it," Jenny said with a chuckle. "And thank you very much. It's a date."

Luke made a face at the sound of the word, raced back to the truck, and climbed into the passenger seat. Mike started the engine, and they disappeared down the road.

"OK, God," Jenny said aloud, "if you are weaving a plan for me, where does that child and a horse show fit in? Or are you just pulling my leg?"

. . . .

"A date? Cool!"

Jenny smiled to herself as she listened to the response of her friends. She hadn't yet told them the "date" wasn't more than ten or that he was proof positive of Mike's marital status. It served them right for being so pushy.

"Tell us all about him," Tia demanded as she kicked off her high heels and put her silk-stockinged feet on the coffee table.

"I know this sounds shallow," Libby said, blushing slightly, "but is he cute?"

"Adorable." Jenny could answer that one honestly. "One of the cutest males I've seen in a long time."

"And sweet?"

"Very."

"Where are you going?"

"To a horse show. He's participating."

"Oh, how wonderful," Libby sighed. "Horses are so beautiful."

"He's an athlete, then?" Tia appeared pleased. "A cowboy?"

"I guess you could say that."

"Is he tall, dark, and handsome?"

"He's dark and very good-looking."

"But not tall?" Tia frowned. "You aren't dating a stump, are you?"

"He comes to here on me," Jenny said, pointing to a spot below her shoulder.

"What?" Both friends leaned forward.

"And he's a child! Now I'll thank you both to leave my social life alone!"

"Oh, Jen, you're teasing us!" Libby chastised. "Shame on you!"

"You deserve that and more, the way you've been pressuring me," Jenny retorted. "I need to move at my own pace through this. I'm sorry if I'm a turtle and you are both hares, but it is my life, you know."

"OK, OK, maybe we deserved it." Tia rolled her eyes. "And now that you've gotten your point across, you'd better tell us more. Where did he come from?"

"He is Mike's son. You saw them together in my yard."

Now she really had Tia's and Libby's rapt attention.

"So it is true," Tia moaned. "Mike is married?"

"And he never said a word!" Libby sounded truly disappointed. "Bummer!"

"That should teach you two matchmakers a lesson," Jenny continued. "From now on, live your own lives, not mine!"

"But our lives are boring," Tia admitted. "At least we can feel good if we help you."

Jenny shot her a glare that sent Tia's hands into the air in a gesture of surrender. "All right. No more sticking our long but very attractive noses where they don't belong. We can still pray for you, can't we?"

"Don't you dare quit." Jenny sighed. "I haven't been doing a very good job of it for myself lately, and I think it's your prayers that have been keeping me afloat."

"Let's do it now, then," Tia suggested. She sat up straight and reached out to grab her friends' hands. Libby scrambled to the edge of the couch, and Jenny perched on the corner of the coffee table. "Dear Lord, help Jenny to grow through this painful time and to know that you are her protection, as you so faithfully promised in Psalm 62. We praise you for wanting to give to your children in abundance. Help us to never take our eyes off you. Give us the faith we need to believe. We're weak, but you are strong. Give Jenny strength to work through the loss of her husband and her lifestyle. Help her to trust that you want far more for her than she could ever even imagine on her own. And help Libby and me to be the friends she needs. Amen."

Saturday morning Jenny was actually nervous as she prepared to drive to the fairgrounds. She wondered what to wear and settled on jeans, a white T-shirt, and a navy blazer. Not too casual, not too dressy. For some reason she didn't want Luke to feel embarrassed by his guest—especially after the boy had so graciously reached out to her. As she was going out the door, she turned back and grabbed an apple from the fruit bowl on the counter. She'd always heard horses liked apples. Luke's friendship couldn't be bought, but she could always try with his horse.

The 4-H arena was easy to find, marked as it was with the big

green-and-white cloverleaf, which symbolized the organization
and the four Hs—head, heart, hands, and health. Horse trailers
littered the large parking lot, and families intent on grooming
and exercising the lovely animals were everywhere.

Luke appeared out of nowhere and grabbed Jenny's hand.
"You came!"

"I said I would, didn't I?"

"Dad thought you might not. He said I shouldn't be disappointed if you didn't show up. He said you'd been having a hard
time lately."

"Oh, he did, did he?" Had she become so unreliable that
Mike felt it necessary to warn his child of her unpredictable
nature? A pang of regret went through her. What kind of
person had she allowed herself to become? Certainly not the
one she wanted to be.

Luke tugged on her hand. "Come on. I'll show you where to
sit, if you hurry up."

He'd saved two seats at the center of the arena. A small cowboy
hat had been placed on one to denote "taken."

"My dad always sits here 'cause he can see everything that goes
on." Luke practically pushed Jenny into the seat. "I have to go.
Somebody is watching Sunshine for me. See you later." And he
disappeared into a gaggle of other young cowpokes.

Jenny felt as out of place as a mouse at a cat show, but she
rather liked the sensation. It was time she stopped haunting the
places she and Lee had gone together and started gathering some
new experiences.

The youngest children performed first. Jenny had almost
figured out what the judges were looking for in each category
when she felt a warm body sink into the seat beside hers. She
was surprised and a little dismayed to see Mike, dressed in
chinos and a white shirt, settling in next to her.

"Good. Luke's age group hasn't started yet." Mike flipped
through the program. "Are you enjoying it so far?"

"What are you doing here?" Jenny asked ungraciously. She hadn't expected to see him here.

"I always come to Luke's shows."

"But Luke said you couldn't come today and that no one would be here to watch him. That's why I agreed to attend." She hadn't expected to feel so sour about this. Of course, she hadn't expected to see Mike, either.

"My meeting ended early. I'd rather that he not expect me and have my coming be a surprise than tell him I'll be here and then disappoint him because someone is too long-winded to know when to be quiet." He smiled at her. "He's a great kid, isn't he?"

"About that . . . it might have been nice to have told me you were married and had a child. I know you are very tight-lipped about anything personal, but to omit the fact that you have a family? Isn't that carrying things a little too far?"

"I don't have a family. Just Luke."

"But what about his mother?"

"Shhhhh. Here they come." It was as if Mike hadn't even heard her. "Luke really loves that horse. They look great together, don't they?" Mike leaned forward with anticipation, his dark eyes fixed on one boy and one horse.

It was easy to see why Luke's horse was named Sunshine. She was a glorious golden palomino with a pale cream mane and tail. Jenny knew very little about horses, but even she could see that Sunshine's head was fine and well shaped and her body confirmation picture-book perfect. What's more, the boy on her back was beaming like sunlight too, with a pride so chest-swelling that it was a wonder he didn't just float right off the horse.

"What a beautiful creature!"

Mike chuckled. "She's my childhood dream horse. Many nights I went to sleep thinking about an animal just like her. I guess that's why when Luke wanted her, I couldn't resist."

Another surprise. Who would have thought the naughty child,

rebellious teenager, and sullen young man would have had dreams such as these?

Before she could talk herself out of it, Jenny took a deep breath and dived into deep water. "Mike, where is Luke's mother?"

He didn't even turn to her until Luke had completed his first round in the arena, warming up for the Western Pleasure class. When he did, he shrugged. "I don't know."

"You fathered a child and misplaced his mother? Excuse me?"

"I didn't misplace her. She left." His eyes were cloudy when he looked at her. "We lived together but weren't married, Jenny. She was angry when she got pregnant and wanted an abortion. I wouldn't let her, and she stayed until Luke was born. She was gone by the time he was a month old."

He watched the shock and surprise register on Jenny's features. "I never said I was well behaved, Jen. Not even for a moment. I did a lot of things wrong, including fathering a child out of wedlock."

His expression turned rueful. "Now perhaps you can understand why my father doesn't know what to make of me. He still keeps me at arm's length, waiting for the next bomb to go off. He trusts that I've repented and God's forgiven me, but he still doesn't trust me very much.

"I've got to be a good father. For my son's sake and for my own. Someday I want my own father to trust me."

"Why—"

Mike already knew what she was about to ask. "I was a troubled kid. I didn't like being singled as a PK—a preacher's kid. Or, as we say in intellectual circles, a TO—theologian's offspring. I rebelled. Gave my dad a great head of gray hair. When I showed up with Luke, I was afraid I'd give him a heart attack as well. Still, Dad never knew what drove me, how his expectations for me to be good seemed to compel me to be bad. There was a part of me he never understood."

Mike sighed and scraped his fingers through his hair. "So I

decided that if I were so smart about what made bad little boys tick, then I'd better apply the knowledge where it would do some good."

"And now you are parenting Luke."

"It seemed like a good idea at the time." A wide grin spread across his features. "And it's been a great idea ever since. I love being a father, Jenny. I'm planning to do everything in my power to show Luke that God is active in his life before he gets into the messes I did."

He took Jenny's hand and gave it a squeeze. "If anyone knows about God's forgiveness, it's me. He's had to forgive me for a lot, but he's never flinched once. My father was right about our Lord being an awesome God. I wish I'd listened earlier."

Jenny had a hard time keeping her attention on the show ring even though it was obvious that Luke and Sunshine were far and away above the others in their skills. Boy and horse seemed like a single graceful creature most of the time. But it was Mike who truly amazed her. While she'd insulated herself from all but Lee and her friends and church, the boy once voted "least likely to succeed" had triumphed not only spiritually but in other ways as well. Had she been so myopic all these years? It was becoming painfully clear that Jenny's priorities had been badly skewed. She had focused on her marriage, to the exclusion of other things equally important. She'd let it come between herself and God.

Had she forgotten this passage in Matthew? "I was hungry, and you fed me. I was thirsty, and you gave me a drink, I was a stranger, and you invited me into your home. I was naked, and you gave me clothing. I was sick, and you cared for me. I was in prison, and you visited me." Jenny felt sorrowful. Direction for her life had been there all along, and she had disregarded it. Instead of reaching out, she'd drawn inward, hoarding her love for Lee alone.

Lessons, lessons, lessons. How quickly she had learned them

since Lee's death! It was as though God had so much to say to her that every day revealed another insight.

Jenny bit at her lower lip. Libby would say God was moving in her life right now, that he wasn't as far away as Jenny thought. More confused than ever, Jenny turned to the arena and willed away the tumult in her mind.

CHAPTER ELEVEN

*The dandelion has been called "the tramp
with the golden crown."*

—ROBERT L. CROWELL

Jenny heard voices as she came out of her bedroom, towel-drying her hair. Libby and Mike were having a conversation in the kitchen. The table was set for a meal, and Jenny could smell Libby's famous fall menu—beef stew and biscuits.

They were laughing as Jenny entered. Mike looked up at her, and his features softened. "There you are. We've been waiting for you."

These communal dinners had become a regular part of their lives as the season changed and fall threatened the summer heat with cooler nights and shorter days. The garden was at its glorious best now. Occasionally Ellen joined them for a meal. Other times it was Luke or Dorothy. The BFF's extended family was growing.

Jenny's heart leaped at the gentleness of Mike's voice and the warmth in his eyes when he looked at her. It seemed like an eternity since someone had greeted her so lovingly. Even Lee, she'd begun to realize, had been less attentive the last months of their marriage. It made her both angry and sad to think of the guilty burden he'd carried secretly.

Because it had been so gradual, it wasn't until recently that Jenny realized Lee had been pulling away from her. Secrets and lies—the breakdown of communication—had all become so much more apparent in hindsight. Could she have done something if she'd known? That was a question she couldn't— wouldn't—ask herself. It was too late now to change the past. Besides, the present was sitting before her, looking at her with kindly eyes.

"Hey, you two! Are you having fun without me?" Jenny asked brightly. It was an effort to be upbeat, but it felt good.

"Not as much fun as we'll have now. I've arranged a contest— with prizes and everything." Libby looked mischievous.

"Now what? I've fallen victim to your contests before."

"But with this contest I've reached my all-time high. Look at this." Libby held out a lemon meringue pie so perfect it could have been artificial. The pointy peaks of meringue were perfectly browned, while the base remained a creamy white. The crust was obviously homemade, and Jenny knew what kind of squeeze-fresh-lemons-and-beat-as-you-cook-till-your-arm-falls-off method Libby used.

"My favorite," Jenny murmured. "Let me at it."

"Not unless you win the contest. Then you can have it for dessert. Otherwise you will get pudding from a box, and Mike will have the pie."

"I'm beginning to like this contest." Mike leaned forward in anticipation.

"You don't get many home-cooked meals, I take it?"

He grimaced. "I do, but I have to cook them."

"What's the contest?"

"You see before you my stupendously tasty beef stew." Libby

gestured grandly at the white casserole dish on the table.
"Tonight there is one small difference, and whoever can pick out
that difference will win the pie!"

"No fair," Mike protested. "If you've put some secret seasoning
in there and expect me to identify it—"

"Nope." Libby lifted the cover off the pot, and steam rose
around her. "There is one piece of pork in this beef stew.
Whoever finds and identifies it wins!"

They both stared at Libby as if she'd lost her mind. The stew
was thick with meat, vegetables, and aromatic gravy.

"That's like looking for a needle in a haystack," Jenny complained.

"Exactly. Have at it."

Jenny hesitated, but Mike grabbed a serving spoon and began
digging in the stew, eyeing each piece of meat as he found it.

"What are you doing?" Jenny demanded.

"Winning a pie."

"Not that easily, buddy." Jenny grabbed her fork and pushed
his spoon aside.

Gravy was splashing onto the table and elbows were jabbing
when Libby broke up the food fight. "This meal is to eat. Shall
we say grace?

"Dear Lord, thanks for food and thanks for friends. And thanks
for the opportunity to have a good laugh once in a while. Amen!"

Within seconds Jenny and Mike were back at it, studying each
piece of meat to see if it were fool's gold or the real thing. Libby
insisted on dishing up the stew in bowls to put an end to their
enthusiastic mining project.

"What if you gave him the pork?" Jenny complained. "Then
there'd be no way for me to win."

"Watch every piece of meat he puts into his mouth."

"Then how can I eat mine?"

"That's your problem. A contest is a contest."

"And why did you dish up your own?" Mike asked. "What if you
eat it yourself? Do you have plans to take the pie home again?"

"*Au contraire.* I happen to be the expert. I can pick out the pork in a heartbeat."

"Then it's oddly shaped," Jenny concluded. "Otherwise she couldn't tell with all that gravy on it."

That started the searching process again, and soon they were all laughing so hard they could hardly eat. It was Mike who speared a large triangular-shaped piece of meat and held it up for Libby's inspection. "This is it."

Libby held up her hand for a high five. "Good job. You know your protein."

She went to the counter for the pie. To Jenny she gave a dish of chocolate pudding.

Mike was nearly finished with his second piece of pie when he told Jenny, "Stop staring at me and eat your own dessert. I won fair and square."

Jenny glared at Libby. "I don't want to play with you anymore. Your games aren't any fun."

"Sore loser," Libby said cheerfully as she gathered her utensils. "I have to go home anyway. Even though it's been wonderful dining with you two, my parents need dinner too."

"You aren't going to make them do this, are you?" Mike asked, looking as if Libby's sanity might be in question.

"No, of course not. They have to mud wrestle for their dessert." With a wink and a wave, Libby disappeared out the door.

Mike and Jenny both burst out laughing.

"Have you seen Libby's parents?" Jenny asked when she could speak again. "They are sweet, frail old darlings that, given a mud pit, would plant a garden."

"I really can't go there. It's too bizarre for me." He studied her speculatively. "But I could share my pie if you were really nice to me."

"How nice?" Jenny's eyes narrowed.

"Make me some coffee and come sit with me on the couch?"

"Can I have a big piece of pie?"

"I'll cut them, you pick one."

"Fair enough." Jenny pulled out her espresso machine while Mike cut the pie and found Jenny a plate.

"You did take the biggest one," he observed when they were settled on the couch.

"You're eating your third piece!"

"A small one. Two of mine equal one of yours."

They both realized at the same moment that they had fallen into a Libby-inspired grade school camaraderie, and they laughed again.

Mike put down his plate and leaned back on the couch, extending his long legs out in a sizable stretch. When his arm came down on the back of the couch, it rested precariously near Jenny's shoulders.

They were quiet, neither anxious to break the friendly warmth of the moment.

Finally Mike said, "I'm glad I found you again after all these years."

"Libby, Tia, and me?"

"Yes. But especially you."

Jenny didn't know what to say. Was it their friendship that was so important? Or something more? Because she'd loved Lee Matthews for as long as she could remember, Jenny had not become proficient in flirting or other games single people play. She felt an overwhelming shyness flood over her.

"I'm glad you found us too." She turned to look at him and saw gentle amusement in his expression, which bolstered her to say more. "In fact, your work on the garden has been a real gift to me. I find myself looking out the window or wandering through the yard, checking to see what's blooming or what needs watering, and it reminds me that it is a beautiful world in which we live. I lost track of that for a while, and your garden gave that realization back to me."

"It's your garden, Jenny. Not mine. But if you'd like to think of it as a gift from me, please do. It's the kind of gift I'd like to give."

"What does all this mean?" Jenny asked.

The perplexity in her voice made Mike smile. "What does what mean? The garden? Lee's death? You? Me?"

"Yes. That."

"You don't ask difficult questions, do you?"

"It's just that I feel so . . . stretched . . . in every direction. Pulling and tugging. Happy and sad. Angry and compassionate. I don't know where I'm at anymore."

"Give yourself some time."

She gave a little sniff of frustration. Couldn't he think of anything more original or more helpful that that? Some days time seemed to be what was killing her.

She decided to change the subject rather than argue. "The zinnias and marigolds are fabulous, but the new perennial garden isn't looking good at all. I don't know much about violets or lilies of the valley and even less about sedum and feverfew, but I don't think I've overwatered them. They just aren't what they should be. They certainly aren't doing much growing."

"But they are doing what they are supposed to be doing," Mike said calmly.

"And what, exactly, is that? I thought flowers were supposed to bloom."

"Perennials are like people, Jenny. When they are transplanted from one place to another, it is a big shock to their systems. New earth, being dug up, and having your roots shaken and slammed down in a brand-new place. How can we expect them to flourish immediately?"

"Poor things. They sound like me—shaken to the roots, having life turned upside down, and being in a new life not of my own choosing."

"Exactly. So because of all the trauma they've been through, they go into a kind of sleep. They rest all that stuff happening on top of the ground and take care of their roots. They put them deep and firm and, though they aren't much to look at above ground, a lot is happening down below.

"They appear to be sleeping, and in a way they are."

"What good are sleeping flowers?" Jenny pulled a soft woolen throw from the arm of the couch and tucked it over her lap. She was not yet accustomed to the crispness of fall. Mike rubbed his hand against her arm, as if to warm her. Unconsciously she snuggled against him.

"Give them time, Miss Impatient One. Next season you will see a difference. They'll start creeping outward, growing at the top again because they've found their footing below."

"So by next summer they will look better?"

"Better, yes, but they aren't done yet."

"If I'd known all this, I'm not sure I would have had so many perennials—"

"But the third year will pay off big time."

"Why?"

"Because that's when they start leaping. They'll be covered with a riot of blooms, the foliage will be lush, and the plants will be as beautiful as anything you can imagine."

"Sleep, creep, leap." A smile graced Jenny's features. "I like that."

"It works that way for humans too, you know. You've been sleeping, Jenny. You've needed to regain your lost footing. Lee's death and the discovery of that other side of him was a terrible shock. This sounds corny, but you needed to take time to get your roots organized."

"Then what? I can sprout leaves from the top of my head?"

"Then you start creeping, venturing out into this new life of yours. Putting your toe in the water. You don't have to take any action that doesn't feel comfortable, but you can decide what your new life will be like. You can design a future and decide what you want from life."

"And begin making it happen?"

His smile was dazzling. "That's right. Start leaping."

Jenny, tucked beneath his protective arm and close to his warm strong body, understood—really understood—what he had been trying to tell her. "And if I'm tired of sleeping?" she asked, her face innocent as a child's.

"Then it may be time to start creeping." Mike smiled.

"How?"

"It's always a good idea to consult with God. He's our master gardener, you know. Then go for it. Do whatever you feel is right. Get a full-time job. Start researching a way to start your own business. Move." He paused. "Date."

Jenny looked up at him, and his eyes, so clear and steady, told her exactly what he meant. "Date me."

"I don't know. . . ." Then she rested her head against his shoulder and closed her eyes. He felt so strong and safe and right that it nearly took her breath away. "Well, maybe . . ."

"Good." He said the word so softly that she could barely hear him. A ripple of warmth spread through her.

"But I don't want to be hurt again," she whispered. "I can't be hurt again."

"It takes both sunshine and rain to make a garden grow, Jenny. Too much sunshine, and your yard would be a desert. Rain isn't bad. Sometimes it's exactly what you need."

"I can stand a little rain, but not a lot."

She didn't even know if they were talking just of the garden or of her life as well.

"And just a little creeping?"

"Yes." She could feel his thumb rubbing a warm spot into her shoulder.

"A drive in the country, maybe? Or a trip to the zoo?"

"Maybe that."

"On Saturday afternoon?"

"I think so."

"At two?"

"I could be ready."

"How do you like creeping so far?"

Jenny laughed and snuggled closer. "So far, so good. I think I might learn to like it."

....

"Hi, creeping Jenny, are you ready for a ride?" Saturday, promptly at two o'clock, Mike walked up the sidewalk to the porch, where Tia and Jenny sat on two big wicker rockers.

Tia's expression turned dumbstruck. "Did I just hear you call my friend a noxious weed? My grandfather hated creeping Jenny. He said it grew close to the soil and formed a mat on the ground with such deep roots he could never get it out!"

Mike grinned. "Ask her if she minds."

Tia turned to Jenny for support of her protest, only to see Jenny grinning as widely and goofily as Wonderland's Cheshire cat.

"What's going on?" Tia demanded.

"Jenny has consented to go to the zoo with me today."

"What for? What's at the zoo?"

"Lions and tigers and bears."

"Oh, my!"

"I think you two really are on a trip down the yellow brick road to Oz," Tia said. "Really, where are you going?"

"To the zoo!" they said in unison.

Tia was still standing on the porch looking as if two deranged monkeys had escaped when Mike and Jenny drove away.

Jenny laughed until she had to wipe away tears. "Poor Tia. That will absolutely ruin her day. She will never quit wondering where we really went."

"You do let her boss you around, you know. Of course, that's not new. Nothing has really changed since grade school."

"I know. It's just that I've needed bossing since Lee died. I was like a ship without a rudder."

"*Was?* As in past tense? *Was* but *are* no more?"

She bestowed on him a contented smile. "I am, after all, creeping Jenny."

The zoo was teeming with people when they arrived. Mike bought a bag of peanuts for the elephants and popcorn for Jenny. They stood at the fence around the pachyderm area as Mike tossed peanuts to a protective mother and her calf.

"She's not very generous with those peanuts," Jenny observed. "That baby has only had two."

"Poor trunk control. It's amazing the species is still in existence."

"Trunk control? Is it really—Mike! Quit teasing me."

"Can't. You are too gullible. I'm totally unable to control myself. You make it too easy."

"It was nasty to tell me that flamingo had broken off one leg."

"I would have gotten away with it too, if she hadn't decided to move and put the leg she had tucked underneath herself on the ground."

"I don't know when to believe you when you do that," Jenny chided.

"I do tell the truth some of the time," Mike protested. "Llamas do spit."

"That wasn't my best moment to think you were kidding, was it?"

"Good thing you have quick reflexes, or you'd have llama slobber all over your skirt."

Jenny dug a peanut out of the bag and tossed it to the mama elephant, whose trunk snaked down to make it disappear. "This has been such fun. I can't remember the last time I laughed like this."

"We don't have to quit laughing yet, do we?"

"Aren't you tired of hauling me around, tormenting me with your bad jokes and tall tales?"

"Not yet. Would you like to go for a drive? I know a place

in the country that makes the best ever freshly squeezed lemonade."

Jenny turned her face to the sky and almost felt like she was one of those plants of which they'd talked—soaking up the sun, growing, creeping. Leaping? "Hmmm. Sounds wonderful."

Neither spoke on the drive. Mike open the windows on his new Jeep and turned up the radio, as Jenny felt herself blissfully melting into the seat.

Had this been out here waiting for her all the time she'd closeted herself away? It was almost impossible to believe.

"You know," she said, as they sat on the patio of a tiny guest house sipping the largest, tastiest lemonade Jenny had ever had, "if you'd told me I'd ever have a day like this, I wouldn't have—couldn't have—believed you. I thought I'd died with Lee and all that was left of me was a shell. Then, when I learned about his gambling and his other life, I didn't even want the shell. I thought it would have been easier to die."

Mike swirled his straw in the lemonade, and ice clinked in the frosty glass. "If I learned anything from all my years of rebellion, anger, and acting out, it was that you should never put a period where God has planned a comma."

"And don't bury yourself before you've died?"

"Yes."

"How did you get so smart?"

"The hard way. By doing everything wrong the first time." He smiled. "But eventually God got through even my thick head. I consider that one of his biggest miracles."

"He had to use a jackhammer to do it?"

"Practically." Mike grew serious. "He's there for you, Jenny. I know that feelings can deceive you. You may not *feel* that God's watching over you, but faith isn't feeling. Faith is believing in things not yet seen. Faith is knowledge, not feeling."

Jenny reached out to take Mike's hand and draw it to her cheek. She could feel the heat of his palm and the chill of his fingers from the icy glass. His cologne—an evasive, evocative scent—filled her head. She closed her eyes and gave thanks that this wise, gentle, funny, hardworking man had come into her life.

. . . .

"Are you coming while it's still fall?" Libby tapped the toe of her dress sandal on the foyer floor. She and Jenny waited at Tia's front door while Tia put the finishing touches on an already flawless face. "Church starts at eleven. I'm sure the council debated having it later so you could get there on time, but—"

"Tsk, tsk," Tia clucked, "did our friend get up on the wrong side of the bed today?"

Libby threw her hands in the air. "I give up. She's late, and I get the blame for being crabby!"

Tia gave her friends a benevolent smile and breezed out the door, leaving Libby and Jenny to trail in her dust.

Jenny loved the old church. Built by a stonemason in the early 1900s, it had such a solid, sturdy look about it that it always made her think of Peter, the rock on which God built his church. Stained-glass windows made the inside glow with color, and vibrant burgundy floor runners led them down the aisle.

She looked around as she followed her friends and realized that even though she had continued to attend church after Lee's death, she hadn't made eye contact with a single one of the parishioners. How sad. There were wonderfully warm expressions beaming all around her.

"There is a guest pastor today," Libby whispered.

Jenny nodded as the pipe organ began to play. As usual, because of Tia, they were the last ones to be seated. Jenny relaxed and let the music wash over her.

For a Christian, nothing is really a coincidence, Jenny had decided, but all part of a master weaving done in unpredictable colors and threads, the pattern sometimes all but indiscernible to the naked eye until the work is complete.

It was one of those threads in a most unlikely color that was being woven in the church today, as the speaker chose 1 Corinthians 15:51-57 as his Scripture:

> But let me tell you a wonderful secret God has revealed to us. Not all of us will die, but we will all be transformed. It will happen in a moment, in the blinking of an eye, when the last trumpet is blown. For when the trumpet sounds, the Christians who have died will be raised with transformed bodies. And then we who are living will be transformed so that we will never die. For our perishable earthly bodies must be transformed into heavenly bodies that will never die. When this happens—when our perishable earthly bodies have been transformed into heavenly bodies that will never die—then at last the Scriptures will come true: "Death is swallowed up in victory. O death, where is your victory? O death, where is your sting?" For sin is the sting that results in death, and the law gives sin its power. How we thank God, who gives us victory over sin and death through Jesus Christ our Lord!

It was a passage she'd heard or read dozens of times before. She'd even considered it for one of the readings at Lee's funeral. But today, at this moment in time, when her roots had gone deep enough to steady her and she'd taken the tentative, creeping moves toward new life, God gifted her with a realization that was to change her life.

What a cocky, confident passage that was! There was no fear of death in those words! Only victory and triumph and confidence. It was, in fact, what Mike had been saying all along. Until you come to grips with your own death, you cannot really live.

She had already waited far too long, Jenny realized. Faithful as she'd thought she was, Lee's death had knocked the legs out from beneath her. The images of him bleeding to death on the kitchen floor, the paramedics, the funeral parlor, the vases of carnations, the tears, the loss, the fear . . .

She had begun to doubt. She had felt her fear, not believed with her heart that God's word was true. And until she dealt with her own motality, nothing would change. And the first person she had to talk to was God.

Jenny prayed through the sermon, the hymn, and the offering. Then she prayed through another hymn, special music, and the benediction. Only Tia shaking her shoulder brought her out the conversation she was having with God.

"Are you all right?" Tia's dark eyes were wide with alarm. "Did you feel faint? Is that why you didn't stand up?"

"Oh, no." Jenny looked up at her friends with shining eyes. "I'm feeling better than I have in ages!"

As they left the church Libby spread her arms wide. "Isn't this a beautiful day?"

"Heavenly," Jenny assented. "Downright heavenly."

CHAPTER TWELVE

*Passionflower: a symbol
of faith and piety.*

—*WILDFLOWER FOLKLORE*

Jenny burst into Tia's store so enthusiastically that the lids on all the teapots rattled.

"Careful. I'm not insured against human tornadoes." Tia looked up from her bookwork and plucked the reading glasses off the bridge of her nose. She sat at an antique writing desk, working beneath the glow of a small banker's lamp. A single rose in a crystal vase was the only ornamentation on the desk.

Across from Tia sat Libby, as rumpled and cozy looking as Tia was meticulous. Libby was wearing wrinkled cotton hiking shorts, heavy socks and boots, and a white long-sleeved blouse. Her hair was tucked under a billed cap, and an unruly ponytail poked out from the hole in the back of the cap. She held a mug of steaming coffee in her hands.

"Were you going for a study in contrasts, or does it just come naturally?" Jenny asked.

"One project at a time," Tia intoned with a weary note in her voice. "Once you are up and running, then I'll work on Libby's wardrobe."

"You will not. I like my clothes," Libby objected.

"For hiking and hippie revivals, maybe, but you do have to realize, Libby, that some of your clothes are older than dirt," Tia scolded.

"Many are gifts from you, I might add." Libby sipped her coffee complacently. Left to her own devices, Libby was totally unmaterialistic. Because she was as slim as the day she'd graduated from high school, she could still wear clothes from her senior year—and often did.

"Are you two going to sit there all day, or are you coming with me?" Jenny demanded.

"Is that a request or an order?" Tia asked. "And aren't you looking perky today?"

"It's a request first. Then, if you turn me down, it's an order. And thank you very much, I do feel perky today." A clerk from the shop drifted up with a mug of coffee for Jenny. Thanking her, Jenny breathed deeply of the rich aroma. "Mmmmm. Chocolate raspberry. We can take the coffee with us."

"And where are we going on this impulsive expedition?" Tia tried to act bored but was obviously delighted with this cheerful change in Jenny.

"I want to go shopping for tombstones."

Tia's face fell, and Libby sagged in her chair. "Jenny!" they moaned together.

"Not that."

"Yes. That. Come now or miss the fun."

Tia and Libby exchanged a glance, gave a mutual sigh, and stood up in unison.

"I don't like the sound of this," Libby fussed. "You aren't having a bad day, are you?"

"I'm having a perfectly wonderful day, thank you. Come on. I left the car running."

Behind her, Jenny could hear Tia whispering to Libby in what she thought were tones Jenny couldn't hear. "I've read that people who commit suicide sometimes get very peaceful and happy once they've decided to do it. Do you think she's—"

"Quiet, Tia. She might hear you!"

"Don't be quiet, Tia; I already have. And no, I don't plan to do myself any harm. Just the opposite, in fact."

"I'm sure that happens a lot while you are picking out tombstones," her friend retorted dryly, but they both got into Jenny's car and allowed themselves to be spirited to the local granite and tombstone facility at the edge of town.

When they arrived, Jenny jumped out of the car and began looking at the vast selection of modest to extravagant headstones. Some were polished to a high glossy sheen; others were more matted in appearance. There were black ones on a bronze base, colored granite, rusty reds, and many shades of gray.

"Oh, pretty!" Jenny gushed as she saw a creamy ivory headstone with angels, wings spread, seeming to watch over what would be someone's final resting place.

"Tell me I'm having a brain fade and this isn't happening," Tia moaned.

Libby, being slightly more practical, asked, "Are you looking for a double stone for you and Lee?"

"Oh, no. He gets his own. I get mine. After all, we are born alone and die alone. It seems only fair to be buried alone."

"Fair. The woman said this is fair." Tia pressed her fingers to her temples. "Libby, do you have any aspirin?"

"I do." Jenny dug in her purse and handed Tia a small bottle. "Take it with water like your mother told you to do."

"I'm having an out-of-body experience," Tia groaned.

Just then an unctuous-appearing salesman approached. "May I help you?"

"I need a headstone for my husband's grave," Jenny said matter-of-factly, as if she were buying a new washer and dryer.

"He was very meticulous and tidy and my high school sweetheart. Do you have something that would reflect that?"

"Something simple, perhaps. Then you can choose an epitaph that is meaningful to you."

Jenny studied every stone from every angle as if she were buying a new car. Every so often she would ask Libby or Tia, "Would Lee like this?"

Her friends just stood gape-mouthed, wondering what had come over her.

"Here it is!" Jenny planted herself in front of a silvery headstone, which gleamed with flecks of refracted light from the sun. "I'll take this one for my husband." She spun around and pointed at the creamy marble one. "And that one for me."

Tia's jaw dropped, and Libby covered her mouth with her hands.

"Jenny, no!"

"Chill out, Tia. I'm not planning on using it any time soon!

"Have you slipped totally off your rocker?"

Jenny grinned. "Do you mean am I a slice of bread short of a loaf? Rowing with only one oar? Missing a light in the attic?"

"Frankly, yes."

"Maybe if you sat down for a bit," Libby suggested. She looked so worried that Jenny burst out laughing.

"Relax, both of you. I *want* to do this. I want to face my own mortality. It's the only way I can really, truly accept Lee's death. When he died, it shook me to the core. The faith I was so proud of having contained more pride than faith. God got me through the funeral, but then I let go of his hand.

"It was Mike who finally made me realize that I'd begun thinking of death as the unknown—something to be feared. That's not so. God told us he was going to heaven to prepare a place for us.

"Besides, Lee died. I didn't. My life is still to be lived, and I want to live it for God. Until I face my own death and come to grips with it, I can't really live. This is my opportunity to grow and thrive here on earth and to prepare for eternity as well. Therefore, I'm getting ready to live by facing my inevitable death. It's as simple as that."

"Simple?" Libby breathed.

"Let me get this straight," Tia muttered. "Once you pick out a tombstone, you're going to feel better?"

"Much better." Jenny turned to the salesman. "I'll be back later with the information I'd like engraved on my husband's stone. My friends can help me with the wording."

"Now we're doing epitaphs?"

"Just one, really. I already know what Lee's will say. It's mine we have to work on."

"How about 'She died a lunatic, but we loved her anyway'?" Tia asked. "Or, 'Her mind went years before her body; may they both rest in peace'?"

"I'm serious about this, you know," Jenny said calmly.

"I'm beginning to understand," Libby said sweetly, although puzzlement was still clear on her features. "How about 'She was loved by all who knew her'?"

"That's very nice, Lib, but that glorifies me. I want the glory to go another direction."

"How about a Scripture verse?" Tia suggested. "Something like Philippians 1:6: "I am sure that God, who began the good work within you, will continue his work until it is finally finished on that day when Christ Jesus comes back again."

"Tia, that's wonderful! God's work began in us with the Holy Spirit and will be finished when we meet God face-to-face. I think my tombstone should talk about Christian growth. I've got enough of it to do!" Jenny jotted down the verse on a small note-pad she carried in her pocket.

"Now what? Dare I ask?"

"I'll bet I know," Libby said. "Music."

"Right, but we'll do that over lunch. I have a hymnbook and sheet music in the car," Jenny said.

"Cool," Tia groaned. "Dirges and donuts?"

Jenny giggled. "I was thinking more like dirges and duck under glass."

"Too expensive," Libby joined in. "How about dirges at the deli?"

Jenny pulled into a small restaurant that specialized in home-made soups and pies. She gathered the music and tucked it under her arm before walking to the door. Tia and Libby followed her, still stunned by their friend's behavior.

Libby finally whispered to Tia, "I hate to say it, but she's really making a lot of sense."

"Not you too!"

"Christians shouldn't fear death. I like the idea of embracing it and moving on."

"Embracing it is one thing. This—"

"Is my way of embracing it," Jenny interrupted. "You two will have to whisper more softly if you don't want me to hear how crazy you think I am."

"Actually, you aren't crazy," Tia admitted. "You're sounding more sane than you have in a long while."

When they were seated at the table, Libby said, "This feels like a turning point for you, Jenny. You are different—peaceful, even joyful. Am I correct?"

"Now that you say it that way, yes. It occurred to me that although I wasn't happy about the secrets Lee harbored or the fact that we had no chance to resolve them before he died, I still could feel joyful. Real joy and happiness are two different things. God gives us joy and peace in the midst of trouble and unhappiness. Now that I have experienced it, I don't want to lose it again."

Although the waitress and the patrons of the café did look at their table from time to time when the trio broke into raucous laughter over some silly quip or comment, no one seemed to find it terribly odd that the three women would occasionally start humming or burst into song. By the time lunch was completed, so were Jenny's music selections.

Libby dug a tissue out of one of her many pockets and wiped her eyes. "I've never laughed so hard over funeral music before."

"It's a send-off, a celebration," Jenny corrected her. "In New Orleans I once saw a funeral procession go by. Musicians were following the casket and playing the most wonderful jazz. That's the kind of music we should play when we know someone's gone to heaven to be with God. What a send-off!"

"Got that. New Orleans jazz band." Tia pretended to write it down. "This isn't going to be cheap, but it's going to be fun."

"I've got it!" Libby burst out. "I know what we'll say on Jenny's tombstone. 'She put the fun back into funerals.'"

Jenny only smiled. Facing death was worth it. Her place in eternity settled, all she had to look forward to now was the future.

Mike was at the house when Jenny returned. He was sitting on the porch, intently studying a dandelion about to go to seed. He looked up when Jenny neared, and the pleased smile he gave her made her cheeks feel warm.

"I thought dandelion season was over," she commented and dropped gracefully to the step beside him.

"They're tough little fellows. Persistent too. They grow in every temperate region in the world."

"I wonder why they are so successful at growing when nothing else can." Jenny leaned against Mike's knee to look at the yellow-headed intruder.

"God's design. See these little florets that make up the head? Every single one will produce a tiny thing that looks like a parachute, each of which is attached to a seed. When you go like this—" he blew at the head, and it seemed to magically disappear—"it sends out a couple hundred parachute-propelled seeds in every direction. Poof! More dandelions."

"When Tia, Libby, and I were kids, we'd pick dandelions and blow the heads off. If we could get the head off in three puffs, that meant our mothers weren't looking for us yet. But if we left any seeds on the head, then we'd run home as fast as our legs would carry us. My father said when he was a boy they would do the same thing to predict how much a girlfriend or boyfriend cared about you. If all the seeds blew off in one puff, she loved you very much. If many were left, well, let's just say it might be time to get a new friend."

Mike got up and picked another fuzzy-headed dandelion that had gone to seed. "Blow on this. You only get one chance."

Jenny obeyed. Mike studied the remaining seeds. "Hmmm. Eleven. Wow."

"What's wow?" Jenny said with a laugh.

"Legend has it that the number of seeds left tells you how many children you'll have."

Jenny laughed out loud. "I didn't know a little weed could come in so handy."

"It's a pretty useful weed, actually. The greens are a good vegetable. Lots of vitamin A. The roots can be roasted to make imitation coffee, and the milk in the roots can be used to make latex. Never judge a book by its cover or a flower by its name, Jenny."

"Or a man by his reputation?" Her upturned face glowed as she looked at him.

"That too." Then he slapped his hand on his thigh. "I almost forgot. I brought you flower boxes for the porch. Come and see."

The activity woke Spot. He had been sleeping on the porch floor on his side, his feet sticking straight out from his body. He was sleek and healthy looking and no longer cowered when strangers came near him. He was healing too.

The flower boxes were a riot of color, a crazy quilt of blooms. "I used all the stuff that was left over and threw it together. Sometimes nature's way is the prettiest, even though we try very hard to make things symmetrical and perfect. If you cover these at night to protect them from frost, they should look good for many weeks yet," Mike explained. His hand grazed Jenny's back as he walked her past the planters, and Jenny found herself walking unusually slow so that occasionally his palm rested on her back.

"The mix might seem a little strange, but when I began looking at what I'd used, I realized it was there for a reason."

"What do you mean?"

"Look at the geraniums. In folklore they stand for triumphing through persistence. And over here, I planted a few forget-me-nots," Mike added. "They symbolize focus."

"Persistence and focus? My two strongest qualities?" Jenny said, jokingly.

"It's a good thing you have lilac bushes," Mike observed, smiling. "They mean a return to clarity."

"Thank goodness! That means there's hope for me?"

Mike looked at her with an expression so gentle Jenny thought she might melt. "A good deal of hope, Jenny."

. . . .

"Who called this meeting, anyway?" Tia groused. She was painting her toenails with her feet propped on Jenny's coffee table. "I wanted to give myself a full pedicure tonight, and now I have to settle for this."

"Who is going to see your toes anyway?" Libby asked. Her polish wardrobe was made up of one bottle—something clear with a nail strengthener in it.

"I am, that's who." Tia wiggled her toes. "I know they're pretty, and I think about it when my feet start to hurt."

"Quit wearing those weird shoes, and your feet won't hurt. Then you won't have to polish."

"Libby," Tia said in a grieved tone, "my shoes are in style!"

"So are mine." Libby flopped the heels of her Birkenstocks.

"I hate to break up this profound intellectual discussion," Jenny said, "but I have something to tell you."

"You've met a man!" Tia gasped.

"You've got a date!" Libby added.

Jenny threw her hands in her hair. "Just the opposite!"

That statement left Tia and Libby puzzling. "Huh?"

"I think I'm finally on the road to letting go of one—man, I mean."

"Who?"

Tears came to Jenny's eyes. "Lee."

Now she had their complete and total attention.

"What do you mean?" Libby asked.

"Lee is gone. Even though he wasn't at all who I thought he was, I loved my husband like I promised to—for better or worse, for richer or poorer, in sickness and in health. Gambling is a sickness, an addiction. I forgive him, and I've put it all at God's feet now. Lee will always be in my heart and in my memories, but he's gone and I can't get him back. I'd give anything to talk to him again, to tell him that I loved and have forgiven him, but it can't happen this side of heaven."

Jenny drew a shaky breath before she continued. "You were right, both of you. God does have a plan for me. I don't know what it is yet, but I don't even know how to pay my bills right now. I have to live on trust that he'll show me what is right. All I know now is that it's time to let go and move on as best I can."

Her expression filled with anticipation. "If my going through the grief and pain I've experienced can show others that they can make it through their own trouble, then maybe it's been worth it. Because God carried me through this, I'm living proof that he can and will do it for others. I know that I want to give myself unconditionally to him so that I can glorify him through my life."

Jenny drew another shaky sigh. "For a long time I identified myself only by my relationship to my husband. Now I'm my own person. I don't need a husband in order to feel whole. God made me. I just want to reflect him now."

"Oh, Jen . . ." There were tears in Libby's eyes, and the tip of Tia's nose got red.

"It's OK. Really, it is. I was always more than Lee's wife, but I didn't acknowledge it or embrace it. It's time for me to step out on faith and see what God has in store for me, to find out who Jenny really is."

"I don't know what you will find for yourself," Libby murmured, "but the Jenny I know is one of the truly beautiful people in the world. You are lovely on the outside but even lovelier on the inside, where it counts. I don't care if you end up stuffing widgets into gizmos in a factory or becoming president of the United States, I love you. I'm glad God gave you to me as a best friend."

"Amen to that!" Tia chimed as they wadded themselves into a group hug and rocked and cried until Tia lost her footing and almost pulled them all over on top of her.

"Thanks for sticking by me, ladies," Jenny said.

"How does it feel?" Tia asked.

"How does what feel?"

"To have turned a corner? Made a first step? Found a light at the end of the tunnel that wasn't a train?"

Jenny thought about Tia's question. How did it feel?

"I feel . . . light . . . airy . . . inside. Like a load has been lifted. I'm not grieving any less, but the pain has changed. It's not so all-consuming as it once was. I feel like there is room inside me again. I'm not all filled up with sadness."

Jenny chewed at her lower lip. "And I feel very, very frightened, as though I'm stepping off the edge of a cliff and counting on God to build me a bridge as I go. I'm trusting that he won't fail me, but I'm scared of heights."

"Makes sense to me," Libby commented. "And when I look at your face, it is as though someone turned the lights back on."

"So he's a master electrician too," Jenny murmured.

"Who? What?" Tia asked.

"God, of course. He turned the lights on inside me. He's giving me back my zest for life. I'm seeing beauty again." She looked out the window at her bountiful garden of flowers. A humming-bird was feeding at a bottle Mike had hung from a shepherd's crook near the riot of flowers.

"I am so grateful that I feel as though I could burst," Jenny admitted. "I'm a survivor! Me! Can you believe it?"

"Jenny, you were wearing God's life jacket all along and just didn't notice."

Jenny smiled. Master gardener. Master electrician. And now, a life jacket. It was a versatile God she loved and who loved her, no doubt about that.

After her friends left, Jenny walked through the garden and into the gazebo. Again, she found something Mike had added—little cast-iron lanterns holding candles ready to be lit. Every time she thought the garden was perfect, he added just one more touch, one more evidence of his thoughtfulness that enhanced its beauty.

The tears that came to her eyes surprised Jenny. For the first time in months, they were tears of joy. Her choices seemed limit-less now. Her world, brand-new. Once she had thrown herself at God's feet and asked him to take over her life—really take over—everything had changed. Lee's betrayal became God's to deal with. Jenny was left with only the job of loving Lee's good memories while God provided her with the ability to forgive and forget the bad ones. The world was her oyster, and she had it by the tail.

Jenny laughed out loud, a tinkling giddy laugh of glee. But oysters didn't have tails! She could even laugh at herself again—mixed metaphors and all—a gut-deep laugh that was as healing as any tonic. It was only when she remembered her precarious financial situation that the glow dimmed. But she would keep praying. So many times over the years she'd heard her mother say, "God's never late, Jenny, but he's seldom early either." She would have an answer to prayer, she just knew it. But for reasons of his own, God wasn't rushing in to rescue her quite yet.

CHAPTER THIRTEEN

*Sunflower: signifies haughtiness,
perhaps because of its height.*

—*WILDFLOWER FOLKLORE*

Jenny was so nervous she was afraid she'd throw up. Her attorney looked far too serious as she sat on Jenny's couch, holding an untouched cup of tea. Jenny knew Carla was here to tell her it was time to take action on her financial situation. Jenny acknowledged that she'd been playing ostrich, burying her head in the sand so she didn't have to face the problem, but it was unfair to ask her parents and Tia to bail her out any longer.

"Well?" Jenny whispered tentatively.

"It doesn't look good, Jen. Something drastic has to happen soon."

"Drastic?" Jenny echoed, not liking the sound of that at all. "Like what?"

"You'll have to find a full-time, well-paying job. Immediately, if not sooner."

Jenny's heart sank. She loved working in the bakery with Mrs.

Meyers. It was such a joy to see people happy with the cakes she'd made for them. Mrs. Meyers said she had a natural talent for decorating—especially with flowers—and Jenny had even started doing the magnificent fondant-covered wedding cakes that were so popular now.

"You will have to pare back your living expenses."

"But I hardly spend anything on myself now! Libby is always bringing food into the house, and I get leftover items from the bakery and the catering service. I haven't bought any new clothes in months. I've even started using a fan instead of the air conditioner."

"But you have a double mortgage on your house."

"Please, Carla, don't start on the house. My garden . . ."

The attorney sighed and took the reading glasses off the bridge of her nose. "I know, Jenny. I understand. But I'm here today to tell you that I've set up a meeting with your bank and a credit counselor. Your bills are current, and you do have some insurance money due you, so you aren't about to be evicted, but we do have a project ahead of us to make you solvent."

"When do we start getting ready for this, Carla?" Jenny felt a surge of bile in her throat. Who would ever have believed that she would be reduced to this?

"I've blocked out adequate time next week. We meet with the bankers the following Monday. I'm confident we can pull everything together by then."

"Good." Jenny stood up. "That will give me time to do what needs to be done."

"I think I've got most of your figures from past income tax statements. Tia's accountant has supplied me with those figures. Now if you will just give me an idea of your monthly living expenses. . . ."

"I can't talk about this right now, Carla. There is something I have to do first."

"Is it more important than this?" The attorney sounded annoyed.

"It is. At least to me."

"What is that?" Carla looked puzzled.

"I need to pray. Specifically. With details. And with my friends. I'm a big believer in intercessory prayer. It will be no problem to get the information you need, but I feel very strongly that I have to go to God for the ultimate solution."

"I hope God is a good businessperson and mentor, Jenny, because you need one."

"He is. He's good at everything as long as you let him have full control." Jenny smiled a radiant, comforting smile. "Don't worry. He'll work it out."

Carla looked doubtful and frustrated, but by now she was accustomed to this side of her client. "Fine. I'll go ahead with what we need for the meetings. You pray." As she was going out the door, she turned back to Jenny. "And you'd better tell God he's got less than a week to get his job done."

As soon as Carla was gone, Jenny sat down at the phone and began to dial. She called Tia, Libby, Ellen, her pastor, the head of the prayer chains at work, and every other Christian prayer warrior she could think of. Then she sat down on the couch and prayed too.

The doorbell jarred her loose from her reverie.

It was Tia and Libby, with Mike in tow.

"We decided that we'd pray together," Tia announced. "And we found Mike outside hanging lanterns in your gazebo, so he's here too."

Jenny was puzzled. "Lanterns? But there's no electricity to the—"

"There will be by Tuesday," Mike said.

"I can't pay for it. Didn't they tell you what we're praying for? A way out of my financial predicament!"

"It's on me."

"Michael Adams, quit giving me things! I feel so guilty."

"Then give me something in return."

Jenny's shoulders relaxed. "What could I give to you?"

"The pleasure of working in your yard. Of having an excuse to see you everyday. It would be pretty selfish of you to take that away from me." His eyes were dancing with laughter. By the expression on her features, he knew he'd won.

"Whoever gets this house next is going to love the yard," Jenny warned.

"Think positive!" Libby ordered. "You can't pray for help not believing that you'll get an answer."

"Maybe God's answer will be no. 'No house for you, Jenny Matthews,'" Jenny pointed out.

"When he shuts a door, he opens a window," Tia intoned. "Come on, we're wasting time."

They sat at the small round table in Jenny's dining room, clasped hands, bowed their heads, and prayed. Spot, who never missed a chance to be next to Jenny, collapsed at her feet in a warm heap. She buried her toes in his fur and lowered her head.

It wasn't until Jenny's stomach started to grumble that she realized it was nearly two o'clock and no one had had lunch. "Food-for-the-body break," she murmured. "I'll make some sandwiches."

"Marathon praying," Libby observed as they all stood up to stretch. "If we did this instead of spending time planning wars and retaliation, think how much better our world would be."

Mike wandered into the kitchen, where Jenny was putting together ham on buns. He moved close to her and put his hand at her neck and kneaded out the knots that had formed there from her bowed head and the intensity with which she had prayed. "How are you doing?"

"Good, now." Jenny practically purred as she leaned back into the warm hand and felt the ache in her neck and shoulders recede. With his touch it was as if a bit of Mike's own strength moved out of him and into her.

....

"Now what?" Libby asked after lunch.

"Wait," Jenny answered. "'I am counting on the Lord; yes, I am counting on him. I have put my hope in his word . . .'"

"Psalms," Libby said. "Good choice." She stood up and kissed Jenny's cheek. "I'd better see how Mom and Dad are doing. Call me later, OK?"

Jenny showed all three of her friends to the door. Mike hesitated a moment, waiting until Tia and Libby had disappeared. "Are you going to be all right?"

"Why shouldn't I be?"

"Just checking." He gave her a little lopsided grin. "Did you ever think you'd be praying with Naughty Mikey, son of poor Pastor Adams?"

"No. Praying for him, maybe, but never with him."

Something flickered in Mike's eyes. Indecision? Wishfulness? Something Jenny couldn't name. Then he leaned over and kissed her forehead. "Hang in there, kid." And he left.

Jenny stared at herself in the hall mirror for several moments, focusing on the spot where Mike had kissed her. She felt embarrassingly like a teenage girl who'd shaken hands with her favorite star or musician and vowed never to wash that hand again. The spot still felt warm to her overactive imagination, and she could remember the feel of his breath against her cheek. Gathering her arms around herself, she squeezed herself in a self-made hug. Then, feeling only slightly giddy, Jenny took her Bible and went outside to the gazebo to read.

....

"Jenny, it's me, Carla."

"Oh, hi. I was just getting up. . . ."

"Have you done whatever you said you had to do yesterday?" Carla meant the prayer, of course.

"Yes."

"And? Did whatever it was help?"

"I don't understand."

"Did you figure out how to get some money? Did you find a full-time job? Did you discover a solution to any of the problems we discussed?"

"Not yet," Jenny admitted.

"Then I've got to take the next step."

"What is that?" Jenny didn't like the determined tone of Carla's voice.

"I have a potential buyer for your house."

"But I'm not selling the house!"

"Jenny, don't be thickheaded. This party wants to see it. The couple both happen to be gardeners. They have plenty of money. This might be a perfect match for both of you."

"How could selling my home be a perfect match for me?" Jenny asked.

"You know what I mean. May I bring them over?"

"Now?" Jenny was horrified.

"Yes. They're leaving town this evening for a few days and want to take that time to decide on a home. Yours is the last they'll be looking at."

"But—"

"We'll be there in half an hour. Just keep telling yourself that this is for the best, Jenny." The line went dead, but Jenny held the receiver in her hand for a long time, staring at it as if she'd never seen it before. Carla was actually doing it—taking steps to sell her house! Though Jenny had told Carla she might consider selling the house "at a later date," this wasn't nearly "late" enough.

Jenny was in the front yard when Carla and the middle-aged couple arrived. She'd taken a walk through her gardens and for the first time regretted their beauty. How could anyone resist this house now? It was more beautiful than ever before.

"Jenny, these are the Sampsons, Irene and Ben. I'm sorry I gave you so little notice, but—"

"We are leaving town," Irene said, "and when she mentioned that you liked to garden, I thought we should take a look."

"Irene and I are avid gardeners," the balding, genial-looking man said. "But never have I seen anything quite as attractive as this!"

"It's not really my doing," Jenny demurred. "I have a friend who is a landscape architect. He and my late husband are the masterminds behind the project."

Did the bushes have to look so thick and green? Or the flowers so bright and perfect as they spilled out of every corner of the yard? Seeing through a stranger's eyes for the first time, Jenny fully realized what an amazing thing Mike had done for her. And now it might no longer be hers.

It took Carla twenty minutes to entice the Sampsons into the house. They were more interested in some of the exotic things Mike had planted and were fascinated by the topiaries he had added.

It was just as Jenny had feared. The house was "perfect" and the yard "fabulous." Even Spot got accolades as he lay stretched out like a rug in front of the door. The Sampsons, by all accounts, were delighted with the find to which Carla had introduced them.

Miserably, Jenny followed them from room to room, wishing she hadn't cleaned or chosen a particular wallpaper or decorated that wall with faux painting. The more compliments she received, the gloomier she became.

Showing the bedroom was most difficult of all. It was such a private and personal space to be invaded by shoppers. But it all seemed out of Jenny's control. Carla and the Sampsons were practically negotiating a closing date by the time they reached her kitchen.

"Have you settled on a final price yet, Jenny?" Carla asked.

Jenny looked at her blankly.

"I'd like to give Jenny some time to think about this," Carla said. "What day did you say you'd be returning?"

"But if Jenny decides to sell, we want to have first chance—"

"Don't worry." Jenny finally found her voice, which had been stuck at the back of her throat. "I promise that this house won't be sold before you return."

Having eased the Sampsons' minds, she managed to scoot them out of the house. After they had driven away, Carla turned to Jenny.

"Well, well, looks like you have a buyer already!"

"Carla, I'm not ready to sell the house."

The attorney frowned. "Then what will you do? You can't afford to live here either."

"I don't know. I'm waiting for an answer."

Carla sighed pityingly. "The power of prayer, right?"

Jenny's chin came up. "Yes."

"You have until the Sampsons get back from their trip, Jenny. You'd better let God know that right away."

"He already does," Jenny said with a sigh.

....

"So, are you going to sell it?" Tia asked. She and Libby had ridden their bikes to Jenny's house, hoping to dislodge her from the front porch, where she had taken up residence these past few days.

"I don't want to."

"That wasn't what I asked." Tia swung a long tanned leg over the porch rail and straddled it like a riding horse, just as they had done as children when they played cowboy games.

"I don't know. I'm waiting for God to let me know."

"And if you don't hear from him by the time the Sampsons return?"

Jenny fought back tears. "He'll let me know. I'm sure of it."

"If worse comes to worse, you know you can always live with me," Tia said gently.

"Or us," Libby added. "My parents love you like you are their own."

"Thank you, both of you."

Mike pulled into the driveway just as Tia and Libby were mounting their bikes to leave. "Maybe you can cheer her up. We certainly failed," Libby whispered.

"Not likely. I've already tried. Every time I say something, she starts apologizing about the yard, saying I worked for nothing. She refuses to accept the fact that I've enjoyed it and that's enough."

"At least she's hanging tough with God this time," Tia observed. "She's come a long way in a short while."

"Good luck," Libby added as they pushed off.

Mike meandered up the steps to where Jenny was sitting. Spot opened one eye to see who was disturbing the peace now, saw Mike, and gave one lavish thump of his tail on the porch before closing the eye again.

"Waiting for a telegram?" Mike sat in the wicker chair across from her.

"Something like that." Jenny studied him. *A heavenly one.*

Mike's arms were brown and sinewy. He was trim and fit, an outdoor man who seemed more at ease in nature than he did in the confines of a house.

He noticed her staring and laughed. "Glad that I'm of such interest to you, Jenny."

"Oh." She blushed. "I've been staring. I'm sorry." With a sigh she admitted, "I've been pretty self-absorbed lately."

"Not self-absorbed, just involved in ensuring your own survival." The smile lines around his eyes creased, and Jenny realized just how very handsome he was.

"What if God's answer is no, Mike? Then what? Where do I go?"

"He'll probably let you know that, too, eventually. I've never found God to rush in with excess information at a time earlier than you need it, though."

"Tell me about it." Jenny tried to laugh. "Want some lemonade? a cookie?"

"Thanks but no thanks. I have to pick Luke up at the riding arena in twenty minutes. I just thought I'd stop by to see how you were doing."

"I've never been to your house," Jenny said. "I just realized that."

"Luke wants you to come for a picnic," Mike told her. "Maybe this weekend."

"Do you have a garden like this one?"

Mike tipped back his head and gave a rippling laugh of amusement. "You've heard the comment 'The shoemaker's children have no shoes'? That's me, I'm afraid. Luke mows the lawn, and I keep things from being an embarrassment around there, but no more."

"You should have done all this work for yourself instead of for me."

"Do you enjoy your yard?"

"It's the most peaceful, wonderful place in the world."

"Then it was good that I did it for you."

Jenny put her hands to her forehead. "What's going on, Mike? What am I supposed to do?"

"God wants you to trust him, Jenny. To wait for him to answer. You are doing all you can right now."

. . . .

That was small comfort the next afternoon when Carla called to say the Sampsons were returning the following Monday afternoon. Also, they had put a generous bid on the house "just in case." It was a bid far higher than the price Jenny and Carla had agreed might be reasonable for the house.

"I've never seen two people so excited about a yard, Jenny.

They raved about it to me several times on the phone. Even my secretary is getting tired of their calling to see if you've made up your mind yet." There was a long pause. "Have you?"

"I'll know before they return, Carla, that's all I can say."

"I know, I know. It's in God's hands now."

"Right."

"OK. You know how to find me when you have your answer."

Jenny stared at the phone a long time after she'd hung up. Hopelessness and despair seeped into her. Where was God when she needed him? He always seemed to slip out the back door when—she stopped herself. She wasn't going to think that way again. That was exactly what Satan wanted her to think.

Desperate for a diversion, she went into the house and got her gym bag.

Jenny had been on the exercise bike long enough to peddle to China when Mr. and Mrs. Meyers came in to do their daily routine.

"You certainly look as though you've had a workout, my dear," Mrs. Meyers said, observing Jenny's red face and damp hair.

Something in the gentleness of her tone brought tears to Jenny's eyes and, unexpected as they were, they fell across her cheeks before she had any way to stop them.

"What is wrong, child? You seemed down in the dumps the other day, too, when you came to decorate cakes."

Because she considered the Meyerses friends as well as employers, Jenny found it easy to pour out her story about the house, the yard, the Sampsons, even the impatience she felt at waiting for God's answers. Before she knew it, she found herself in the snack bar of the complex, being fed orange juice and an energy bar by the two elderly people.

"If anyone knows about waiting for answers to prayers, it's us," Mr. Meyers said. "With my wife's arthritis the way it is, we know she can't keep on decorating cakes much longer. You've been a real lifesaver at the store for us, Jenny. Worse yet, our catering director gave us notice yesterday that she and her husband are moving to England. Now my wife will have more rather than less work because I'm certainly not capable of planning parties and meeting the public like that. Put me in the back room with a stack of ledgers or a rolling pin and I'm fine, but—"

Suddenly something sparked among them, and all three looked toward the ceiling as if to see if a light had come on in the room. Then they looked at each other, and three jaws dropped open in amazement. They all began to talk at once.

"I could help you with the catering. I'd love it. And I'll do all the cakes."

"Are you any good at keeping books?"

"We'd like to travel, to get away."

"We could expand, do larger parties. I've seen ideas for cakes that would blow you away."

"Weddings, birthday parties, conventions . . ."

Finally they all burst into laughter.

It was Mrs. Meyers who said, "I think, my dear, that God has just spoken."

. . . .

Jenny was humming when she arrived at Carla's office.

Carla looked up from her work when Jenny entered. "What on earth has happened to you?"

"Me? Nothing. Why?" Jenny sat down in the chair across from Carla's. Jenny was wearing a pale yellow dress not very different in color from the ringlets of her hair. Over it was a cornflower blue jacket, which mirrored the color of her eyes. And on her head Jenny wore a jaunty summer straw hat with a band of yellow and blue.

"You look marvelous! Jenny, you're ten years younger than when I saw you last week! What on earth did you do to yourself?

A spa? If so, you have to give me the name. I'm signing up for a lifetime membership!"

Jenny's tinkling laughter filled the room. "He answered, Carla! He answered!"

The attorney looked puzzled for a moment. "Who—oh, God?"

"Yes!"

"Tell me everything," Carla ordered. "This I've got to hear."

Jenny took a deep breath and began. "Do you remember Mr. and Mrs. Meyers? The people I work for part time?"

"You told me about them."

"I ran into them this morning at the health club. They were talking about Mrs. Meyers's arthritis and how they felt so tied down at the bakery—"

"Jenny, it's your problem that I'm interested in, not theirs."

"But their problem solves mine! I'm going to manage the bakery and catering service and continue to decorate cakes as well. They said they'll pay extra for every catering job I do myself. It's a very profitable, well respected business with great potential for an ambitious owner." Jenny paused for breath. "And if we're all still in agreement in one year, we'll work out a contract for a deed so I can be buying the business while I work there!

"Until then, the Meyerses want to pay me enough to keep me from losing my house. They've felt moved by God to help someone. Can you believe it, Carla?"

"Jenny, this might sound good, but—"

"Here are the figures. All of them." She pushed a slip of paper across the desk and sat back.

Carla studied the figures with narrowed eyes. Then she penciled out some of the numbers herself. "Hmmm. It just might work, Jenny. These people have been more than generous with you."

"They've been like surrogate parents, Carla."

"Yes, I see that."

"God has been generous too."

Carla tapped the end of her pen on her desk and studied the woman across from her. "OK, I'll admit I was wrong. God is a good businessman after all. But he certainly didn't give you any extra time to relax."

"It doesn't matter now. Things are working out better than I'd ever dreamed. I love it at the bakery, and my cakes are already very popular. New customers have heard of me and are requesting my work. The catering will be a blast. I've already asked Libby to help me when she can. I'm no cook at all compared to her. Besides, that will be a good job for her because she can work around her parents' needs and the time she spends at Tia's store."

"Frankly, I can't believe it all fell into place." Carla was still puzzling over the numbers.

"It's a promise," Jenny murmured.

"What's a promise?"

"God gives his children more than they could ever dream of for themselves. It says so in Luke."

"OK, let's have it," Carla said with a smile. "Educate me."

"If you give, you will receive. Your gift will return to you in full measure, pressed down, shaken together to make room for more, and running over." Jenny smiled. "A heaping plateful of goodness."

Carla studied her. "You're sure of that, aren't you?"

"I am. I've had proof."

"Every prayer of yours wasn't answered," Carla pointed out. "You haven't forgotten that, have you?"

"Every prayer is answered. Sometimes God says no. Lee is gone. This is part of the plan for what is left of my life. I believe that with all my heart."

"Congratulations, Jenny. You have just saved your home and found yourself a career." Carla stood up and reached across the desk to shake Jenny's hand. "And it couldn't happen to a nicer person."

Jenny practically floated down the steps to the car. It was hard for her to understand now why she had doubted. But, she reminded herself, it was a day-in, day-out job, turning things over to the Lord. The trick was to give him her problems and then refuse to take them back. And second-guessing! She was a master at that, worrying that God wouldn't make the right choices for her life or that he'd deny her something she really wanted, even though she knew all he desired was the very best for her.

The weeks and months since Lee's death had been a humbling experience. Jenny knew now more than ever that faith was a relationship with a living God—an active person, a best friend. To doubt that friend was to find dissatisfaction and confusion. But when she stood close enough to hear God speak, all things changed.

She was humming when she arrived home. As was so often the case these days, Mike and Spot were waiting on the front step. Today Luke was present too.

"Hi, guys. What's up?"

"We're gonna have a party!" Luke crowed. Spot jumped up to dance on his hind legs in celebration.

"What for?"

"'Cause Tia called Dad and told him that Libby had called her 'cause you'd called Libby and told her that your lawyer had told you that your news was good," Luke announced in one gigantic run-on sentence. "And I don't know what the news is but I don't care 'cause Dad said we could grill steaks at our house and eat ice cream till we throw up!"

Jenny looked at Mike with a raised eyebrow.

He shrugged unrepentantly. "So I'm an indulgent parent. Good news is worth celebrating."

"It is, isn't it? I'd love to come."

"Spot too?" Luke asked.

"What would a party be without him?"

For as much time as Mike spent at her house, Jenny had never been to his.

She wandered through the public rooms of the house admiring the huge windows and indoor plants, which led seamlessly to the perfect expanse of lawn and greenery outside. "This is like a personal greenhouse! If I lived here, I think I'd sit and admire the view all day long."

"Not quite. This is a thirsty bunch of critters I've planted. Watering them is a full-time job."

"My job in the summer," Luke said proudly as he carried a pitcher of fresh lemonade to the table. "Are the steaks done, Dad?"

Mike glanced at his watch. "To perfection. I'll pull them off the grill on the way to the picnic table."

Jenny was impressed by the vast redwood table, set with a red-checkered tablecloth, festive dishes, colorful flatware, and filled with salads, breads, and a mound of steaming baked potatoes. "I had no idea you were such a homemaker, Mike."

"Move over, Martha Stewart." He put a steak the size of a small country on Jenny's plate. "Actually, I went through a serious domestic phase when Luke was younger. Thought having a single father might seriously damage him somehow, so I decided to learn to be both mother and father. I found out I liked cooking and creating order."

His expression turned impish. "Pretty amazing for a guy who used to love creating chaos, huh?"

"Were you really so bad?" Jenny asked as she put sour cream and chives on her potato. "Maybe my perspective on you was skewed because I was such a Goody Two-shoes."

"Yes. I was bad. Angry. Resentful. A real nasty dude." Mike glanced at Luke. The boy had left the table to dine with Spot, out of earshot and under a nearby tree. "And, since we're talking about it, I have some good news too."

"You aren't a nasty dude anymore?" Sitting here outside of this graciously appointed home on a perfectly manicured lawn, watching a charming, well-raised son, her question seemed ludicrous. It seemed unthinkable that Mike had ever been anything but what he was today. Of course, she knew better. She'd grown up with the old Mike.

"I am when I make Luke do his homework before he goes out to play. And I am when I say he has to go to Sunday school, even if he has a sleepover the night before."

"You're downright heinous!" Jenny teased.

"I've turned into my father, Jenny."

"And is that so bad?"

"At one time I would have thought so. The worst thing that could possibly happen. But not anymore. That's my good news."

"Oh?" She leaned back to study him.

"I've been watching you, Jenny. I've been observing how you've worked through the anger and resentment and betrayal you experienced because of Lee. It changed me."

Jenny straightened, sensing that Mike was saying something very, very important.

"If you can let the past go, then I certainly can. Dad and I have spent too many years skirting the real issues, being cordial but not close. I spent a long time with my father over the past weekend. We hashed out what transpired between us, laid it all on the table, and decided that it was all old news. We're finally *friends,* Jenny! For the first time since I was Luke's age I can actually say that!"

Mike laid his hand across hers on the table, and she felt the heat of his skin and the tremble of emotion down to his fingers. "Watching God work in you allowed me to open up and invite him to work in me too."

"Oh, Mike—" The words caught in her throat. What had she

told her friends? That she wished to glorify God through her life. When Mike's wish had been fulfilled, hers was as well. Astounding. The loose ends of their lives were being knit tidily together by heavenly hands.

And she'd thought for a time that God wasn't even listening!

CHAPTER FOURTEEN

Take thou this rose, O rose,
Since love's own flower it is,
And by that rose
That lover captive is.

—13TH-CENTURY WANDERING SCHOLAR

"How does this look?" Tia held up a misshapen wad of raw meat for Jenny's inspection. Tia was wearing a white apron over her jeans and sweatshirt; a hair net clamped her dark hair to her head and spread a web of fine crisscrosses over her forehead.

"Frankly, both you and that hunk of burger look like something created by Dr. Frankenstein," Jenny said. "That doesn't even resemble a meatball!"

"It's made of meat," Tia argued.

"It does look a little like a hockey puck," Dorothy Matthews said optimistically. She, too, was decked out in a white apron and hair net and, like Tia, wore plastic gloves on her hands.

"What's the theme of this party?" Libby wondered. "Maybe we should make all the meatballs in the shape of hockey pucks."

"It certainly is true that you get what you pay for," Jenny muttered. "Especially in hired help." She moved to the meatball-production line—Dorothy and Tia—and patiently showed them for the umpteenth time how small and round a cocktail meatball had to be.

"I think we're ready to start cutting these things," Ellen called out. She and Libby were spreading a mixture of cream cheese and jalapeños into softened tortillas. The entire catering kitchen was awash in party food in different stages of completion—baby cream puffs were cooling on racks, while Jenny finished mixing the chicken-salad filling. Two kinds of barbecue sauce burbled on the stove—sweet and sour for the meatballs, barbecue for five pounds of tiny smoked sausages.

"I'll do that while you start the cucumber sandwiches." Jenny surveyed the ordered chaos. "Do you think the alumni board at the university will be satisfied with the food? Will we have enough? This is my biggest catering job yet."

"There will be enough food to feed all the alumni from 1920 on," Tia predicted. "And they'll all love it."

"Mrs. Meyers said that if this is a success, I should get some really good catering jobs. It is a function that she and her husband have been bidding on for years and have never been fortunate enough to get."

"Is that why we're working for you for practically nothing? So you can give your product away?" Tia scowled.

"Think of it as a loss leader in your store, Tia. Once your customers see what you can do, they'll be back for more."

"Who'd a thunk it?" Tia said. "Shy, sweet Jenny—a business mogul? Amazing!"

Jenny sat back and surveyed the scene. The catering kitchen was full of gleaming equipment, and through a large window she could look directly into the bakery, where employees were busy serving customers. She'd added an espresso machine and a few wrought-iron tables and chairs to an underused spot near the front window, painted murals of Paris streets on the walls, and begun serving not only their usual bakery goods but also sand-wich croissants and homemade soups.

That part of the business had become popular so quickly that Jenny was now looking into purchasing the building next door to make into a bistro. Lee's sister, still feeling sad about all the years that she and Jenny had missed being friends, seemed determined to make up for lost time by helping Jenny every chance she could. They had even discussed adding Dorothy's skills to the mix by hiring her to manage the bistro around her teaching schedule.

Jenny still decorated most of the cakes herself but could see that the time was soon coming when she'd have to hire someone to help her full time. Jenny was so particular about the cakes— each a work of art in its own right—that she had feared she wouldn't be able to find anyone who could do the work as she wanted it done.

Then Ellen told her that as a young woman attending college in London she'd had a job at Harrods in the kitchen of the food court doing, of all things, decorating cakes. She had demonstrated for Jenny her ability to make a fondant frosting so smooth and perfect that Jenny had known on the spot whom her first choice as pastry chef would be when the time came.

"Jenny, did you say that Mr. and Mrs. Meyers wanted to turn the whole business over to you?" Libby asked. A dusting of flour on her nose made her look ten years old again.

"As soon as I can swing the payments. My attorney wants me to get more established before I take that step, but it won't be long. Besides, the Meyerses want to travel part of the year but would be willing to take over the bakery for a couple months so that I could have time off for myself."

"God is good," Libby said softly.

"He's given me more than I could have dreamed of. This business is far more exciting, complex, and profitable than anything I could have thought up as a gift to myself." Jenny gave Libby a squeeze around the waist. "And my friends even more so."

Libby turned around to smile at her friends, and Jenny noticed a vaguely worried expression in her eyes.

"Lib? Is something wrong?"

"I'm just so happy for you, that's all."

"But are you happy for you?"

Libby glanced at the others. All were engrossed in their work. "It's nothing I didn't expect. Mom and Dad are spending more time in clinics and physicians' offices than ever before. Memory, eyesight, hearing—all gradually fading. It's just hard to watch." Her eyes filled with unshed tears.

"Anytime you need help, call me," Jenny ordered. "I'm my own boss and have plenty of good help. I can sit with your parents while you get a massage, shop, nap—anything. You were here for me. Now it's my turn to be here for you. That's what being Best Friends Forever is all about."

"Hooray for BFF," Libby said with a laugh. "A support system without equal."

"Hey, you two! Knock off the blabbing and get to work!" Tia gave them a glare and held up a perfectly round meatball. "And look at this baby. Perfect, huh?"

"We can't be shown up by Tia," Jenny said aloud. "She can't even boil water, and she's outdoing us. And remember, ladies, the sooner we finish, the sooner we go out for lunch—on me."

. . . .

"I certainly haven't seen Mike around lately," Tia observed as they drank the double-tall lattes Jenny had made for them for dessert. Dorothy and Ellen had already excused themselves to do afternoon errands.

"He's been busy. Luke tells me about it. They are planting trees right now. I guess October and November are a good time for that."

"Is something wrong between the two of you?" Tia asked bluntly.

"I don't think so," Jenny said slowly. "I'm just not sure. He doesn't call or come by much, but when he does, he's the same as usual."

"But Luke makes up for it," Libby observed.

Jenny laughed with pleasure. "He is a darling child, even though he would like to be attached to me at the hip."

"You are his mother figure," Tia deduced. "That kid thinks you walk on water."

"I know of only one person who did that," Jenny said with a chuckle. "But I do agree that Luke and I have become very close. Mike is a wonderful father, but sometimes a little boy needs a woman's touch."

"A woman's cooking, you mean?"

Jenny laughed again, remembering the amounts of food the child could pack away. "Maybe so. Luke says during his dad's busy season they live on peanut butter sandwiches and TV dinners."

"You could fix that," Tia said, her voice heavy with implied meaning.

"Don't try matchmaking, Tia. Mike has never indicated that he's interested in anything like . . . that."

"So he's a gentleman, that's all. He's giving you time to heal, to get over the pain of Lee's death. He's perfectly aware that the first anniversary of his death is nearing."

Jenny looked at her friend doubtfully. She didn't know if she agreed. Something was holding them apart, but she wasn't sure what. She glanced at her watch. "Excuse me for a moment, will you?"

She escaped into the office and closed the door. After turning on a small lamp that softly lit the room, Jenny dropped to her knees in front of the couch she kept there for resting during some of the night-long cooking sprees she did for clients. She buried her head in her hands and began to pray.

"Father, thank you for the friends you've given me. They are so loving and such willing workers. They reflect you in all they do. You have blessed me, Lord. My friends, the Meyerses, this business, a new life. You have allowed me to put Lee's life into perspective as well. I didn't marry a perfect man, but he was mostly a good husband to me—an imperfect woman.

"I've come through dark times, Lord. I finally see a light at the end of the tunnel. I'm ready to move on with my life. And, despite all my friends and this business, I'm lonely, Lord. I ask for a mate of your choosing. A love that can last a lifetime. I'm not interested unless he has your stamp of approval, God. Give me the faith and the strength to put this request into your hands and leave it there, Father. You give me even the faith I need to believe. Amen."

She arose from her kneeling position and brushed the front of her skirt. She was lonesome. She wanted a mate. Mike rested on her heart and mind, but if he was not the man God had in mind for her, she would have to pull away. She sighed. This faith stuff was difficult. She had to remember that the rewards were great.

Her mind exhausted and her head unsure, Jenny went to start her afternoon projects.

....

"Dad?" Luke was sitting on Jenny's porch swinging his legs and watching Mike clean out one of the flower beds.

"Yes, Luke." Mike's tone was patient, in spite of the fact that Luke had been grilling him all morning about things that were none of the boy's business.

"Why is it again that I don't have a mom?"

Mike stood up, tipped back on his heels, and studied the boy with undisguised impatience. "What has made you so interested in my marital status all of a sudden?"

"Just wondering." Luke gave his father an innocent, almost

angelic gaze. "My friends have mothers. At least most of them do."

Mike threw down his spade and strode to where his son was sitting. "All right, explain yourself."

Luke didn't even flinch. "It was just a question, Dad."

"I know that. What I'm wondering is, who put it into your head? A mother has never been a big concern of yours before. Who has you asking these questions?"

Mike would have backed down if he hadn't seen a spot of color appear in Luke's cheeks. So he was right. Someone was putting the boy up to this.

"Luke . . ."

"They aren't hurting anything, Dad. And I do want to know—"

"They who?"

Luke's shoulders sagged. "Tia and Libby. Especially Tia."

"I should have known." Mike raked his hands through his hair before sitting down by his son. "And I take it that the three of you decided that meddling in my life and Jenny's was perfectly acceptable behavior."

"Something like that. Tia, Libby, and Jenny are BFFs, you know."

It was Mike's turn to look startled. How did Luke know about that? He decided to play dumb. "BFFs? What are those? Something like UFOs?"

"No, silly. Best Friends Forever. It's been that since they were little girls."

"What else did they say?" Mike settled back, thinking that this might turn out to be very interesting.

"That you were a naughty little kid and that I am much better behaved than you ever thought of being."

"True." Mike could hardly deny the truth.

"And that you turned out lots better than anyone expected you to and that now you have potential."

"Potential for what?" Mike was almost afraid to ask.

"I don't know. They wouldn't say."

"Thank goodness for small favors," Mike muttered.

"I think they want you to marry Jenny," Luke deduced. "Then she'd have a husband, you'd have a wife, and I'd have a mom."

"Have they consulted Jenny about this?"

"No. Just me."

"Figures," Mike mumbled, making a note to himself to read those two meddlers the riot act next time he saw them. "Luke, from now on you are not allowed to play with Tia and Libby. They're a bad influence on you."

"But they're grown-ups, not little kids!"

"All the more reason to avoid any more conversations with them. They're worse now than they were as little kids. Believe me, I've had experience."

Luke sighed and kicked at the miniature lilac near his feet. "Dad, this is the first time I've ever thought that you aren't much fun."

Mike tousled the boy's hair. "Hey, I'm a dad. It's my job." And he went back to work, wondering what Tia and Libby were up to now. He was a big believer in the saying "Where there's smoke, there's fire," and Luke was just full of smoke today.

By evening it seemed Luke's smoke had turned into something more—a fever. He was glassy-eyed and restless and chose to lie on the couch rather than go with Mike to the stables to groom Sunshine. This finally scared Mike into action. Until now he had never seen the boy too ill to visit the horse.

He went downstairs to call a doctor, but before he could dial, the doorbell rang.

It was Jenny.

"What are you doing here?"

"That's a nice welcome for someone who is personally delivering the cake you ordered," Jenny chided. It was then that Mike noticed the cake box in her hands. Through the see-through plastic window he could see an elaborately decorated cake with a theme of skyrockets, sparklers and generally colorful fireworks.

The word *SURPRISE!* was scrolled through the middle of the cake.

"I'm sorry I didn't get it here sooner, but the delivery van had already left when I discovered your order by the till. Fortunately I had extra cakes baked, and I finished this as soon as I could. I hope it's not too late."

"For what?"

"For your party, of course. Why else would you order a cake like this?"

"What party?"

"I'm sure I don't know. You are the one who ordered the cake. Aren't you going to take it?" Jenny thrust the cake toward him; instinctively he reached for it.

"But what am I going to do with it?"

Jenny gave him an impatient look. "Serve it at whatever you ordered it for, of course!"

"But I didn't order a cake!"

She cocked her head to one side. "You didn't? It was your name and address on the order form."

"I don't know anything about this cake, Jenny. I didn't order it and—"

"Dad? Who's here?" From the top of the stairs Luke's voice was little more than a croak, but when he saw Jenny framed in the doorway, he came padding down to greet her. His hair was tousled, his cheeks flushed, and his slim body shivering. "Hi, Jenny!"

Then he caught sight of the cake. "Oh, no! I forgot!" Tears began to streak down his cheeks.

"Luke, are you sick?" Jenny went to the boy. "Child, you are burning up."

Mike looked from his young son to Jenny and back again. "Did you order this cake?" Luke's lip wobbled, and he looked as though he were about to burst into a wail.

Jenny shot Mike a stern look. "I think you should call a doctor."

"I was just about to when you—"

"Then what are you waiting for?"

Mike, shaking his head, put the cake on the floor and went to the telephone. He wasn't sure what had happened, but he did know that Luke, Tia, and Libby had been behind the cake. Why?

It was a question Mike didn't get to ponder again until much later. At his description of Luke's condition, the doctor told him he would meet them at the emergency room to look at the child. Within minutes, Mike and Jenny, with Luke curled on her lap, were on their way to the hospital.

"Luke, are you sure you don't want your own seat? You are almost as big as Jenny."

"No," came the muffled answer from a face buried in Jenny's shoulder.

"He's OK," Jenny murmured. "I don't mind. We're buckled in." She was absently stroking Luke's hair. "He's burning up."

At the hospital, things shifted into high gear. Luke was spirited away for tests, and Mike and Jenny were left sitting helplessly in the waiting area.

"What do you think is wrong with him?" Mike asked. "He was fine this morning."

"The doctor will tell us as soon as he knows," Jenny soothed. "Luke's in good hands."

"Just a few hours ago we were having this crazy conversation." Mike stood up and began to pace. "When I get my hands on Tia and Libby, I'll—"

"What do they have to do with this?" Now Jenny was confused.

"They put him up to ordering that cake. Or maybe they ordered it for him. Your friends are schemers and connivers, Jenny. That was their way of getting you to my house tonight."

"Why didn't they just tell me to come, if you were having a surprise party?"

"That's just it. I wasn't. If my hunch is correct, *you* were my surprise."

Mike prowled the room restlessly, muttering to himself. "All that talk about 'Why can't I have a mother?' business. That's their doing too. I can feel it."

"Mike," Jenny finally asked, "are you sure you're feeling all right? You aren't making very much sense, you know. Has anyone checked your temperature?"

He glared at her and kept pacing. "Those two are worse now than they were back in school. Then they were all talk. Now they get an idea and they have the means to implement it. Getting a little kid to be their accessory—"

"Mr. and Mrs. Adams?" A nurse entered the waiting area. "The doctor will see you now."

Mike and Jenny exchanged a glance, but neither made an effort to correct the nurse's error. Instead they followed her through a maze of corridors to a small room where Luke lay on a table.

"Mike, hi." The bespectacled doctor reached out a hand.

"Hi, Doc." But Mike's eyes were on his son. "Luke, how are you doing?"

"Not so good, Dad." Tears were shining on Luke's cheeks.

"It looks like we have an inflamed appendix," the doctor said. "It needs to come out tonight. The paperwork will be ready for you to sign shortly. I'm going to go check on things now and will be back in a few minutes."

As soon as the doctor left the room, Luke began to cry. "I don't want to have surgery, Dad!"

"No big deal, kid. I had mine out. How about you, Jenny?"

She snapped her fingers. "Just like that. You'll probably feel a lot better than you do now."

"But I'm scared."

"That's normal. We're all a little frightened of the unknown," Mike said softly. "Sometimes the familiar—even if it is uncomfortable—seems more acceptable than taking the risk to make your life better. But you and I have talked about this. About God's promises and—"

Luke waved a dismissing hand. "I know about that, Dad! I'm not afraid of dying. I'm just afraid of dying before I know for sure that Jenny's going to be my mother!"

If an orderly had not come in at that moment with a cart to move Luke to surgery and if a nurse hadn't arrived with consent papers, Mike and Jenny might both have fallen over in shock. As it was, there was barely room left for them to remain upright.

Mechanically Mike signed the papers, kissed his son on the forehead, and wiped away the tears from his cheeks.

"Is she, Dad? Going to be my mother? We haven't found anyone we like better, have we?"

"I didn't know we were looking," Mike said helplessly.

"I've been."

"I didn't know."

"You ask her while I'm gone, OK? Let me know when I wake up." And in a flurry of white and steel, Luke was rolled out of the room.

Mike stared at Jenny as though she'd punched him in the stomach.

"You'd better sit down," Jenny said, "before you fall down."

He nodded dumbly and sank onto a stool. Jenny watched him with amusement. "Your boy is a few jumps ahead of you, I see."

"Not jumps. Miles. Light-years, even."

"Maybe it was the fever talking," she suggested gently. "Don't be embarrassed."

"I'm not embarrassed," Mike said. "But I think I'm the one who is scared."

"He'll be fine."

"Oh, I'm not worried about Luke. I know he'll be OK. He has an excellent doctor and he's a healthy kid. It's you who frightens me."

Jenny took the comment in stride. "I know my hair doesn't look great, but—"

"Seriously, Jenny. It's easy being single, not having anyone who depends on me for emotional support, not having anyone to disappoint."

"You have Luke."

"That's different. He is part of me. Caring for him is as natural as caring for myself. Until just now, I thought I could practically read his mind. But—" Mike cast his gaze toward the floor—"I disappointed my parents so much and so often that it made me afraid that I could never do any better than I did for them. I vowed I'd never again intentionally hurt someone who loved me. I broke their hearts over and over before I finally got it right." He looked at her, and she could see the pain in his eyes. "I promised myself I'd never inflict that on another person, Jenny."

"What makes you think you would?"

He gave a small, humorless laugh. "My track record. The confidence I never really inspired in my own parents. The rebel in me."

"It seems to me that rebel has grown up, Mike. And turned into a pretty wonderful human being."

"*Wonderful* is an elastic sort of word. It can be stretched in a lot of directions."

"All of which include you."

A nurse came into the small room. "Mr. and Mrs. Adams? Would you like to wait in the family room? It's more comfortable there, and coffee and television are available. The doctor will call on the phone in there to let you know as soon as the surgery is done."

Mike stood up, unfolding his long, lean body, and held out a hand to Jenny. Gratefully she took it. Her legs felt a little weak. She wasn't sure what was going on but knew it was significant. She would have to wait to ask Mike about how Luke was involved with Tia and Libby. He wasn't making all that much sense now anyway, with Luke in surgery.

An hour passed. Mike spent most of it with his head in his hands, praying. The second hour, he paced. Every few minutes he'd stop in front of Jenny and ask, "What's taking so long?"

Before she could respond, he'd begin pacing again.

"Mr. and Mrs. Adams?" A nurse stood in the doorway. "The doctor just called from surgery. Things have taken a little longer than usual. There have been some complications."

Mike was in the woman's face in a heartbeat. "What complications?"

"The doctor will call here as soon as he can. He'll explain—"

Jenny was afraid Mike was going to grab the poor woman and shake the information out of her, so she jumped up and clung to his arm. "Thank you. We'll wait."

"Why'd you do that?" Mike shook her off as he turned to her, his eyes frantic.

"Because she wasn't allowed to tell you more, that's why. We'll have to wait for the doctor."

Mike sank onto the couch and threw his head back until it rested on the wall. Jenny took his limp hand and held it between her own.

After what seemed an eternity, Luke's doctor entered the room, still in surgical scrubs. Mike jumped to his feet.

"He's fine. You can relax now, Dad."

Mike took a step backward and exhaled. "What went wrong?"

"The appendix ruptured before we got to it. Took us longer, but Luke's resting well now. He's a spunky kid. He'll be fine." Then the doctor took Jenny's hand. "You've got a fighter for a son, you know. You'll be able to see him as soon as he is out of recovery."

Mike stared at the door through which the doctor disappeared. Finally, his eyes focused on Jenny. "Well, Mom, shall we find out if we can see our son now?"

Jenny's cheeks turned pink. "The people here assume a lot,

don't they? I suppose we should have corrected them the first time they called me Mrs. Adams."

"I'm not sure."

She turned to look at him. "What?"

"I think," Mike said softly, "that instead of correcting them, we should correct us."

"I don't understand."

"If we look so much like Mr. and Mrs. Adams, maybe that's who we should become. What do you say?"

Jenny was speechless.

Mike, however, was not. "Luke did want to know if you were going to be his mom."

"That's because Tia and Libby filled his head with crazy ideas!"

"Maybe they were the right ideas." Much to Jenny's astonishment, Mike dropped to one knee right there on the waiting-room floor and said, "Jenny Owens Matthews, will you marry me?" He paused to smile. "And be a mother to my son, Luke?"

At Jenny's delighted nod, two nurses standing in the doorway began to clap.

"That's the best yet," one nurse said to the other. "The only thing more exciting that's happened in that waiting room is a knife fight. And all that meant was that we ended up with more patients on our shift!"

Mike and Jenny looked at each other and burst out laughing. A cake purchased under false pretenses. A ruptured appendix. A proposal of marriage that could top a knife fight. The unusual combination seemed to promise an exciting beginning for a new life together.

*Carnations—The pink, a small cousin of the carnation, was named
not for its color but for its scalloped edges (i.e. "pinking" shears).
The pink later became a symbol of marriage and married love.
In paintings, newlyweds were shown carrying pinks.*

—ROBERT L. CROWELL,
The Lore and Legends of Flowers

"Do I look fat?" Tia tipped back the wide-brimmed straw hat she
was wearing and studied her reflection in the full-length mirror
in Jenny's bedroom. Tia wore a pale lavender floral chiffon dress.
Multihued flowers cascaded across the filmy fabric, making Tia
herself look like a magical garden.

Libby and Jenny exchanged amused glances. "Fat as a twig, my
dear," Libby said. "How about me?" She was wearing a diapha-
nous dress identical to Tia's, only in a soft mint green.

"A reed along the riverbank," Tia responded poetically. "But
nothing like our bride here."

Jenny's cheeks turned rosy, reflecting the pink of her dress so
pale and delicate that she felt as though it—and she—were made
of gossamer.

"Ellen did a beautiful job with the flowers, didn't she?" Jenny
touched a pale rose picked from her garden, which was now part
of her bouquet. The bouquet was a riot of the sweetest colors in

bloom and tucked everywhere with one of her favorites, the tiny carnation. She raised her eyes, and her friends saw tears in her eyes.

"Don't get weepy on us now," Tia ordered. "This is going to be the most beautiful wedding ever."

"I can't help it," Jenny said, her voice awed. "God has blessed me in so many ways that it is hard to take it all in. You two, Mike, Luke, my job, Dorothy's and Ellen's friendship, the garden. The day Lee died, I died too—or thought I did. But my winter has passed—both a literal and a figurative one. And now—"

"Now spring is back with all its new life, and the most drop-dead gorgeous groom and the world's cutest groomsmen are waiting for you downstairs."

Jenny frowned. "Grooms*men?* I thought Luke was Mike's only attendant."

"Oops." Tia clapped her hand over her mouth.

"Who?" Jenny demanded.

"A friend of the family," Libby interjected. "That's all we're supposed to say if you ask."

Jenny rolled her eyes. "Can't even my wedding day be without surprises?"

"There certainly aren't many. You catered your own reception, are holding it in your own yard, and planned every detail. If Mike wants a second groomsman, he should have that right."

"OK, OK, but—" Then the harp and strings began the music downstairs, and Jenny knew it was time.

"Yee haw!" Tia cheered. "Let's go get these sweethearts hitched before they chicken out."

"Decorum, Tia, decorum. That's the watchword of the day," Libby reminded her. "And don't forget Mike's ring."

In a flurry of perfume and chiffon, Jenny and her attendants made their way down the stairs.

All the furniture had been removed from the living room to make room for a lavish buffet table and ornate ice sculptures. There were flowers everywhere. It seemed fitting, after all, considering what had brought Jenny and Mike together. White wooden folding chairs made an arc of seating in the room, and linen-topped tables were scattered here and there, all displaying lush floral arrangements from Jenny's garden. Never had flowers been put to such loving use.

The music changed, and Libby positioned herself at the French doors open to the garden. Slowly she took her first step outside the house and down the aisle. Tia took her place in line.

Jenny stepped behind Tia and waited. As she did so, she closed her eyes and prayed. "Dear heavenly Father. Thank you. All praise to you. You brought me through a wilderness to a beautiful land. I ask that you be the centerpiece of our marriage and guide us every step of the way. Without you in our lives we are nothing. With you we can be everything. Gather your angels around us and keep us safe—Mike, Luke, and me. Be with us every step of the way. Amen."

When Jenny opened her eyes, Libby was halfway down the aisle on the brilliant white runner the ushers had rolled out. Now it was her turn, Jenny realized. With a deep breath she stepped out toward her new life.

Everyone was smiling, eyes shining, faces glowing as they watched her come down the aisle through the center of the yard. Her parents were beaming with joy. Carla was openly dabbing at her eyes, as were Mr. and Mrs. Meyers and the dozens of friends and coworkers who had come to see Jenny and Mike united in marriage. Jenny could smell the freshly mown grass and the fragrance of the garden as she glided down the aisle. Mike's father, her father-in-law-to-be, smiled beatifically from his pastoral post at the garden altar.

As she neared the front, she noticed that the smiles were wider, and a few of the guests seemed on the verge of laughter. Her eyes sought Mike's for reassurance.

He was there at the front—tall, strong, and incredibly handsome, with that impish naughty Mikey Adams expression on his features. Puzzled, Jenny's gaze slid to Luke. He was standing so straight and proud he looked as if he might burst. The love in his eyes nearly took Jenny's breath away.

And then she spotted Mike's other "attendant." Sitting as erect, alert, and still as she had ever seen him, was Spot. He'd been scrubbed and brushed within an inch of his life. He wore a black bow tie just like the ones Mike and Luke were wearing, and his tail fanned a gracious welcome to his mistress as she came down the aisle.

A thought occurred to Jenny then. Life had changed forever. No more somber times, no more lies. She was marrying naughty Mikey Adams and, she realized with delighted trepidation, would shortly become poor Mrs. Adams, wife of that creative genius and societal rebel whose upside-down sense of humor would keep her on her toes day and night.

Jenny's step hastened. She couldn't wait. The best days of her life were yet to come.

Judy Baer lives in North Dakota and raises quarter horses and buffalo. She is also an amateur sled dog musher. She is the mother of two grown children, Adrienne and Jennifer.

Judy began writing in 1982 and to date has published more than sixty books. During her career she has been the recipient of numerous awards, including Woman of the Year in 1995 for the North Dakota Professional Communicators' National Federation of Press Women, and the Concordia College Alumni Achievement Award in 1997.

Jenny's Story is Judy's first full-length Tyndale House novel. Previously she was the lead author for the Tyndale anthology of romance novellas entitled *Reunited*.